HEART OF ROCKS

A NOVEL

JIM TRAINOR

UpNorth Press

Heart
of
Rocks

A Novel

For Ron, Damon, and Bob

Let's slip out the side door of sorrow
Round past the watchman of worry
And make for the green fields beyond.

Steven Charleston

Chapter 1

At his feet, a muted yellow and orange carpet of rotting leaves was the only color in this otherwise black-and-white landscape. Declan Lewis drew a deep breath, filling his lungs with the cold, twilight air, then gazed up into the skeletal branches of leafless trees stretched like desperate arms into the grayness. In the stillness, he wondered if this was what it felt like to not exist.

But his shivering confirmed that he was still alive. Even with the Pendleton wool shirt under his Patagonia down jacket, one of the few nice things he still owned, it was not enough. It would be turning colder tonight, expected for Wisconsin this time of year, so it was just as well that Perch Lake Campground would close tomorrow for the season. It was nearly deserted. As far as Declan could tell, the campground host was the only other camper still here, probably the only person for miles.

A good night for a campfire, but he had no firewood. He'd seen the stack of shrink-wrapped bundles for sale over by the campground host's RV, on his way to his daily hike, but he'd make do without a fire. Gazing into the dancing flames of a campfire was good for pondering, remembering, discerning—things he could do without.

The warmth of an RV appealed to him though, but he'd have to get by in his old mummy bag and his tiny tent, remnants from his college backpacking days, set up ten yards away from his rusted-out Corolla. The sleeping bag and tent had gathered dust for years, but since he left Chicago six months ago, he'd used them every night.

An hour later, Declan lay on his back in the tent, the hood of the mummy bag pulled tight around his face. Even with all his clothes on and a wool blanket over the down bag, he might be cold tonight.

Bedtime had been a challenge for over a year, and if he allowed memories to get a toehold in his mind, he'd toss for hours. But tonight, the dark and the quiet helped the toxic memories recede beyond some far horizon, and the longed-for sleep came quickly.

A clicking sound jolted him awake. He stayed still and listened, but there was no further sound. But he was sure about what he had heard—this wasn't part of some dream. Someone had opened the door of the Corolla.

Chapter 2

"What a steaming pile of—," Julia groaned, as she slammed down the lid of the laptop. She leaned back and stared at the ceiling, shaking her head. She'd been working on the page all afternoon, ever since she'd finished cleaning the last outhouse. The last outhouse was where this page belonged.

She imagined Ernest Hemingway hunched over his noisy old Underwood, dimly illuminated by a 25-watt gooseneck lamp, hunt-and-pecking on his manuscript for *The Old Man and the Sea*. Maybe he'd lean back in disgust at the page he'd just created, then grab it by the top edge and rip it from the typewriter. He'd angrily crumple the page, then hurl it toward the corner in the general direction of the waste basket. Maybe there'd be a dozen such crumpled pages there on the floor, a memorial to his failure. For Julia, ripping the page from a typewriter would be so cathartic right now, much more satisfying than punching the delete key.

Julia poured an inch of Scotch from the bottle that shared the small dinette table with the laptop. It was an expensive fourteen-year-old Oban, the only classy thing in her old RV. As the smoky fire warmed her insides, she recalled a line attributed to Hemingway that a novelist should write drunk and edit sober. Maybe that was her problem: she wasn't drunk—this was her only drink of the evening. She pondered what old Ernest would have to say about the novel she was working on.

She turned her attention to the memo on the refrigerator, attached with a colorful *Kettle Moraine State Forest* travel magnet. She pulled the sheet down and studied it again—*Perch Lake Campground Closing Checklist.* She'd perused it several times during her month as campground host, but tomorrow she'd put it into action. Although she'd been a host at many campgrounds over the past few years, she'd never been the last host of the season.

Tomorrow she'd leave, and the problem was her next hosting gig—in the Florida Keys, which was great with winter coming on—didn't start for another month. Not really a problem, she thought. She was excited about her first trip to the Keys, and she relished the thought of vagabonding for the next month.

Julia scanned the list. *Return Mule with unsold firewood bundles to park office.* She'd miss the Mule, as the state-park folks called it. Like a cross between a golf cart and an Abrams battle tank, it was really a John Deere Gator utility terrain vehicle, a slightly domesticated version of an all-terrain vehicle, with seating for two and a small cargo area. It was awesome for patrolling the campground and hauling firewood and cleaning supplies.

Final cleaning of fire pits—Ugh, the messes some people left. *Final cleaning of outhouses.* This was her least favorite job, and it had gotten harder since the pandemic—wiping down the surfaces with antiseptic cleaners and mopping the floors. *Walk through campsites for lost items, trash, etc.* It was amazing what people left behind: smart phones, jewelry, various clothing articles and once even a laptop. All these went into the lost and found at the park office. *Check security on flush toilets & shower.* The shower had been closed for two weeks—required by the possibility of freezing weather—so no big deal. The list went on with several other, mostly trivial, tasks. But she wanted to do it right.

Unless that one camper had trashed out his site—he seemed like a quiet, keep-to-himself kind of guy—the last day would be a breeze, and maybe she could be on the road by noon.

Campground hosting was a mostly solitary job, except for the daily interactions with the campers, and that part was usually enjoyable. These folks were her community, and she would do what she could to ensure they had a great time. But it wasn't always easy. Quieting noisy groups after hours was the worst— more than once she'd had to call the police on campers who'd become loud and confrontational after a night of too much drinking. Then there were the endless questions, most of which could be answered by just glancing at the brochure they'd been given at the park office. *How do I recognize poison ivy? Are there snakes around here? Where's the trailhead to the lake? When can I run my generator?*

All in all, camp hosting was quite a bit of work for no salary, just a free campsite in the forest. Was it worth it? Many would say no. But there was this beautiful wilderness and all those nice people. Best of all, there was often little work between about ten and three, when new campers would be arriving, and this left plenty of time to work on her novel. Of course, it was worth it.

Work on her novel? She cast a wary glance at the laptop. Why did she keep doing this? She took another sip of the Oban. That recent class at Madison had been a low point, and there had been a lot of low points. *Write to Your Potential*, put on by the University of Wisconsin Extension. She often found writing conferences and workshops during her camp-hosting gigs, and she'd really gotten fired up last year at a writer's workshop in

Jackson, Wyoming, while she hosted in Grand Teton National Park.

Things were going well at Madison, too, until she met with an instructor who was critiquing her writing sample, the most dramatic part of a thriller she was drafting. The instructor sat across from her at the small table, shaking his head slowly, avoiding eye contact. She gripped the edge of the table, preparing herself to be crapped on. Finally, he said something like, "So, Ms. Evans—oh, wait, Ms. Marshfield-Evans…" He let out a quick cynical laugh. "You say you're writing a thriller. But, to write a thriller, you actually need to include something that's thrilling." Now, he looked her in the eye, but only for a second. "Don't want to deflate you, but this"—he held her writing sample up like he was preparing to toss it into the trash—"is about as exciting as Velveeta." Julia had done her best to hold it together but hadn't been very successful.

Damn, she didn't need to relive that now. "Need to actually include something that's thrilling." Maybe that was her problem. Although she'd known her share of despair and disappointment, she'd experienced little in the thrilling department. And the way he even mocked her name. Julia Marshfield-Evans. Lord, he'd seen through that, too. She was just plain Julia Evans, but had added the "Marshfield" (she'd lived for a while in Marshfield, Wisconsin) to make her name more author-like, like Julia Spencer-Fleming or Taylor Jenkins-Reid, who obviously knew something about thrilling.

She closed her eyes and listened to the night. Total quiet, just the distant whine of a siren, probably out on I-41. She raised the lid of the laptop and brought up that problematic page, as the siren was now a little louder. At least, something thrilling may be happening out there tonight, she thought.

She turned her attention to the last paragraph as the sound grew louder. She stopped and stood, realizing that the emergency vehicle was coming into the campground.

Chapter 3

Declan's first instinct was to jump from the tent and confront the intruder. The last thing he needed now was to have his car stolen. But that instinct quickly gave way to caution. Who would be out here in this deserted place? Maybe they have a weapon. Breathing hard, he tapped 911 into his phone and whispered his report of the intruder. Off the phone, he lay in silence, pondering what to do.

It could take a while for the cops to show up, and he wasn't going to lie there while some jerk absconded with his car. He unzipped the front door a few inches and peeked out—the tiny tent had no windows. In the darkness he could see nothing. He pulled on his glasses, which quickly fogged up from the cold.

For a moment, he stood beside the tent, shivering, considering his next move. He leaned down toward the fire pit and found a branch—a weapon, if he needed it. He eased up to the car from the rear, staying in the so-called blind spot that drivers worry about. Everything was still. Maybe he really had dreamed about the sound. His gut churned with a sudden misgiving about having called the police.

Then he saw it. The edge of the passenger door protruded a half inch from the body of the car—it wasn't latched. Someone had opened the door, then gently closed it to not make a sound. Most likely the intruder had found nothing of value and left. There was little harm they could do to the interior of the old car, anyway. But he'd check to be sure. Silently sucking in a deep breath, he eased the door open and shone the light from his iPhone flashlight into the interior. Nothing going on.

As he started to close the door, there was a sudden movement in the back seat and a head shot up. Declan jumped back, his heart in his throat. Long gray hair encompassed the person's withered face. It was an old woman.

This was about the last thing he expected to see. Declan spun around, checking his surroundings again—the old woman could be a decoy to distract him while an assailant snuck up from behind. Nothing. He turned back to the woman, huddled in the darkness of the back seat. The interior of the car reeked of body odor. "Who are you?" he demanded, with as much authority as he could muster.

The woman was silent. She appeared to be shaking.

"You broke into my car. Get out." He stood back, but the woman remained in the back seat.

She said something, so softly he couldn't make it out.

Declan leaned closer. "What?"

"I'm cold."

The woman wore a thin cloth coat and hugged herself as she shivered. This was some homeless person out here in the middle of nowhere, trying to find shelter on a cold night. Some pathetic soul, who could've been him. Even in the darkness, he could see a desperation in her face that he recognized. That look could crumple him now if he let it. "Look, you shouldn't be in my car." His voice had lost its authority. Peeling off the Patagonia jacket, he said, "Here, take this."

The woman quickly pulled it on.

"Wait here," he said. He hurried back to the tent, leaned in, and pulled out the wool blanket that covered his sleeping bag.

The woman didn't hesitate to accept the wool blanket. She mumbled some words.

"What?" He still couldn't make out her features, as she cowered in the back seat.

"Thank you."

"Are you feeling warmer yet?"

"A little."

"Who are you?"

No answer.

"Look," he said, "when I heard you open the car door, I called the cops. They're on their way, but don't be afraid. I'll explain to—" He couldn't finish his words, as the woman leapt from the car and bolted into the woods.

"Wait," he called out, but she was gone, taking with her his wool blanket and Patagonia jacket.

Chapter 4

When Julia arrived in the Mule, a black-and-white Washington County Sheriff's cruiser had already pulled into the campsite, headlights on and red lights flashing. A cop was talking to the camper. No one else was there. Her quick scan of the site revealed nothing amiss. The camper looked to be okay. What was a cop doing here?

The officer shot Julia a questioning look as she approached them. "I'm Julia Evans, the campground host," she said. He was a big guy, in a means-business uniform, with all kinds of equipment belted to his hip, including a large pistol. His silver badge sparkled in the red flashing lights.

The cop turned his attention back to the man. He cradled a small notebook in one hand, a pen in the other, ready to write. "You said someone broke into your car?"

"Yes, but it's okay now."

"What do you mean it's okay now?"

"It was just a homeless person, who was cold, looking for a warm place." The camper's breath misted in the air. He wore a plaid wool shirt, which was not enough for the cold night. It was hard to make out his features in the strobe lighting, but she remembered him from the other day, when he hiked past her site. He was a good-looking guy, maybe some kind of professional person. The lights from the cop's car flashed in his glasses.

"He was in your car?"

"She. Yes."

"Was it locked?"

"No."

The deputy gave his head a slow shake. "Was anything taken?"

"I don't think so."

"What was she doing way out here?"

The camper shrugged.

The cop turned to Julia. "Did you see anyone around this evening?"

Julia glanced from the cop to the shivering man, pulling her own jacket tighter. "No, I just heard your siren."

He turned back to the camper. "So, where'd she go?"

"I don't know," the camper said. "She just took off when I told her I'd called the police."

The cop did a slow three-sixty, peering into the encircling darkness. "So, she could've gone anywhere. I'm sure you didn't get her name. Right?"

The man shook his head.

The cop tapped his pen against the notebook, clearly annoyed about being dragged out to the boonies for nothing. "I don't see any indication a crime was committed." After a pause, he added, "It's going to be cold tonight. Did she have enough warm clothes?"

"Probably. She's got my wool blanket and my down parka."

"She stole those?"

"No, no. I gave them to her."

The cop exhaled a deep breath, then tucked his notebook into a pocket. "Anything else you want to tell me?"

"I think it's okay now."

The cop backed away, like he couldn't wait to get out of here. "Okay. You all have a nice evening."

Julia and the camper stood in silence, as the cruiser, flashing lights off now, slid away into the darkness.

The man turned to Julia, hugging himself and shivering. "Sorry you had to be dragged over here. Really wasn't a big deal."

"You look cold."

"Yeah, she ran off with my blanket and my Patagonia. That jacket cost three hundred bucks."

"Sorry for your loss." The words came out more sarcastic than she'd intended. "You going to be warm enough tonight?"

The man looked around. "I may have to sleep in the car, run the heater."

"Look, I've got a couple extra blankets over at my place. Why don't I run back and bring them over?"

"That's not really necess—actually, that would be nice. I'm leaving first thing in the morning; I'll drop them off then, if that's okay. In fact, why don't I just walk over to your place and pick them up, save you a trip."

"Come on, hop aboard the Mule. I'm Julia."

"Thanks," he said. "Declan."

The mule rumbled back to Julia's RV. Julia kept both hands on the wheel, aware of her awkwardness. After all, she was out here in the dark middle of nowhere with this stranger. He could be an axe murderer, for all she knew. She was normally very cautious around the campers. All kinds of people could be in the campground. She was always careful not to let on that she was a single woman, out here all alone. That's why she kept two folding camp chairs set up around the fire pit at her site. She knew nothing about Declan—isn't that an Irish name? Maybe it was hearing that he'd given his blanket and his three-hundred-dollar jacket to a woman who broke into his car. Or maybe she needed to experience something thrilling. Or maybe she was just a damn fool. She'd been a fool in her life, but not for a while. She prided herself in not being a fool.

Yet, when they pulled up to her RV and she hopped off and hurried to the door to fetch the blankets, she turned and said, "You look cold. Maybe some hot chocolate?"

Chapter 5

Was she inviting him in? Declan stayed seated, but then she opened her door and gave him a little head nod.

The interior of the RV was surprisingly spacious. He'd noticed it before, as he passed her site almost every day on his way to the Perch Lake Trail. It was one of those smaller units built on a heavy-duty Ford pickup chassis, a big F350—he guessed it was about twenty-five feet long. "Why don't you sit there?" she said, gesturing toward the bench seat at a small dinette table. She peeled off a bulky parka and tossed it in the corner, then put a cup of water into the microwave. Papers and books and a laptop occupied almost all the surface area of the table, so he kept his hands in his lap.

"This is nice," he said, while Julia focused on the settings on the microwave. She was slender and tall, but it was hard to judge her age. Her hair was tucked up under a Packers logo ski cap, and a gray flannel shirt hung loosely over blue jeans and nondescript running shoes.

"About your fancy jacket. Be sure to stop by the office tomorrow before you leave. It's unlikely, but maybe someone will turn it in."

"I'm heading out early, probably before they open. Anyway, I'm guessing the jacket's gone."

Julia shot him a glance, while her hands were still on the microwave controls. "Yeah, you're probably right, but why don't you give me your cell number and I'll leave it with the office when I head out. If I'd lost a three-hundred-dollar coat, that's what I'd do."

Declan struggled to find a blank sheet of paper in the chaos on the table.

Julia turned toward him as he was scribbling. "Sorry for the mess, that table is also where I do my work."

"What do you—" His words were cut short, as a massive animal appeared from the rear of the RV and bounded toward him. Declan backed against the wall, suddenly unable to breathe.

"Nivvie, sit," Julia commanded, and immediately the huge dog sat, still focusing its wolf eyes on Declan.

Declan eased out of the booth, where he felt trapped by the drooling canine, and stood, then slowly backed away.

"Nivvie?" was all that he could get out.

"Yep, that's David Niven. I call him Nivvie. He's a Redbone Coon Hound." Julia was still fussing with the microwave, seemingly unconcerned with the probably-lethal menace that he was facing.

Declan edged toward the door, trying to avoid any sudden movements. Nivvie eyed him carefully but remained where Julia had ordered him to sit. Declan scooped up the two blankets that Julia had set by the door, then slowly pushed the door open. "Maybe I'll skip the hot chocolate," he blurted. "I'll drop these off tomorrow." Julia started to respond, as he stepped out into the night, closing the door quickly before the dog could charge him.

Walking back in the darkness, now warm with the two blankets around his shoulders, he was still shaking from his encounter with the hound—hound of the Baskervilles? Sure, he'd made a rude exit, but he felt no guilt—there was little that he felt these days. The primordial fear that the dog—David

Niven? (Who names a dog David Niven? Wasn't that some old-time actor?)—had spurred in him was the first real feeling he'd experienced in months.

That dog had scared the crap out of him. Yes, it was irrational. The dog was a pet and most likely gentle, but that reasoning comforted him little. Encounters with dogs always brought back that attack when he was seven. He'd never been able to shake the image of the next-door neighbors' Doberman that he saw through the fence every day. Huge, with its fierce yellow eyes, its sleek black fur, teeth bared, saliva drooling from its jaws and ears sloped back like it was ready to attack. But Declan was safe on his side of the fence, until that day the dog burrowed beneath the fence, then charged him, sinking its teeth into his arm. His parents had been on the scene immediately, and the wound turned out to be superficial. But the terror he'd experienced—he never recovered from that.

Declan was finally back in his sleeping bag, beneath the two blankets, in complete darkness. He still wasn't completely warm, and he wished he had that hot chocolate.

Chapter 6

Julia had finished scrubbing and disinfecting the outhouses. The worst part was over. Now to the campsites themselves. Of course, there was only one campsite to tend to, so her work would be easy, and she could probably be on the road soon. Declan was already gone. When she'd stepped out of her RV to take David Niven for his morning walk, her two blankets had already been returned, neatly folded next to her door. He'd left his campsite spotless. No trash anywhere. He hadn't had a fire. The bed of ash in the black-iron fire ring still bore the rake marks from when she'd cleaned it last week.

The campground was completely quiet. No red squirrels chortling in the trees this morning. Probably too cold. No birds chirping, although she had seen a pair of cardinals earlier—they always cheered her up. She'd heard that there was at least one pair of pileated woodpeckers, and she'd spent the last month watching for them, without any luck.

This guy Declan was an odd one. The way he'd bolted from her RV last night. She'd encountered people who didn't care for dogs, but an adult so terrified—weird. She looked over at Nivvie, her sad-eyed hound, leashed to the Mule because coon hounds are known to bolt if they catch the scent of wildlife. It had been a mistake to invite a camper into her RV. It crossed boundaries. Hot chocolate? In retrospect, her cheery attempt at hospitality made her cringe. She wouldn't make that mistake again.

The main thing Julia liked about her camp-hosting gigs was the time she got to be alone in the wilderness. Some people had asked her if she ever got lonely during these hosting stints. But how could she be lonely, surrounded by woods teeming with life and beauty? The wilderness to Julia was not a mysterious place of hardship and danger, with fierce creatures ready to sting, bite or eat you. It was a place of peace and comfort. The soothing melody of the breezes through the pines was more glorious than any symphony she could imagine.

It had not always been that way. Just three years ago, she was living in a simple three-bedroom house in the middle of Milwaukee suburbia. She'd been there for twenty years, ever since she and Gary got married. She watched Jenny grow up there, packed lunches for school, ferried her to after-school events in the Odyssey. Had a flower garden and worried whether the asters were getting too much water. She'd had a nice kitchen that they'd finally remodeled with granite counter tops, white cabinets, and new stainless appliances. She and Gary had worked for months planning that, before dipping into their savings to make it happen. She'd had a part-time job for years as an admin for a financial management company, but she had little interest in financial stuff. It was the people, her coworkers and the clients, who she loved.

She had just turned forty when Jenny headed off to Stanford on a full-ride scholarship. Julia had harbored hopes that Jenny would settle on Madison, so she'd be nearby, but Jenny wanted to move far away from the place she'd known all her life. Not so much to get away from mom and dad—or so she said—as to test her wings, to seize her big opportunity. Julia could not deny her daughter's desire for a big opportunity, but now her only child was gone. Suddenly her whole world—her stable world of well-nurtured asters, stainless-steel appliances, the reliable Odyssey—was shaky. In her mind, she was at a crossroads: too young to be old, and too old to be young. She needed a big opportunity, too.

Yet, Julia was made of tough stuff, and she would plow ahead. But soon after Jenny left for college, Gary broke the news that he was leaving her for Marylin Shubert, a family friend and one of Julia's coworkers at the financial management company. Apparently, their affair had been going on for years. Geez, how could she not have known? So, just like that, Gary was gone. Apparently, this was Gary's big opportunity.

The months that followed were the worst of her life, lying awake, listening to the big trucks out on I-94 and pretending it was the ocean. Then one night, three years ago, she settled on a new course. Why pretend she was hearing the ocean, when she could leave and go to where she really could hear the ocean? Although she'd worked in finance for years, she'd applied little of that expertise to her own life, but now she had a plan of sorts. Soon, they'd sold the house, sold the old Odyssey, and she combined her proceeds with about half her meager savings. It was enough to purchase the used Winnebago Minnie Winnie. It was old, a 2015 model with 80,000 miles. Twenty-five feet long. It was all she could afford, but it was perfect for her new life, whatever that would turn out to be.

At the same time she bought the Minnie Winnie, she also got Nivvie, the ideal partner for her big opportunity. Found him at the humane society—the staff thought he was about two years old. A friend suggested the name David Niven, because the dog displayed a certain refined dignity, just like the vintage movie star, even though he was from the pound.

This new life was perfect for the new Julia. But there were times when she missed her old home, a reliable place that was always there at the end of the day. And a reliable man who was always there at the end of the day, too.

The fire ring at Declan's campsite was clean, but she ran the rake through it anyway, as she pondered her life. The rake snagged something, probably a piece of trash that Declan had left. She reached a gloved hand down to pick it up. Not just a piece of foil or a beer can but … what the hell? The rake fell from her hands.

Chapter 7

Declan hadn't gone far. He'd headed out early since he couldn't sleep anyway. He left the blankets at the camp host's door and considered also leaving a thank-you note but figured he'd already made enough of a fool of himself. Best thing he could do was split.

Now, he sat in the Perkins near the interstate, only a few miles from the campground. He was down at the end of the counter, away from the other diners. He always chose the counter, because a booth reminded him of how alone he was.

Sipping a black coffee, while he waited for his manager's special, he pored through Google Maps on his phone, pondering where he'd go next. He'd stayed in Wisconsin since leaving Chicago six months ago, drifting from one campground to another, but now he'd have to head south, where the nights would be survivable for a guy who no longer owned a Patagonia down jacket.

A good day's drive could get him to a state park down in northern Missouri. The state parks usually had the best scenery and hiking trails, and hiking was about the only thing that brought him peace these days.

He'd just spent five nights at Perch Lake, part of the Kettle Moraine State Forest, which cost twenty bucks a night for a non-electric site. More than he wanted to pay. With no income, he was slowly draining his modest savings. What would he do when that ran out? He'd been successful, so far, at pushing that scary question away.

Declan had become good at pushing away unpleasant thoughts. Sitting at the counter with a hot refill of not-bad coffee, amidst the upbeat white-noise ambience of laughing voices, clinking dishes and rustling newspapers should be a good time for reflection, but any reflection would naturally lead him through the painful sequence of events of the last few years. His career crashing and burning, a marriage that had cooled, and worst of all that look, as she turned her eyes toward him one last time. Camping raised questions he could handle. Nothing more challenging than finding a level spot to pitch his tent.

Yeah, that state park in northern Missouri would be his destination for today. Five hundred miles in the old Corolla. The farthest he'd traveled in a long time. After that, where would he go? He could head east, but even though he'd spent the last few years in Chicago, he wasn't a city guy. Maybe he'd head west. See some mountains. But truth was he wasn't really interested in going anywhere.

And, anyway, that decision could wait. He was in no hurry to get anywhere, except away from the cold. He took another sip, just as his manager's special arrived: two eggs and toast for two-ninety-nine. He leaned back, savoring his privacy, much needed after the night he'd had. That woman breaking into his car and making off with his jacket. The cop grilling him amidst the flashing lights. And that big dog, threatening him.

Declan had just placed his napkin on his lap and raised his fork when the voice interrupted him. "Beautiful day, huh?"

He turned toward the voice, already resenting the interruption. The man had just taken a seat at the counter, two seats down from him. Declan didn't need to answer this. A nod would suffice.

The man now turned his swivel chair toward Declan. "You been camping at the park?" He spun the swivel chair back and forth. "Yeah, I think I saw you. I was there yesterday."

Really? Declan thought. He hadn't seen any other campers. He said nothing.

"Did you hear the cops come into the campground last night? What the hell was that about? Kinda disturbed the quiet, if you ask me." He drummed his fingers on the Formica, while he continued to swivel his chair.

Why's this guy so antsy, wondered Declan. "Yeah, I heard it. Nothing much, as far as I could tell." He had no reason to mention the woman or provide this nosy guy with any information. He gave a shrug, then focused on getting jam onto his toast.

"Kind of a long ways for cops to come out for nothing much. I'm guessing it was important." The man took a quick sip of his coffee, eyeing Declan from over his cup, like he knew he was holding back. "Maybe they were looking for that old woman who was running through the campground." He glared at Declan like he expected a response.

He'd had enough involvement with this guy already. "Don't know anything about that."

"So, where you headed today?" He continued to watch Declan, then added, "Oh, hell, I'm sorry, that's intrusive, don't mean to be prying."

He was a normal looking guy. Had a shaved head, like many young men these days. Short beard. Levi's and a gray sweatshirt with a UCLA logo. Long way from home, thought Declan, but he didn't comment. Could've been a camper, but he was certain there were no other campers there last night. Almost certain; the campground had several loops. "Not sure yet, just exploring," he said.

The man nodded, dropped a bill on the counter and stood. "Well, happy trails." With no further words he left.

Declan returned to his manager's special and had just lifted a fork of over-medium egg to his mouth when his phone beeped, startling him. He rarely got phone calls.

"Mr. Lewis, it's Julia the campground host."

He set down his fork and sighed. "Don't tell me you found my jacket."

"Actually, no, the office hasn't opened yet. But I found something else."

"Yeah?" He didn't need to get chewed out because he'd left the site a mess. "I really tried to leave my campsite clean."

"Oh, it was spotless. No problem, but I have to ask you if you left anything in the fire pit."

Declan was silent for a moment. "I don't think so. What did you find?"

"You're certain?"

He rotated the coffee mug and watched the ripples on the black liquid surface. Was this payback for his awful behavior last night? "Yes, I'm certain." He continued to fiddle with the mug. "So, what did you find?"

She started to speak, but then she stopped. He heard her exhale a deep breath. "Actually, I'm not sure I should discuss this over a telephone connection ..." Then there was more silence.

Declan picked up his fork again and considered the runny egg. "Look, I'm trying to eat my breakfast, and I'll repeat, I didn't leave anything in—"

"Are you still nearby?"

He took a bite of the egg. "Why?"

"Maybe we can talk. Look, this is weird, and I'm not sure what to do."

He shook his head, as he looked around, as if someone might be listening in on this crazy conversation. After all, this was a woman who'd named a dog David Niven. While chewing, he said, "I'm getting ready to head out, don't have time to—"

"I understand, but I don't know who else to talk to. There's no one at the office. The state park hotline isn't answering, and I …" She was going a mile a minute. "I really need to talk this through with someone, and you were the most recent camper here. It'll just take a few—"

He set the fork down again. "I'm only a few miles away from the campground. You still there?" He silently chastised himself for bad judgment, feeling himself cave.

"Standing at your campsite, actually."

"I'd like to finish my breakfast. Guess I could be there in a half hour."

"Good. See you then."

He tried to rationalize his bad decision. There could be no harm going back. He could still be down in Missouri before evening. He turned his attention to the work at hand: polishing off the manager's special.

Chapter 8

Julia turned the canister over in her hand again. Good thing she always wore work gloves to do her campsite cleaning. She was already worrying about fingerprints. It was just a small metal cylinder, smaller than her balled-up fist, with a screw cap on one end. What had stunned her were the words on the label affixed to the cylinder.

TOP SECRET

Property of **USANETC**

Fort Huachuca

Do not remove from this room.

She'd already been back to her RV with the cylinder to do some online research and, after a deep breath, to unscrew the cap of the cylinder.

Now she was back at the man's campsite, poking through the layer of ash in the fire pit, looking for further evidence, as his Corolla pulled into the site.

Declan stepped out of the car and, even before greeting Julia, cast a wary eye at David Niven.

"Don't worry," Julia said, "I've got him leashed up."

Declan came only about halfway to the firepit and stood there fiddling with his car key, like he wasn't planning to stay long. "So, what did you find?" He was a tall, rangy guy—over six feet for sure.

Julia had thought this through. The obvious conclusion was that Declan had left the canister there. But why would he drive away, leaving it here? That was part of the purpose of her call: to hear his reaction when she mentioned her discovery. He'd seemed clueless during their phone conversation, which was reassuring, but that didn't mean he wasn't involved with this object. Perhaps a top-secret object. Of course, the canister could be a fake, part of a kid's spy kit. Maybe his reaction would give her a clue. If he was associated with a top-secret object, maybe he could be dangerous. She shot a glance over to Nivvie, just a few steps away. She could unleash him in a second.

"This," she said, holding up the canister. Her instinct told her Declan could be trusted, and she trusted her instincts. The look on his face, his awkwardness, impatience, curiosity—not the look of a criminal she'd just exposed. And why had he called the cops last night if he were holding on to a stolen secret? Nonetheless, she'd be careful. She glanced over at Nivvie again.

Declan squinted and stepped closer. She held the canister up toward him, so he could read the writing, but didn't want to hand it over to him. She watched him as he studied it. The wireframes gave him an educated appearance. He looked serious. His shaggy hair bore some gray at the temples. Early forties, she figured.

"Fort Hua …not sure I know how to pronounce this," he said.

"It's pronounced *Wah-chew-kah.*"

"Impressive you'd know that."

Julia gave out a little laugh. "I didn't. I just looked it up."

"So, where the hell is Fort Huachuca?"

"Way down in southern Arizona, close to the Mexican border."

"And USANETC. What's that?" He was still focused on the canister, looking up at her only briefly.

"It stands for US Army Network Enterprise Technology Command. According to Wikipedia, it's an organization that has oversight of the Army's cyberspace. Planning, deploying, defending—all that kind of stuff."

"Top secret—that's like national security business. So, this could be important." Now he leaned closer. "And you found it here in the fire pit?"

"Yep."

"Maybe this thing is fake, like some novelty or toy?" He touched his chin with his forefinger, like he was thinking it over. "I mean, does the government keep top secret information on physical media that can be stolen? Isn't that something they did in Austin Powers movies? I mean, wouldn't they keep their info in the cloud?"

"That's what I thought, too, but I found one site that said some agencies still keep their secret data on physical drives, in safes, in secured rooms. Too much worry about hackers, I guess."

"So, I still suspect this is fake. I'll bet you can get one of these online for ten bucks." He let that hang in the air for a moment. "But if it's real." He was silent again. "Then someone removed this from a safe, then removed it from a secure room and then, I'm guessing, removed it from a secure lab. Inside job, right?"

She nodded.

"It does look authentic, I must admit," he said. "But seriously, we're in a campground in Wisconsin. I can't imagine any far-fetched explanation for how a secret government object would be out here." He took a step back, like he was ready to head out. "Have you looked inside?"

"Yes. Maybe I shouldn't have, but I did. There's a strange kind of flash drive inside."

He looked at her with raised eyebrows. "And let me guess, you stuck it in your computer to see if you could read it."

"Of course."

"And?"

"Nothing happened. Probably has some kind of encryption or something. My laptop couldn't even recognize that I'd inserted a new drive."

"Or it really is just a toy."

Was he making fun of her? Maybe he should be. Maybe she was just a silly camp-host woman living by herself in the woods, ready to believe anything. She stood up straighter, fighting off her tendency to doubt herself.

Declan looked around the campsite. "Funny I never saw it, but then I didn't use the fire pit. I wonder how it got here. I mean, obviously, somebody put it here. Could it have been accidentally dropped?"

"That seems unlikely."

He rubbed his chin, stubbly from a week's lack of shaving, between his thumb and forefinger. Now, he looked her in the eye. His eyes were large and blue behind the wireframes. "Hmm. Okay, let's assume for a minute that it's authentic. If someone placed it here intentionally, they were expecting it to be found. If they'd just wanted to get rid of it, they could have tossed it anywhere out in the woods."

"Do you think the homeless woman might have put it here?"

He seemed to consider this. "She was hardly the type who'd be carrying top-secret things around with her."

"But she did run when you told her you called the cops."

"Sure, but that was probably because she just didn't want to be dragged off as a vagrant."

"You and she were the only people around here."

He was silent for a moment. "I can see how you might wonder if I'm involved in this."

Julia just smiled. Then she said, "Okay, here's a scary thought. This thing was obviously stolen. Maybe someone left it out here for some other contact to pick up. Might be a good place to do that kind of thing."

Declan pursed his lips. "Maybe, but that seems risky. And, why would they pick an occupied campsite, when there are dozens of empty sites all around here? How could they be sure that some camper or you wouldn't find it? Which of course, you did."

Now he stood with arms crossed and eyes rolled skyward, like he was doing some deep analysis. There was one big question left, and she knew it would be coming soon. His eyes returned to hers. "So, what are you going to do with it?"

Julia stared at the canister, as she rolled it around in her hand. "I've given it some thought." She had, in fact, thought this through, while she sat with the canister at her computer. Her first thought was to drop it off at the state park office, where the normal lost and found stuff wound up, but it only took a second to realize this made no sense. If this was federal property, the state park folks wouldn't know what to do with it any more than she did. Same with the local police. They'd be clueless, too. Clearly, she needed to get it to the FBI. A computer search led her to the main regional office in downtown Chicago. She checked out a route on Google Maps, then shook her head. No way was she up to piloting the large Minnie Winnie into downtown Chicago traffic. She leaned back in her chair and stared at the vinyl ceiling of the RV. Well, she probably could make it, but she had a more intriguing idea. She leaned forward and, with just a few keystrokes, checked out another option. Yes, this could work.

While she pondered how to share her new plan with Declan, he said, "I say you take it to the nearest FBI office—must be one in Chicago or maybe even here in Milwaukee—and turn it in."

It's what she expected him to say. "I've considered that, and that's one option, but I've got another idea. Unless you think it's yours—it was found in your fire pit."

"You can do whatever you want with it. I don't want that thing. I say it's yours. You found it." They both laughed, the first time she'd seen Declan laugh. "So, what's your idea?"

She held the canister up before him in her palm. "I want to take it to Fort Huachuca."

He threw his hands up in an I-give-up gesture. "That's crazy."

Of course he'd say that. "If you think through the options," she countered, "and I have, this makes as much sense as anything else. So, I say, why not?" She shrugged her shoulders in a carefree way. "I've got nothing better to do for the next month. I checked out the maps. Four-day drive from here. Lot of cool places to see. Never been down in that part of the country. Have you?" Crazy or not, this was something to help fill the next month. Maybe the canister was just a child's toy, not to be treated seriously, and maybe she was not to be treated seriously either. But she stood firm, looked him in the eye.

"Been to Phoenix a couple of times. Look, you don't know what you're getting yourself into here. You could—" He had an exasperated look, then glanced back at his car, like he might be getting ready to make a run for it.

"Hey, I'm just going to take some missing property back to where it belongs. And one more thing…" she said.

"What?"

"It'll be warm down there."

Declan leaned in toward her, as if to emphasize what he was about to say. "Sure, but did you hear me? This could be dangerous. If this is some top-secret thing, then it's obvious that it was stolen—no other way it could be here. Whoever stole something top secret from the Army is not someone you want to mess with. And the fact that it's here means they either lost it and they're looking for it or they wanted to get rid of it or, worse yet, someone's on their way to pick it up." He cast a wary look around them. "Whichever, this is a patently bad idea."

Declan's firm pushback shook her resolve. Her first tendency was to concede the merit of his argument, to back off from her plan. "Well, I guess maybe you're …" Then she stopped and looked down at the canister again. Maybe it really did contain top-secret information that could affect many lives.

Julia felt the doubt invade her mind like a virus. She looked up into his face. He looked like someone who should be making the decisions. There was intelligence behind those wireframes. His serious demeanor indicated that he was not prone to emotional overreaction. The graying temples, the shaggy hair, the intense eyes—he was probably a professor. And she was just a camp host. She should be hosting. Not deciding what to do about top-secret information. She closed her eyes for a moment and saw her mother, shaking her head in disapproval.

She started to speak again but couldn't get any words out, so she turned and walked over to where Nivvie sat. She leaned down and stroked his head. His big knowing eyes bathed her with trust. Then she looked up at the bare canopy above her, these stark woods that had been her home for the last month. A bird sang from the barren trees. Boldly, even in the face of approaching winter, it sang. It was a Red-eyed Vireo, she noted. Its song was melodic, repetitive, confident, almost defiant. A migratory bird, on its way from somewhere up north to somewhere farther south but stopping here.

She turned back toward Declan. The shaking she'd experienced when she first discovered the canister threatened to return. Maybe a thrilling life always begins with shaking, she thought. She clasped her hand tight around the canister and looked down, planning her words, fiddling with a lock of hair. Then she looked at him and said, "I've planned a route. This thing will be back in its home in four days. That's what I'm going to do."

"So you're willing to throw caution to the winds."

She straightened. "I'm not throwing anything to the winds. But neither am I going to curl up into a fetal position and hide under a rock. So maybe I get down to Arizona only to find out this thing is fake. There'll be a little momentary embarrassment, but I'll have had a great trip. It's worth it."

Declan shook his head slowly, like he was disappointed in her poor judgment. "I can't stop you from doing whatever you want to do, but again, I say this could be dangerous." Even in his obvious frustration, his voice remained at a soft, steady level, but he seemed like the kind of guy who never raised his voice.

"Maybe, but who's gonna know I've got it? There's no one around here except us, and I'm gonna be out of here in ten minutes. Sure, I'll keep my eyes open, but I think it's going to be safe." It's also going to be thrilling, she thought. That word—thrilling—had been churning through Julia's brain ever since she'd found the canister. "I want to head out as soon as I drop off the Mule. Maybe make it to Missouri by tonight."

"Missouri?"

"Yeah, maybe northern Missouri, then head out across Oklahoma or Kansas. Then the Texas panhandle, New Mexico, and on down into Arizona."

"So, you've already scoped this out."

"Of course." She smiled. "Me and Google Maps."

With hands on hips, Declan stared at the ground, again shaking his head like maybe he could rid himself of the insanity he was hearing.

"So where are you headed?" she asked. "Home?"

"Uh, no. Actually, I don't know. Some place warmer. Tell you the truth I was thinking about going to Missouri tonight. There's a state park north of KC that sounds pretty good. But, uh …" He trailed off there, as he shot a glance over at David Niven, leashed to the Mule.

Julia shifted her weight from one foot to the other. "Don't get the wrong idea, but maybe we could travel together. At least down to Missouri. Split the cost of the campsite, save some bucks. I'm self-contained; there'd be plenty of room for your tent. I mean, you follow me, or I'll follow you. I'll keep David Niven on a leash."

"Thanks for the offer, but I'm thinking I'll just head out on my own."

"Okay," Julia shrugged. She turned toward the Mule. "So, Nivvie, let's hit it." She needed to do something thrilling. She was ready to roll.

Chapter 9

While she waited for the call, Alana Selkirk knelt by the planter box containing the Heirlooms. Frost was predicted tomorrow night, so these would be the last tomatoes of the season. The Heirlooms were odd—prized for their great flavor, but they were ugly things. Not round and smooth like most tomatoes but irregular with ribbed surfaces. Large and robust, nothing delicate about them. She plucked the largest Heirloom from the vine, still green but beginning to show traces of yellow and red. She'd let it ripen in the house; otherwise, the squirrels would get it. Yes, the non-initiated might overlook these tomatoes, even reject them, not realizing that under the surface their flavor was superior. She stroked the tomato gently and held it close.

The Heirlooms were just like her. So long unappreciated, but that would soon change. Just a year ago, before she met Mr. Tucker, she was still in her wallowing period, terrified, often enraged. She'd had no idea what to do. The only person in her life, her dad, was still confined to that depressing county home—Ocean Pines. She hated euphemisms. Ocean Pines: hardly a good description for the smell of urine, moaning, hallways filled with vacant-eyed residents slumped in their wheelchairs.

Then she met Mr. Tucker in the vegetable section at Whole Foods. She had looked up and there he was, standing across from her, appraising a yam. He was a small man with receding hair, horn-rimmed glasses—he looked like a seventh-grade

English teacher. But that assessment would be selling Mr. Tucker short, way short.

"Miss Selkirk," he said, "It's good to finally meet you."

Alana had recoiled. She'd never seen this guy before. But over the next few weeks, always in the vegetable section at Whole Foods, she learned more than she had ever dreamed. She knew she was headed for new things the second time they met, just a week after their first meeting, when Mr. Tucker handed her a purse. "Just a small token of my appreciation. Let's call it a down payment."

Down payment for what? Out in the parking lot, Alana discovered that the purse was packed with hundred-dollar bills. Thirty thousand dollars. She felt her knees wobble, and she had to lean up against her car. She envisioned her father in a fancy new apartment far away from the urine stench and her on a path toward the retribution she longed for, that she deserved.

Yes, she'd come a long way from that fateful day, three years ago, when she decked Regina Ketchum. She'd never punched anyone before in her fifty-seven years, but she handled it like a pro. A right cross that Regina never saw coming. And Regina deserved it. All that sucking up, week after week, those cutesy smiles and sexy little gestures that she was allowed to substitute for competence. What an idiot her boss, Dr. Walsh, was. Regina got the promotion, and Alana, with all those years as a top security specialist in the Pentagon, was left hung out to dry. She'd never regretted her outburst for a moment, even though she was immediately fired. "We should have seen it coming," she'd heard one of the managers say. Even before she decked Regina, she'd been sent to that anger management course, which was a colossal waste of time, and she'd been disciplined for verbal outbursts in the past, but this time—to hell with that. Remembering the blood pouring out of Regina Ketchum's nose still made her smile.

Her naive fantasies were about all that kept her going following her termination, after running home to Albuquerque to be near her dad and as far away from DC as she could get. Ultimately, those fantasies—imagining how it would feel to stand at Dr. Walsh's desk with a Glock in her belt—had just made her feel worse.

But then Mr. Tucker appeared at Whole Foods and offered her a path forward. A new project that she would lead and she would design, a project that would extract all the sweet revenge she craved. And today would be her shining moment: the delivery would be made—her victory complete.

She cradled the ugly Heirloom tomato like it was her baby, just as her phone beeped. She almost jumped, ecstatic to hear that announcement of success. She laid the tomato gently on the ground beside her and listened carefully to the man. After a long time, she said, working to stay calm, "What do you mean it's gone?"

She felt the tears build behind her eyes. Was it all coming undone again? She picked up the Heirloom and cradled it in her hand. Then in a sudden burst of fury, she crushed it with brutal force, its juice spurting everywhere like blood gushing from a severed artery.

Chapter 10

The GPS said it was eight hours down to Wallace State Park, in northern Missouri, almost all of it on interstate—the straightest, fastest route to get from somewhere cold to somewhere warmer. A monotonous drive, allowing lots of time to think. Thinking wasn't what Declan wanted, so he'd had the radio cranked up almost from the moment he left the campground. First a raucous country station from Milwaukee, then a classic rock station from Chicago. Then, across the brown farmland between Rockford and Des Moines, he picked up only a few static-filled stations with farm reports and conservative talk shows.

It happened on the long stretch beyond Rockford, when he glanced into the rear-view mirror and saw her. It was Emily's face in that window at the ER, locking eyes with him. His Corolla veered into the adjacent lane—thank God there was no traffic—and he struggled to regain control of the vehicle. That final image of his wife, her eyes radiating helplessness, had been a frequent companion the past year and a half, but he'd recently hoped he'd broken free of its haunting.

What was he doing out here? During his camping phase of the past six months, he'd wandered from one campground, roadside rest or Walmart parking lot to another. He'd had no specific destination; his only goal was to keep moving, keep finding places to hike, which was the only activity that brought him any peace.

It was almost two years since Emily died and over six months since Conor's restaurant closed. A rational man like Declan knew he should be recovering from his grief, and maybe he was. He had been in the deepest pit of his life, and maybe he was climbing out of it. Or was he just getting used to being in the pit? He was still running from those crippling memories, that was certain. He knew what he was running from but had no idea what he was running to. There was absolutely no place he really wanted to be.

Across the Iowa state line, he merged onto I-80 for the straight shot west into Des Moines, where he'd cut south toward Missouri. Afternoon sun streaked across the farmland, which stretched on forever, punctuated only by billboards, an occasional off-ramp to some town he couldn't see from the interstate, and the rest stops every forty miles or so.

He pulled into one of those rest stops and slid into a parking spot next to the doggie walking area. As he stepped out of the car, there, immediately in front of him, was Julia walking David Niven. Apparently, she hadn't spotted him, focused on encouraging the dog to do his business. He hurried toward the restroom, not wanting another encounter with this woman. But when he exited the restroom, he walked right into her, almost knocked her over. He caught her shoulders to keep her from falling. In the moment of contact—her face was just inches from his—he felt the heat of her body, her warm breath on his face, and the softness of her shoulders in his hands. He had not been this close to a woman in a long time, and he felt a surprising response stir in him.

He immediately let go of her shoulders and stepped back quickly, flustered. "I'm so sorry. Are you okay?" he said.

Julia looked surprised. She backed up a step, then brushed her hair back with the sweep of a hand and licked her lips. "I'm fine."

Declan cleared his throat, looked around for David Niven, but apparently she'd already put him back in the RV. "Yeah," he said. Not a terribly profound response, but what do you say in a chance encounter at a place where you both stopped to pee?

"So, how's the drive going so far?" Julia asked politely.

She'd had the Packers ski hat on when he saw her this morning, but now her brown hair was tied back in a ponytail behind the smooth fair skin of her face. Although he avoided eye contact, Declan noted that her green eyes were warm and curious. A few lines radiated from the corners of those eyes. Probably in her mid-thirties. "Enjoying the scenic stops," he said, looking around at the bathroom building. Good Lord, did he just make an attempt at humor?

"So, another four hours for me. You mentioned a nice state park in Missouri. Found Wallace on my AllStays app, looks like a nice place. That where you're headed?"

He didn't know what the AllStays app was, but he now regretted mentioning that state park. "Yeah, probably," he said.

"Well, okay, guess I'll be heading out." She looked down, obviously not wanting to revisit his earlier rejection of her invitation to caravan. She turned toward the parking area.

Sometimes your mouth says things that are not sanctioned by your brain. "A few more hours still to go. I guess we could travel together." Maybe he was remembering the blankets that kept him warm last night. Maybe that was it. Or was it her breath on his face? He'd hardly talked to another person in the last six months. Now he was offering to head off to Missouri with this crazy woman. As they walked toward the parking area together,

he wondered how anything could happen to him that was worse
than what had already happened to him.

Chapter 11

Maybe the key to a thrilling life is to be open to opportunities and new avenues for exploration—be spontaneous. Julia hadn't always been good at that, and maybe that's why the comments from that writing instructor in Madison stung so much. But no one could deny that she was being spontaneous now, heading off to the desert of southern Arizona, carrying a probably stolen top-secret object. And now, on top of that, she was traveling with a mysterious man she'd just met last night. All this could easily terrify her, but what kept her going was she was doing exactly what she needed to do to produce a good novel.

Julia knew she was born to be a novelist, even though she'd received little validation that she had the necessary gifts and skills. Sure, she'd only started writing seriously three years ago, after finally overcoming the paralyzing grief and anger from Gary's departure. But, geez, she'd self-published two novels already, after she'd been unable to find an agent for either of them. But she had little skill or interest in marketing, and the poor sales for both books got her down to the point where she was tempted to give up. But something kept her going. She attributed this to being truly destined to be a writer.

Admittedly she had little professional preparation to be a novelist—it'd been over twenty years since her last English class—but she remembered reading that Tom Clancy wrote *The Hunt for Red October* while working as an insurance agent. Yet she had persisted in honing her skills. A whole cabinet in the Minnie

Winnie was dedicated to writing, from how-to books on plot development, point of view, dialogue, character arc, and so on, to reflections from writers about the processes they embraced to practical books on self-editing to finding a publisher. And her notes from the writing workshops near her campsites were dog-eared. She was convinced that she was a better writer now than when she started, and she was determined that her new book, another thriller, would be her breakthrough. Maybe her new adventures would ensure that.

These were the thoughts coursing through Julia's brain, as she climbed up into the cab of the Minnie Winnie. She looked in the rearview mirror to verify that Declan's Corolla was back there—it was.

She was starting up her rig when she heard a shuffling sound behind her. She glanced back into the living area. David Niven was already curled up at the foot of the bed, asleep. She rose but stayed in the driver's area, gripping the back of the driver's seat tight. Something or someone was back there.

Her first impulse was to escape through the driver's door, but she waited. No further sound. Had she imagined this? Perhaps the sound had come from outside.

She reached down and picked up a windshield ice scraper and clutched it like a gang member readying for a knife fight. She stepped back into the RV. Nothing was amiss but immediately she was almost overcome by a foul odor. It wasn't like anything she was familiar with from Nivvie. She had just turned back toward the cab area, when she detected motion above her in the over-the-cab sleeping area. Holy crap, someone was up there. Julia jumped back, ready to flee the RV, when the person sat up.

Julia knew immediately who it was. The Patagonia jacket was the giveaway. Backing away from the smelly woman, she barked, "Dear God, who are you and what are you doing in my vehicle?"

The woman said nothing.

Julia pushed open the side entry door, in case she needed to leap for safety, then she opened a vent above her head and turned on a ventilation fan. "I need you out of here. Now."

The woman looked at Julia helplessly but didn't move.

She shot a glance toward the small bathroom in the RV, which she never used, in order to keep the black-water tank clean. "Have you been using my bathroom?"

The woman looked down. Stringy white hair fell around her wrinkled gaunt face. She was a pathetic looking thing.

Julia paced around in the small living space. Declan was waiting behind her, no doubt wondering why she hadn't backed out yet. She pulled out her phone and punched in the last number from her "recent calls" list. When Declan answered, she said, "So, I found your three-hundred-dollar jacket."

"Huh? Where?"

"It's on the woman who took it. And she's here in my RV."

"Oh?" There was a pause. "What are you going to do with her?"

"I was hoping you might have some genius answer."

In a moment, Declan was at the open side door to the RV. Peeking inside, he said, "Yep, that's her. How'd she get here?"

Julia stood next to the open door, so she could breathe fresh air. "Your guess is as good as mine. Probably snuck in while I was cleaning up your campsite."

"What's your name?" Julia asked the woman, who still sat on the bunk.

Silence.

"If you won't tell me, I'm going to throw you out at this rest stop right now." Julia crossed her arms over her chest to project authority.

"Elizabeth," the woman said.

"So, what are we going to do with her?" Declan asked again, as he surveyed their surroundings. Nothing but empty farmland stretched to the horizon in all directions.

Julia took some solace that he said "we" and not "you."

They stood in silence, pondering their next move, while Elizabeth stayed perched up on the overhead bunk. Julia cast a disapproving eye back at Nivvie, who was still curled up at the foot of the bed. "Some watchdog you are," she said.

Chapter 12

Declan welcomed the quiet, after more interaction than he'd wanted today. At least the woman was riding in the RV with Julia. Elizabeth? Was that her name?

It had taken a while back at the rest stop, but they'd hatched a plan. They agreed they couldn't just abandon Elizabeth in the middle of nowhere. They toyed with the idea of calling the police but then decided they'd drop her off at a homeless shelter in Des Moines, which they'd be passing through in a couple hours. Julia had located one close to the interstate. That seemed like the most humane thing to do with this sad creature.

Elizabeth had watched their discourse in silence from her nest in the over-cab bed, but when they'd settled on a plan, she spoke up. "Please don't."

Declan and Julia had turned toward the woman.

With her head down, Elizabeth mumbled, "I heard you say you're heading south. I have a cousin in Kansas City. If you could just take me there." She shook her head like she was trying to shake loose something painful from her mind. "Plus, it's so cold here. I need to be where it's warmer." She flashed them a brief glance with hollowed-out eyes. "Please."

"Look, Elizabeth," Julia said, "You hardly have a strong bargaining position here. You broke into my RV. That's a crime, and you're damned lucky we haven't just called the cops. That's still a possibility."

Elizabeth looked down again. "I know," she said, wringing her bony hands, while she shook her head. After some silence, she said, "I didn't mean to break in. I know it's wrong, but I didn't have anywhere else to go. I was so cold."

Of course, they'd both wilted. It would have taken a heart of rocks to deny the poor woman. Julia had checked Google Maps. "KC's just an hour beyond the campground. I suppose I could drop her off there tomorrow."

Declan said, in a hushed voice that Elizabeth could no doubt hear, "This isn't a good idea. We know nothing about this woman. She could be dangerous. Having her in the RV with you for another two hours is a bad enough idea. Having her spend the night in here is unacceptable." His eyes penetrated into her like his common sense needed to be acknowledged.

Julia looked away from Declan's piercing gaze, back up to Elizabeth. Sure, there could be danger, but she wasn't going to let that stand in the way of doing the compassionate thing. She looked back to Declan. "We'll take her to Kansas City," she said.

I-35 south from Des Moines was nearly deserted, and with Declan following the RV, the driving didn't require much concentration. The scenery was more brown fields, with few distractions. He kept the radio off now, enjoying the quiet.

At one time, Declan traveled a lot. He and Emily made car trips all over the west. They met at Berkeley, where Declan was in grad school in physics and Emily was in her third year of a music major. What they had most in common was that neither one of them was particularly ambitious. This was not a harsh judgment. Just a fact that seemed right to him now, as he rolled across the empty miles of southern Iowa. While other students were hitting the books over the weekends, Declan and Emily were often camping on the beach in Mendocino or cross-country skiing in Yosemite.

He first saw her at a winter camping class—six evening sessions at the North Face store in Berkeley—that would culminate in a weekend snow-camping trip in the Sierras. Declan had gone to learn about winter wilderness survival, building snow caves, snowshoeing techniques, and so on—not looking for romance. They hadn't spoken to each other during the first two classes, but after the third class, Declan remained at the store, shopping for a new sleeping bag rated for winter use. Turned out, Emily had stayed at the store, too, also shopping for a new bag. Their initial conversation had centered around sleeping-bag technicalities: should they go for down or synthetic fill? Would it be light enough to carry on a backpack? Was it waterproof? But as Emily trailed a finger across the smoothness of one bag's ripstop nylon cover, Declan began thinking about trailing a finger across the smoothness of Emily's arm. By the time the snow-camping trip came around, after the sixth class, they would be sharing the same tent.

He could still remember her in that North Face store, like it was yesterday: her robin's-egg-blue sleeveless blouse, the tight jeans and white tennies. The shoulder-length straight hair, simple and no-nonsense. Her face was pale with a faint smattering of freckles, and her eyes—oh, those eyes—were large and blue and innocent. Even after all the years of life together, it was still that image of Emily testing the loft of a mummy bag at the North Face store that was his mental avatar of her. Those eyes were also what he remembered from the last time he saw her, through that window, as they wheeled her away. He still had that sleeping bag, but he no longer had her.

Lord, he should be moving past the grief. Aren't people supposed to be getting better after so long? Did he want to get better? Or was the wallowing a comfortable place to hide? He knew those were valid questions but had little interest in exploring the answers. One good sign, maybe: he was heading out on a long trip, the first time he'd travelled so far since Emily got sick.

Declan switched on the radio, but all that came in was some guy ranting about how vaccines aren't needed. He palm-slammed the power button off.

They made one more stop on the drive down to Wallace State Park, for gas and potty breaks and a refreshment of the supply of snacks that Julia kept in the RV, which she referred to as the stash. Declan cringed every time he had to put gas in the Corolla—a little more cash being sucked out of his drying-up savings account.

It was while they walked together back from the small convenience store that Declan noticed something odd. Elizabeth stopped suddenly, her gaze locked on a black sedan parked nearby. She started to turn, perhaps to run, but then she gathered herself and continued to the RV.

South of the Missouri state line, the farmland became interspersed with patches of thick woods. By the time they left the interstate and headed down the narrow two-lane toward Wallace State Park, they were engulfed in heavy woods, in the last days of stunning Fall colors.

Declan waited for Julia to back her RV onto the concrete pad, which she handled quickly and expertly. Then he parked the Corolla in front of the RV. Few words were needed, as they went about the work of setting up camp. Julia plugged into the electric power pod and checked the leveling of the RV, while

Declan set up his tent. Elizabeth had exited the RV and sat at the wooden picnic table, with a blank look on her face.

After she hooked up the RV, Julia came toward Elizabeth with a towel, a bar of soap, and some clothing, then pointed toward the shower house nearby. Then she headed over to the camp host's site, where she chatted a while, probably comparing notes, returning with a bundle of firewood.

Declan opted for a walk around the campground, nearly empty in late October, even though it was a beautiful evening. It felt strange being here with other people. He'd been alone for so long. He thought about Julia's crazy quest to take the top-secret canister all the way to Arizona. It made no sense at all. Not to mention being dangerous. But it wasn't his problem. And who, in fact, was this Elizabeth and why had she done that double take at the gas station? He recalled the guy in Perkins asking about the old woman. Had he been looking for her? Sure, he had a tendency toward paranoia or maybe he was just appropriately cautious. At least he'd be heading in a different direction tomorrow, away from this craziness.

By the time he got back, Julia had a fire going and her two camp chairs set out. Elizabeth again sat at the picnic table, her hair now wet and stringy. She had her old cloth coat and the Patagonia on over the fresh clothes Julia had given her. David Niven was on a long tether attached to a leg of the picnic table. Sleeping.

Nodding toward the RV, Declan said, "You're pretty good at backing that big thing up."

Julia, leaning toward the fire and rubbing her hands together, looked up with a smile. "I am now, but I wasn't always." She stood and turned toward him, hands now on her hips and grinning, like she was ready to share a story. "When I first got the Minnie Winnie about three years ago, it was pretty embarrassing. I think I was at Devil's Lake. First time I'd ever backed it up and I was having a terrible time getting it into the campsite." Now she picked up a piece of firewood and turned back toward Declan. "Some guy came along and said something like, 'Hey, little lady, looks like you're having a hard time with that baby.' (She made her voice go deep as she mimicked the man). 'Maybe I can give you a few pointers.'" She chuckled, then laid the piece of wood on the fire. "That was the last thing I needed, some mansplaining old guy making fun of me. I said no thanks, I've got it under control, but of course, now I was even more self-conscious." She stood with hands on hips again, watching the new piece of wood catch fire. "So, after several more tries, while the guy stood there laughing, and by now several other campers had gathered for some comedy, I just pulled out and left." She laughed. "I still cringe when I think about that."

Julia seemed confident and comfortable in her domain. She looked like a veteran camper, which she no doubt was: well-worn flannel shirt under a Bean fleece. Levi's and Keen sandals over wool socks. He wondered what her story was.

She certainly wasn't some twenty-two-year-old vagabond student taking a year off from college to see the world. She'd had a life before this, and yeah, there had no doubt been some crap in Julia's life. The difference between her and him was that she seemed to be a survivor, seemed to be able to laugh and enjoy the here and now. She had prevailed, while he wallowed. But right now, her laughter was infectious. And Declan felt like laughing, too, as he headed to the Corolla to get his camp stove and some food.

Chapter 13

Julia finished scrubbing the pot she'd boiled the linguini noodles in and set it to dry next to the small sink. The Minnie Winnie was a tiny space, but it had everything you needed to get by, including an amazingly well-equipped kitchen, with a two-burner propane stove, a microwave, a fridge with a decent-sized freezer compartment, and a stainless sink with hot and cold water. The small kitchen suited her as well as any granite-counter-topped kitchen from the latest episode of House Hunters. She was also pumped because she was on the road again, after a month at Perch Lake, heading out on a new adventure. And this new adventure could be more exciting than any of her previous treks, thanks to the little piece of top-secret cargo, stashed in a safe hiding place in the back.

It had been an odd evening so far. Declan, an evasive loner for sure, had fixed his own dinner, choosing to heat some soup on his Coleman stove, rather than try the pasta that Julia offered to share. Elizabeth had no problem accepting her food. They had sat around the wooden picnic table mostly in silence. Several times it seemed like Declan was about to speak but then had second thoughts and kept silent or offered a few words of polite but inane chit chat. He hadn't even mentioned the mysterious canister. How could he stay quiet on this balmy evening in the woods, under a starry sky?

Elizabeth, who'd sat at the table with them, had also stayed quiet, but Julia had come to expect that from her. Although she had put on the filthy cloth coat and the Patagonia over the clean clothes Julia had loaned her, she looked more presentable after her shower, and she smelled better, too. It was interesting watching Elizabeth eat. Even though she'd obviously been floundering in the bottom of life's barrel, she ate with elegance. Although she was no doubt starving, she'd exhibited the graceful manners of a sophisticated matron.

Julia was determined to keep the mood upbeat, as she stepped out of the RV and returned to the campfire. She invited Elizabeth to take one of the two camp chairs, while she stood. She was putting more wood on the campfire, just as Declan returned from stowing his cooking gear and washing his dishes off at his car. Julia nodded at the unoccupied chair. "That one's for you."

Declan backed away a step. "Actually, I thought I'd turn in early. Got a long drive tomorrow. But that's a lovely fire."

"Oh, come on, it's not gonna hurt you to sit for a while. Go ahead."

Obediently, Declan took the other camp chair. Nivvie, still attached to the long tether, approached Declan, who visibly tensed up. He gripped both arms of the chair, like he was ready to bolt, but then the dog circled a couple of times and curled up at Declan's feet. Declan relaxed his grip on the arms of the chair but kept a wary eye on the big hound.

Julia paced around the periphery of the fire, holding a stick she'd been using to poke the logs, like it was a drum majorette's baton. "So, Declan. What's your story?" She threw the question out there and let it hang in the still night air.

"Not much to say." He peered into the fire, not looking up.

Julia nodded. "Or, not much you want to talk about, huh? Anyway, that's fine. So, where do you think you'll be heading tomorrow?"

"Not sure."

"Maybe stay here another night?"

"I doubt it."

"So, no destination in mind?"

"I'll think about that tomorrow."

Julia nodded, as she continued to pace. "Fair enough. In fact, I'm a little envious you're able to do that. I'd be laying out the itinerary, maybe making reservations. Nice not to have any obli—"

"My wife died."

The silence probably lasted a few seconds, but it seemed like forever. She laid the stick down gently next to the fire pit. "I'm sorry." She knew better than to probe too much.

After more silence, and after it was clear Declan wasn't going to say any more, Julia said, "So, Declan. Don't hear that name very often. Is that Irish?"

"Yeah. My mom said it means man of prayer or something like that." He rolled his eyes.

"So, you're Irish?"

"Hardly. My mom traveled to Ireland once and loved it. So, she gave her sons, Conor and me, Irish names. We were both born in California."

"Where's Conor?"

"He went back to LA, where we grew up."

"Back from where?"

"Chicago. We had a restaurant there. Conor's."

"Had?"

"It folded six months ago—couldn't recover after the pandemic."

"Sorry to hear that. So, you're a chef? Now I understand why you'd rather eat your own cooking."

"Conor's the chef. A good one. I helped him with the books and the business end of things. I'm a terrible cook." Was that the hint of a smile that Julia detected?

"So, what are you doing now?" Julia knew she could be pushing it here, but what the hell?

"Just traveling and hiking and … well, that's about all …" He started to say more but stood instead. He gave Julia a long look that was hard to understand, then said, "Yeah, want to get an early start tomorrow." He nodded at Elizabeth, cast a wary glance down at David Niven and even gave him a nod. Then he headed for his tent.

An hour later, Julia worked at her laptop, while Elizabeth lay in the over-cab bed, staring at the ceiling. Julia kept an eye on her. Several times during the evening, she'd tried to get Elizabeth to open up, with little success. It wasn't like she was intentionally holding back some secret, but more like she was too ashamed to speak. She didn't seem like a dangerous person, just skin and bones, and Julia could no doubt physically overpower her, if it came to that. Her intuition told her that it was safe sharing the RV with this stranger, but she would be careful.

She'd been on a roll. She'd just introduced a new character early in the book, a middle-aged real estate salesman, who's gotten entangled in a shady deal. Divorced and maybe depressed, he's now found himself way out of his depth. She savored the last line of the chapter. *All his other problems paled in comparison to the grim reality before him—two dead bodies, face up, lying at his feet.*

She leaned back and smiled at the page. Definitely not Velveeta. But was it good writing? *Damn, Julia, don't go there.* Don't go to that familiar place where you doubt yourself, where you shrink back. She recalled a funny piece of advice she'd heard at one of those workshops: "Do not place a photograph of your favorite author on your desk, especially if the author is one of the famous ones who committed suicide." This gave her a much-needed laugh.

She looked up at Elizabeth. Now, there would be an interesting character for her novel. But she really knew nothing about her. Lord, how could she be sure that it was safe having this strange woman sleeping in her RV? She felt goosebumps on her arms. Maybe after Julia was asleep, Elizabeth would make her way to the utensils drawer and pull out a steak knife, then head to the rear of the RV. Julia shook her head. She didn't need to get spooked about that right now. Elizabeth seemed harmless, but she was all too aware of news interviews with the neighbor of the slasher saying, "He was always such a quiet type."

Anyway, Julia always took precautions. A woman living on the road alone has to take precautions. She locked the RV doors at night, and she slept with a large pipe wrench from her toolbox. Anybody trying to bother her in the middle of the night would get a face full of steel.

"So, it seems I'm surrounded by people who don't want to talk," she said in Elizabeth's direction. "Starting to take it personal."

Elizabeth turned toward Julia and rose on an elbow but said nothing.

"What's your story, Elizabeth?"

Silence.

"I mean, what the hell, we're two strangers out here in the woods, probably never gonna see each other again after tomorrow. Why not talk?"

Julia could see Elizabeth's lips move, but she made no sound.

Julia stood and faced Elizabeth, hand on hips. "Look, Elizabeth, I need you to start talking. I'm totally ready to toss your sorry ass out right now. So, tell me, how'd you get to the campground last night?"

Elizabeth's eyes widened with panic, but she said nothing.

Julia stepped toward the door and rested her hand on the latch. "Okay. This is your call."

"I rode in the back of somebody's RV. Like this one."

"Who's RV?"

"I don't know. I just climbed in at a gas station."

Julia started to push the door open. "I need more than that."

"I really don't know who it was. It was in Milwaukee. Hid in the back. When they stopped, the man spotted me and started yelling. I jumped out and ran."

"And this was in the campground?"

Elizabeth nodded.

Julia decided not to ask about the canister. "So why did you do get into that RV?"

"I was cold."

"You don't have a home anywhere?" Julia suspected she knew the answer to that.

Elizabeth was silent.

"So where are we dropping you off tomorrow? Do you have an address for your cousin?"

"Huh?"

"Your cousin. The one in Kansas City."

Alarm filled Elizabeth's eyes. She ran a hand through her gray hair. "Actually, he doesn't live in Kansas City. My brother lives in …"

"Hold on. You said he was your cousin. And what do you mean he doesn't live in Kansas City?"

"Uh, my cousin left."

"Where'd he go?"

"Uh … I don't know."

"So, where is this brother?"

"My brother is …" Her voice trailed off.

"You're just lying, aren't you, Elizabeth? Is Elizabeth even your name?"

"Can't you just take me with you?"

Julia leaned toward Elizabeth. Pissed. Pointing a finger at Elizabeth, she blurted, "Look, I don't like to be screwed around with. Got it? I'm tempted to throw you out right now."

"I know," Elizabeth said, looking down and sounding pathetic.

The old pulling-the-heartstrings move, thought Julia. "Look, Elizabeth, I can't have you just moving in with me. A day or two, maybe. But that's all. Got it?"

Elizabeth nodded, like another day or two would be fine, then rolled toward the wall.

Julia turned toward Nivvie, bristling with frustration. The last thing she needed was a homeless person sharing her small space. "You about ready to go out for your final business,

Nivvie?" Outside, she said to the dog, "Well, I took you in from the shelter. Guess I can take one more."

Nivvie cocked his head toward her, his floppy hound ears encircling big brown eyes that seemed to reach right into Julia's soul. She stroked his head. "Nivvie, I'm not sure what I'd do without you."

They strolled around the dark campground. Only a few other campsites were occupied. A few big rigs with panoramic windows through which she could see couples watching large flatscreens. Two pop-up trailers and a camper van. A tent or two. Most everybody was inside for the evening. There was only one campfire, where a young couple sat close, staring into the flames.

Julia pulled out her phone, opened her list of favorites, and tapped Jenny's number. Two hours earlier on the west coast— Jenny was probably having an early dinner, studying or out with friends. Now starting her senior year at Stanford, Jenny seemed to have a large group of friends. Her call would no doubt find her daughter busy and not in the mood for a mom call, but she needed to hear Jenny's voice tonight.

Jenny picked up right away. "Mom, it's not a good time." There was a familiar hint of annoyance in her voice. After a pause, her voice softened. "Is everything okay?"

"Yeah, it's fine, sweetie, just wanted to hear your voice. I know you're busy."

"I'll try to call you tomorrow, okay?"

Julia leaned a hand against the trunk of a large oak. "Sure thing. Just wanted to let you know I'm on the road again, heading to Arizona."

"Great, Mom. Talk to you tomorrow." Jenny usually called every two weeks or so and preferred that Julia not call her—she preferred texting. She was always too busy.

"I love you, darling," Julia said, but Jenny was already gone.

The call had lasted less than a minute, but Julia got to hear her daughter's voice, and that's what she needed right now. Maybe she needed it because of the young couple cuddled by the campfire, maybe it was having Elizabeth crashing in the Minnie Winnie, maybe it was the antisocial Declan. Maybe it was her, foolish her, charging off to yet another destination that wasn't home. She looked down. Her only family from day to day was David Niven. Right now, she could use the real David Niven.

An owl hooted in a distant tree. It was a barred owl, Julia noted.

Last summer, Jenny had joined Julia for two weeks at Pictured Rocks National Lakeshore, where she was hosting at the Hurricane River Campground, one of Julia's favorite places right on Lake Superior. And Julia made her way out to Stanford at least once a year to see Jenny. She'd tried to find a hosting gig nearer to her daughter for the past three years but had never been successful—camp-hosting assignments in places like Yosemite or Pinnacles were almost impossible to snag. And now, Jenny was almost through with Stanford and was talking about grad school. Environmental science—that was Jenny's passion. Maybe Julia's love of the environment had rubbed off a little. She gave Nivvie a gentle stroke on the head.

A senior. Julia had been a senior—English major—when she dropped out at UW Milwaukee, pregnant with Jenny. *Hang in there, Jenny.*

Then there was the canister. Declan was no doubt right; she should have gone to the FBI. She had no business—no, wait. She'd spent too much of her life limiting herself with thoughts like *I have no business* ....

She and Nivvie came to the edge of a clearing, quiet and still. The sky was alive with stars, and a late-autumn breeze caressed her face. The beauty almost took her breath away.

Chapter 14

In that mysterious space between consciousness and sleep, the old tapes played again—the unerasable record of those final two weeks. He was the first to get sick—just sniffles and a low temp. Normally not enough to worry about, probably just a cold. When Emily encouraged him to test himself, he resisted. After all, they'd both been vaccinated and the pandemic was winding down. But a few days later, as symptoms persisted, he gave in and picked up a test kit at Walgreens. Emily decided she might as well test, too, even though she had no symptoms. The tests were positive for them both. Surely, they'd made an error. They tested again. Same result. How could this be? They'd both been so careful. Emily had no symptoms, so if she did in fact have Covid, she'd gotten it from Declan. But in the days ahead, Declan got better, as Emily began to show symptoms. Even then they didn't take the situation seriously. Emily was only forty and such a healthy person, more fit than Declan; surely this virus would deliver no more than a glancing blow to her.

But she got sicker—a low-grade temperature, some nasal congestion, but mainly there were the breathing problems. They had one of those finger-tip oxygen monitors, but it gave erratic results. Mostly, it indicated that Emily's blood oxygen level was low, but, damn, she was so healthy—surely the monitor, a cheap plasticky thing, was defective.

They should have gone to the ER sooner, but they'd seen those awful images on TV of crowded ERs: gurneys lining the hallways, overworked staff, people waiting desperately for access to a ventilator. When they finally went to the ER, Emily was still able to walk just fine, although she was gasping for breath. But there were new medications, and the world was moving on from the pandemic. This would be an inconvenience, not a crisis.

As he slipped deeper into sleep, the familiar dream replayed. The ER staff had wasted no time getting Emily into a wheelchair and taking her back to the examination area. Despite his protests, Declan was not allowed to accompany her. As the automatic door closed behind Emily, Declan pressed himself against the window in the door. Emily turned and flashed him a smile and gave him a confident thumbs up—but there was a haunting knowing in her eyes that pierced his heart.

Declan bolted upright, disoriented and sweating, his head bumping against the low ceiling of the tent. In the darkness, he couldn't get his bearings, and it took a moment to realize where he was. The dream still hung over him like a dark cloud: that look of her face through the window—it was the last time he saw her. She had been admitted, immediately put on oxygen and pumped full of the latest meds. They had every reason to be optimistic. For the next two days, he talked with her almost hourly on Facetime, even though she struggled to breathe. Then she went onto the ventilator, was sedated and unable to communicate until she died a week later. They'd only allowed him to see her, comatose, right at the end.

He never learned how Emily, so young and healthy, vaccinated, had died of Covid. The doctors spoke about unknown comorbidities that were triggered by the virus, but no definite explanation was ever given. Even though she was young, she was just one of a million fatalities, and perhaps the system had wearied of digging deeper. Bottom line—he never found out why she had died.

Declan never figured out how he'd gotten Covid, either, but one thing was clear: he was the poison carrier who had caused his wife to die.

It had been a while since he'd had that dream. Why now? After all this time he should be emerging from these middle-of-the-night horrors. Still breathing hard, he glanced at the luminous dial on his watch. Two-fifteen—he knew it was unlikely he'd be able to get back to sleep.

Chapter 15

Julia held the big platter high, like a waiter in some snooty restaurant, as she emerged from the RV into the sunshine. Elizabeth and Declan already sat at the picnic table, with its red-and-white checkered tablecloth providing the cheery ambiance of a small-town cafe. Elizabeth had risen when Julia got up, early, to take Nivvie out. Declan already had taken down his tent and packed it into his car. He apparently had just returned from the shower, his wet hair matted to his head.

Julia set the platter of French toast in the middle of the table, where butter and syrup and paper plates were already set out. "Don't get used to me waiting on you lazy bums hand and foot," she laughed. "You just caught me in a generous mood this morning."

Declan didn't hesitate in reaching for two slices. If he had any plans to cook up his own breakfast on his Coleman stove, the sight of the French toast apparently vaporized them.

Julia had slept well, despite her earlier concerns about Elizabeth, and was in the euphoric mood that setting out on a new adventure always generated. She'd already booked a campsite west of Oklahoma City and was ready to roll. "Everybody sleep well?" she asked, lifting her coffee cup for a first sip.

Elizabeth nodded while she sipped her coffee but said nothing. She still wore the Patagonia over her old cloth coat.

Declan nodded.

"So, this is a beautiful place, right?" Julia asked, looking from face to face. Hardly the chattiest bunch she'd ever been around.

"It's warmer than where we were yesterday," Elizabeth finally said.

No response from Declan. They ate in silence for a few minutes.

As Declan pulled a third slice of French toast onto his plate, Julia asked, "You said you kept the books for your brother's restaurant. You were trained in accounting?"

"No." Applying butter and pouring syrup apparently were more interesting to Declan than conversation.

She wasn't going to let Mister Personality off the hook. She leaned in his direction, like what he was about to say would be momentous. "Well, what then?"

"Physics," he said, without looking up.

She straightened, eyes widening. "Physics? That's pretty hard stuff."

"Yeah. But I wasn't all that great at it."

"I'm sure you must be pretty smart just to get into a school for physics."

Declan shrugged. "Truth is, I'm not very good at anything."

She took a bite of the French toast. *Not bad*, she thought, silently congratulating herself. "Not good at anything? Seems to me like you're pretty good at feeling sorry for yourself." Oh, sheesh, did she just say that? "I mean, you're young and good looking"—maybe she shouldn't have said that, either—"and you strike me as bright. I suspect you could do anything you want. For example, you—" She stopped. She was babbling now, trying too hard to fix her insult of the morning.

Declan surprised Julia with a laugh. "Guess I deserved that."

"I'd say what you deserve is a refill on your coffee."

Elizabeth stood. "Why don't I bring some more coffee out?"

Julia and Declan shared looks of pleasant surprise. "That would be nice," Julia said.

"This French toast is really good," Declan said.

Maybe her insult had roused him out of his sulk. "Thanks. Everything tastes better out in the woods."

"Maybe," he said, "but I'm sure the French toast at Conor's wasn't any better than this."

"Wow. That's a nice thing to hear."

When Elizabeth returned with the coffee pot, Julia said, "Thanks, Elizabeth. So, tell us a little about your life." Might as well try again to get through to her.

Looking down, while she stirred some creamer into her mug, she said, "I doubt you want to hear about that."

"Of course we do," said Julia. Declan shot her a don't-probe-too-much look. Julia shot right back with a mind-your-own-business look.

After more silence, Elizabeth said, "My life hasn't been easy lately."

"I've never met an interesting person who had an easy life."

"If you knew me, you'd know I'm not that interesting."

"Well, Geez, Elizabeth, I'm trying to know you."

But Elizabeth had gone quiet again.

They ate in silence until Elizabeth stood and collected the dishes and took them into the RV. Declan and Julia exchanged glances again.

While Elizabeth was gone, Julia asked, "So, have you figured out yet where you're heading today?"

"Not yet. Think I'll just get on the highway and see where it leads."

"That sounds charming, but what if you get on the highway that leads to some place crappy?" She looked around. "I mean, not every place is this nice. I'd be looking for something like this."

He nodded in agreement. "I know you're right, of course. I just don't feel like planning much of anything at this point."

Julia pulled out her phone and brought up the AllStays app. "Here," she said, handing the phone to Declan, "take a look at this."

Declan studied her phone.

"Maybe you're not ready to plan anything yet, but at some point you will be. Then this may come in handy." He handed the phone back to her. "For example, I'm heading out to Arizona, so today I plan to make it out to western Oklahoma. Don't want to be on the road for more than six hours, especially after that long drive yesterday. I just consulted this app and found out what my best options are. Really easy."

"I'll keep it in mind." He gazed into the distance, like he was looking for something that was hard to find. Then, he seemed to gather himself and looked at Elizabeth, who had just returned. He cleared his throat and said, "So, you're going to your cousin's place today?"

Elizabeth opened her mouth, but no sound came out. Julia cut in, "Slight change of plans. Elizabeth's going to travel with me for another day or so."

Declan looked at Julia with surprise, then rolled his eyes.

Later, while Elizabeth still sat at the table, staring into her coffee mug, Declan approached Julia, who was folding up the camp chairs. In a hushed voice, he said, "I still think you should contact the FBI about that canister." He looked back to check if Elizabeth was listening in, but she seemed lost in thought.

"You're probably right." Julia looked down at her feet—of course, he was right. Contacting the FBI now would be quick and low risk. She could hand the canister over and be done with it. But it was only three days to Fort Huachuca, where she could return it directly to a security official, get a feel for its place of origin, maybe learn more about what was on the drive. This would be research for a new thriller that would've made Tom Clancy envious. She looked Declan in the eye. "But I spent half my life opening the dishwasher and asking the burning question, are these clean or dirty? I'm ready to ramp it up a notch."

"And you're taking her with you?"

Frankly, it was none of his damn business what she'd decided to do. Yet, it was kind of nice that he was concerned.

"You know nothing about her," he said. "Oh, wait a minute, you do know she's a thief, and who knows what else?"

"Sorry, Mr. Lewis, but what I do is ultimately none of your concern, is it?"

He shook his head like he was deeply disappointed by her poor judgement but added nothing more.

Julia started to say more, just as Elizabeth, who'd obviously heard more than they intended, stepped up to them and peeled off the Patagonia. As she did, the old cloth coat underneath also came partially off, too, and a collection of stuff dumped from its pockets and lay scattered on the ground like the debris from an overturned trash can. She handed the Patagonia to Declan, her eyes cast down.

Declan took the coat, but there was a sudden look of shame on his face. He licked his lips, like he was struggling to find words, but none came out. He quickly knelt and helped Elizabeth scoop up the items that had fallen from her pockets. Then, he stood and backed toward his car. He nodded once, turned and left.

Chapter 16

Declan glanced one last time at Julia and Elizabeth in the rearview mirror, his knuckles white on the steering wheel. He forced his eyes back to the road, hitting the turn signal with more force than necessary. What an ass he'd been. Julia was an impressive woman, out here alone, traveling across the country. Well, maybe not quite alone—she had Elizabeth, which was probably worse than being alone. Julia certainly had an adventurous spirit. Trying to keep everyone else's spirits up, too. Declan and Elizabeth—what a depressing pair for the upbeat Julia to endure. Yes, he'd been an ass. Treated Elizabeth badly and basically ignored Julia. No healthy male would ignore Julia, but he hadn't asked her anything about herself. Did she have a career? Did she have kids? Yes, his wife had died, but how long did that give him the right to treat everyone else like they didn't matter?

As he merged into the southbound traffic on I-35, the image of the French toast surfaced. He almost smiled, then caught himself, his mouth tightening into a familiar line. Had he actually laughed this morning? He'd laughed so seldom recently, it was difficult to tell the difference.

It was pure charity on Julia's part to help Elizabeth. Maybe he should have stayed to help out, and—no, screw that, he didn't need to do anything out of guilt.

Images from last night's dream still stalked him this morning. That chaplain at the hospital, obviously out of his depth, had said empty words to him: "It will take time, but it will get better." In fact, maybe he was getting better, despite last night's dream. He knew all about the various stages of grief—too many times, well-meaning people had explained them to him like he'd never heard of them and somehow this new awareness would help him to "snap out of it," as one patron at Conor's had once suggested to him.

Acceptance. He gripped the wheel, focusing on the steady hum of the tires on pavement. Wasn't that a stage? The therapists talked about healing, a return to normalcy. Normalcy? Acceptance just felt like staring into a fog so thick you couldn't even see your own hands. He flexed his fingers on the wheel, one by one, as if testing whether they still worked. Yeah, acceptance meant finally seeing clearly that your life just... sucked. He blinked hard, adjusted the already perfectly positioned mirror, and kept driving.

What helped him the most these days was hiking. He'd always loved it, ever since high school back in LA, when he and his best friend Glenn got into what they called "bagging peaks." Bagging peaks referred to climbing to the tops of any summit they could find, from the modest mountaintops of the nearby San Gabriel Range to the high peaks of the Sierras, a five-hour drive north. They were fanatical about it. Kept logs and tabulated the elevation gains for each ascent. The word *ascent* was probably euphemistic, as it brought up images of traverses across steep icy ridges, when many of the ascents were little more than walks up fire roads.

Sure, he realized now, bagging peaks was probably a substitute for bagging girls, for which neither he nor Glenn had many skills. By his senior year of high school, Declan had been on only a few dates, but he had bagged over fifty peaks. A worthy accomplishment, but a lousy substitute for even one passionate kiss.

But the experience of the wilderness had gotten into Declan's blood, and it became part of his life. He found a freedom from the stress of the physics problems he struggled with in his college classes. As work had become his and Emily's focus in life, the hiking took a back seat. But in the last year, hiking was the only activity that gave him peace.

With his mind wandering to a high meadow in the Sierras, Declan almost missed the offramp to Missouri 291, just north of Kansas City. Google Maps promised it would take him over to I-70, missing the rush hour mess in KC. When he got to I-70, he'd head east. Maybe cut farther south at some point. Julia had talked about having a plan, but this was as much of a plan as he wanted. He didn't want to drive too far today. If you don't know where you're going, then why be in a hurry to get there? Maybe he could stop around two and still have time for a good hike. Where that would be, he had no idea. Maybe he should have downloaded that AllStays app.

On the two-lane state highway, there was little traffic, and Declan lowered the window to let the warm air blast his face. He switched on the radio, which brought in a classic rock station from somewhere. He used to love rock music, but not since Emily died. It was too much about romance and longing, too heart wrenching. He punched the radio off.

He used to be an interesting person. Wasn't he? Loved music. Good novels. His Kindle, unused for months, was in the back seat, but the battery was now almost certainly dead. And he was passionate about sports or used to be. He'd been an avid Cubs fan, but now, in October, he had no idea if they'd made the playoffs this year.

He had told Julia this morning that he wasn't any good at physics, which made him cringe now. That self-pitying comment had no doubt been the result of his awful dream last night. Truth was, he hadn't been that bad of a physicist, even though his physics career had ended suddenly on a bitter note. He had, after all, made it through Berkeley with a PhD, and that wasn't for wimps. True, his years at Berkeley had dragged on longer than normal, as some faculty had noted with a scowl. But he had been, after all, trying to make a life with Emily, and he had no regrets about those weekend outings that took him away from his dissertation work.

He recalled that one time his thesis advisor called him in for a heart-to-heart chat, as he'd called it, and questioned whether he had the commitment that a career in physics required. He suggested Declan might be better off dropping out of the program, seeking a profession elsewhere that would allow more time for what the advisor called his "extra-curricular activities." Declan had argued that he was cut out for it, that he would work harder, and he did for a while. It took him eight years to finish his PhD, far longer than most of the other students. But his degree from Berkeley got him a position at a prestigious national lab, and he was employed there for years. Right up until the disaster.

The disaster. Declan shook his head and grimaced at the Missouri state highway stretching out ahead of him.

He looked over at the passenger seat, where the Patagonia jacket lay, and shook his head again. God, how humiliating, standing there like the king of jerks, while poor Elizabeth peeled it off. He should have just given it to her. Here he was, so mired in his self-pity that he was unable to show compassion for

Elizabeth, her life devastated by something too dark for her to even speak of it.

And then for her possessions, just crap really, to be poured out everywhere. A few coins, some scraps of paper, even an empty plastic bag. A bag from a pharmacy. Maybe the poor woman was on meds. What did it say on the bag? It had caught his eye. He shook his head; he couldn't remember. But it had caught his eye because it didn't sound like a place in Wisconsin.

A half-hour later he came to the onramp for I-70, but instead of heading east, which would take him to Arkansas and beyond, as he had intended, he took the I-70 West ramp. He didn't really want to go to Arkansas anyway. He didn't really want to go anywhere, except away from the cold. But if he was headed anywhere, maybe he'd head west, where there would be mountains, and the hiking would be better. He should check out some possibilities on a map—that's what Julia would do. Maybe he could be called spontaneous, but that would be too generous. Aimless was a better word.

By four, he was parked in a Walmart parking lot, somewhere in Kansas. His quest for a beautiful campsite near a good trail had been abandoned. He called Conor but got his voicemail. Conor was busy trying to start a new restaurant back in LA, so he rarely picked up nowadays. He left a brief message. Those last days of the restaurant had been difficult. Conor's, which had been a flourishing dining spot, had taken a nosedive when onsite dining became impossible. He and Conor had struggled to be innovative, implementing curbside pickup and even delivery, but none of that made up for the loss of restaurant dining. By the time restaurant dining again became possible, it was too late. Too much money had been lost.

Former employees had scattered. And Declan had been of little help, as he was immobilized with grief.

After he'd wandered through the aisles of Walmart and stopped at the restroom, he was back in the car with no place to go. He drummed the steering wheel in boredom. He picked up his phone, saw he could connect into the store's guest WiFi and decided to download the AllStays app. He would try to find a better place tomorrow night.

After the app downloaded, Declan scrolled through some possible destinations for tomorrow but quickly lost interest. He checked a news site and his email. Nothing there. Played a couple games of solitaire. He started to lay the phone down, but then it popped into his head: the odd name of that pharmacy on Elizabeth's bag. He brought up Google Maps and searched for Sierra Vista. Only one entry was listed—a city in Arizona. He clicked on the entry to bring up the map. His mouth fell open when he saw it. Sierra Vista was the town adjacent to Fort Huachuca.

Chapter 17

Sometimes you need to do something depressing to cheer yourself up. Julia had heard that somewhere but wasn't certain it was true, yet the sudden thought of visiting the Oklahoma City Bombing Memorial began to lift her spirits that were as gray as this Kansas morning. She was used to it by now, this infrequent invasion of despair, pulling the rug out from under her usual positive attitude. What the hell was she doing out here? This single woman in her forties with no family other than a daughter too busy to talk on the phone. This foolish woman, with no income, constructing novels that no one had asked for, that no one would read, that agents would shake their heads at and say, if they said anything at all, "This is about as thrilling as Velveeta."

There wasn't much to distract Julia on the nearly six-hour drive to Oklahoma City. It was all interstate driving across flat grassland down through eastern Kansas. Crossing the brown Missouri River near Atchison and later checking out the distant Wichita skyline from the interstate were the only two memorable experiences along the way. Elizabeth sat up front with Julia, but she spent most of her time staring out the window.

"Let's ramp it up a bit," Julia finally said to Elizabeth, who returned a blank look. "Have you ever been to Oklahoma City?"

Elizabeth shook her head.

"Me, neither. I'd like to see that memorial park where the bombings took place."

Julia felt her spirits rise as she steered the big boxy Minnie Winnie into the heart of downtown Oklahoma City. Yeah, maybe she couldn't write worth crap, but screw it—she could drive an RV into the unfamiliar congestion of a large city. It took some effort, but she finally found a parking lot near the memorial that would accommodate her twenty-five-foot vehicle.

As they walked the two blocks to the memorial, Elizabeth suddenly became talkative. "I've always wanted to see this place," she said, turning her head toward Julia as they walked. "An important part of modern American history."

This unexpected comment from her silent companion caught Julia's attention. "Oh, yeah?"

"Yes. McVey and Nichols were the first domestic terrorists."

Julia's mouth fell open. "They killed a lot of innocent people."

"A hundred sixty-eight, to be exact."

"How the hell would you know all that, Elizabeth?"

Elizabeth shrugged her shoulders. "It's part of our history," she said.

This Elizabeth was a mysterious creature.

The memorial was a somber place. Near the entrance, they passed a remnant wall from the original Murrah Federal Building, where informative displays told how the modern federal office building had been demolished in 1995 by two tons of explosives. Elizabeth lingered longer than Julia at each display, seemingly captivated by the information, even tracing her fingers across the lettering on one plaque. They followed a path into an expansive garden, where the rest of the office building once stood, then along a reflecting pool across an open area. Even though downtown office buildings ringed the area, an eerie stillness cloaked the garden like a thick fog. The few other visitors, like them, spoke in hushed tones. Arrayed along the reflecting pool, a hundred sixty-eight empty bronze and glass chairs represented the loss of the people who died that morning. From far away, perhaps from a neighboring church, a bagpipe played "Amazing Grace."

This place was so peaceful. Was its purpose one of sadness or a quiet proclamation, or maybe hope, that peace would ultimately prevail over the ugliness of hate? Julia couldn't ponder what happened here without her thoughts returning to the canister. Was it authentic government property or some fake novelty, like Declan had speculated? She would assume it was authentic. This tiny thing contained top-secret information— what kind of information? It was obviously stolen. By whom? What kind of hatred might have motivated its theft? Was someone searching for it? Were there terrorists, growing frantic, looking for it now? Was she, in fact, being followed? This place illustrated what happens when hate has its way. Julia looked around at the few people strolling the garden. An elderly couple, arm in arm, the woman reading aloud from a guidebook. A single woman taking photographs. Might one of them be following her? She looked at Elizabeth, who was kneeling to study the crumbled remnant of a wall. How might she be involved? She could be a good character in her new book, a villain completely unsuspected. A helpless, maybe just apparently helpless, old person. How, in fact, did she know that Elizabeth didn't have a loaded Glock stuffed inside that old coat? Oh, for crying out loud, Julia. Yet, it was strange that the quiet, disconnected Elizabeth would come alive and knowledgeable when the subject of the Oklahoma City terrorists came up. A chill washed over her.

Julia stared out across the pool. "It's hard to imagine that morning," she said to no one, not looking at Elizabeth. "Nine AM. All those people, just getting settled into work. Maybe strolling over to the break area to get a second cup of coffee. Thinking this was just another day. Maybe bored, wondering if life was ever going to change. Worried about a million things that ultimately were irrelevant. Never thinking that death was just a few minutes away." Now she looked at Elizabeth. "God, that's so depressing."

"Of course, you can't imagine it. You've probably never seen someone die suddenly." She fixed her eyes on Julia but only for a moment, before she shook her head and looked down. "Forget I said that."

Julia stared at Elizabeth. "Have you?" she said. "Have you ever seen someone die suddenly?"

Elizabeth turned and headed back toward the entrance.

Back in the Minnie Winnie, Julia tried to recapture an upbeat mood. "I'm glad we stopped. That's a very sad place, but I think it was good to see it."

Elizabeth had returned to staring out the window.

It had been a good stop for Julia, getting her focus off herself and her bleak feelings of self-pity.

How would she work this moving stop at the memorial into a story? She somehow needed to capture the solemnity, the sense of tragedy, and yet the sanctity of life. Maybe she should start over with her current manuscript, which suddenly seemed shallow and juvenile.

Why was writing so hard at times? Allegedly, Faulkner wrote *As I Lay Dying* in six weeks while working night shifts at a power plant. Maybe writing was just hard for her.

Two hours later, they pulled into a county campground, spartan and nearly empty, out in the middle of nowhere, but just off the interstate. A few taller trees dotted the campground, but it was mostly covered by thick, head-high scrub brush. Gray and ugly. Weeds grew from the gravel parking pads, and the whole place looked run down. There would be constant road noise from the highway, but once they were inside the well-insulated Minnie Winnie, that wouldn't be much of a problem. At twelve bucks for the night, the site was perfect.

The only commercial establishment within walking distance of the campground was a truck plaza—a gas station with an attached coffee shop and a sprawling gift shop—all of it beneath a tall gaudy sign advertising the Cherokee Trading Post. A huge concrete buffalo, painted in the colors of an American flag, stood out front. "It must be an important place," joked Julia, as they drove past the gift shop. They'd been seeing colorful billboards for the last hundred miles proclaiming, *See the last original wild west trading post, just 43 miles ahead. Clean restrooms.* "We've gotta go check that out once we get settled."

An hour later, they browsed the aisles at the Cherokee Trading Post, a five-minute walk from their campsite. This amazing place offered everything you didn't need or perhaps didn't think was even available. You could purchase a stuffed rattlesnake—Elizabeth leaned close to the glass case, eyes wide, while Julia instinctively took a step back. Nor were they tempted by the rattlesnake jerky. But they were drawn to the beautiful turquoise and silver jewelry glittering under the track lighting. Julia picked up a bracelet, felt its cool weight, then put it back.

There were sequined moccasins, allegedly crafted locally. Cowboy hats galore. Elizabeth grabbed a wide-brimmed one, plopped it on her head, tilted it rakishly, and laughed as she modeled it for Julia. It was the first time Julia had seen her laugh.

They passed a huge display of hunting knives and leather scabbards, then paused to run their fingers over soft buckskin jackets with tassels like the good guy in an old western might have worn. Tacky statues of Indian chiefs and maidens and warriors stood guard over the mostly empty aisles. They wandered past piles of Indian blankets made in Asia. Indian headdresses. Leather belts with ornate cowboy buckles. It wasn't clear if any of this stuff was made by a real Cherokee. Julia snapped a picture of Elizabeth standing next to a life-sized statue of an Indian brave, his brown skin as wrinkled as Elizabeth's.

It was right after she took the photo of Elizabeth that she noticed him. Maybe it was only because the place was nearly deserted or maybe because he didn't seem interested in looking at the merchandise. Had he been following them? When Julia turned toward the man, he stopped and examined some trinket. She stepped closer to Elizabeth. "You about ready to go?"

Elizabeth nodded.

On their short walk back to the campground, they heard a car alarm go off. Julia shrugged. "I hate it when people set those things off. Really ruins the wilderness ambiance, and I—" She stopped, glanced at Elizabeth, then started to run. "Oh, damn," she shouted, "it's coming from the Minnie Winnie."

By the time they made it back to the campsite, the alarm had silenced, and she realized that, most likely, the sound had come from another vehicle in the campground, even though she saw no other campers nearby. She'd never heard such an alarm go off in the Minnie Winnie—she wasn't even sure it had a burglar alarm.

Then she found the Minnie Winnie unlocked. She was certain, almost certain, that she had locked it before they'd gone to the gift shop. She pulled the door open to find Nivvie napping peacefully. She must have forgotten to lock it. Julia moved to the rear of the RV, looking over her shoulder to be certain that Elizabeth wasn't watching, and checked the hiding spot of the canister, beneath the mattress, underneath the water pump housing. The canister was still there. She ran her hand across the heavy pipe wrench next to her pillow. She hoped she'd never have to use it, but she was ready if she did.

Outside, she turned and did a slow three-sixty, surveying the campground. Quiet and empty. Suddenly an old feeling, one she hadn't had for a couple of years, back when she was a newbie at camping, shuddered through her like an ice cube dropped down her shirt. She was out here alone. Quite helpless, ultimately, against anyone who meant her harm.

The image of the guy at the trading post flashed in her mind. She turned to Elizabeth, who was standing by the picnic bench, gazing into space. "Did you see that odd guy in the store?"

Elizabeth shook her head.

"Well, hell, Elizabeth, I say let's not worry about that anymore. Okay? Nivvie here is ready for supper, and so am I."

"Are we going to have a fire?" Elizabeth asked. Apparently, she was starting to like the camping life.

"I didn't see any wood for sale; no campground host. But I still have some pieces left over from last night. So, we're in luck."

Dinner conversation was stiff. Elizabeth either stayed silent or offered meaningless blather, like, "It's nice to be in warmer weather." At least she was making a little effort.

After dinner, they lounged around the fire, while Nivvie curled at Julia's feet, close enough that she could rub his head.

"Tomorrow, we'll make it to New Mexico. I've never been there. Have you?"

"No."

It was what Julia expected from her. Elizabeth had never even asked Julia where she was heading.

Julia had just laid another log on the fire, when a car pulled into their campsite, spraying gravel as it came to a screeching stop, its headlights bright and blinding.

Chapter 18

Julia and Elizabeth jumped to their feet. Declan didn't mean to startle them, but his sense of urgency had not subsided since he left the Walmart parking lot many hours ago.

"We need to talk," Declan said, as he jumped out of the car, not wasting any time.

"What are you doing here?" Julia's voice shook.

"We need to talk. Now."

As Declan stepped toward her, Julia backed away, clearly alarmed. "I said what are you doing here. I thought you were headed east." Her voice was raised, and she had her hands up as stop signs. "And how did you find me?" She looked around like she might need an escape route from this stranger. "Were you following me?"

Elizabeth stood by the table, watching.

Declan took a deep breath. Of course, Julia would be startled. She didn't really know him, and here he comes storming in out of nowhere, unexpected and uninvited. He did his best to sound calm. "I found something." He glanced warily at Elizabeth. "You need to know about this, be—"

"—Look, this is creepy." She backed up another step. "If you've got something to tell me, why didn't you just call me?"

"I tried, but you didn't answer." He had tried her phone several times but got no answer. But then he decided that she'd just blow him off anyway. She seemed sold on this Elizabeth, had invited her to travel with her for several more days. He'd considered calling the police. But what would he tell them? That he'd seen a pharmacy bag? And if he reported that Julia had the missing canister, that could land her in a lot of trouble. No, he couldn't do that. He needed to tell her in person. If something bad happened to her because he hadn't cautioned her, that would be yet one more badge of shame for him.

Julia pulled her phone from her pocket. She shook her head. "Okay, so there's no signal out here." She seemed to calm a bit. "So how did you find me?"

Yes, she needed to know he wasn't some creepy stalker. He took a step backward to give her more personal space. "It wasn't that hard." Well, it hadn't been that easy, either. When Declan had been unable to reach Julia's cell, he remembered that campground app she'd talked about. She'd said she was heading for Oklahoma. He knew she'd be looking for something cheap, and he knew it would be on the route to Fort Huachuca. There were only a few campgrounds that fit this description—he'd already been to two others tonight. The hard part was the long drive. He was staying afloat on adrenalin. When he finished his explanation, he said, "Can you and I take a little walk? I need to talk with you alone. This'll just take a minute."

Julia, with hands on hips, looked down like she was considering if this was safe. Then she glanced at Elizabeth. "We're just gonna take Nivvie for his bedtime walk, Elizabeth. Be right back. You just stay here by the fire." She grabbed David Niven's leash, then approached Declan. "This had better be good."

They strolled down the gravel campground road in total darkness, past a neighboring empty campsite, Julia keeping David Niven between them. Declan stopped and faced her. "I think you may be in danger."

Julia stood with her arms crossed, like she wasn't in the mood for any crap. "Seriously? The only scary thing I see is you storming in here, all panicked. I—"

"—Just listen to me," he interrupted. "When Elizabeth spilled the stuff out of her pockets this morning, one of the things that fell out was a plastic bag from a pharmacy, like the kind medicines come in."

She shifted her weight from one foot to the other. "So?"

"This one was from a place called Sierra Vista Pharmacy."

"Sierra Vista Pharmacy? What's this got to—" Julia stopped mid-sentence. "That's the town at Fort Huachuca."

"Yep."

Julia took a step back and rubbed her chin between her thumb and forefinger, like she was trying to unravel this mess. "So, she knows about the canister. Shit. You think she stole it?"

Declan had been thinking about this all afternoon. "Hard to believe. But she could have been delivering it. I mean who'd suspected a down-and-out old woman?"

"That makes more sense. She drops it in your fire ring for someone else to pick up, then—"

"—Maybe, but that would risk someone else finding it, which of course, you did. Also, if she was dropping it for someone else, why would she hang around in the back seat of my car? I mean, I've had some time to think through these scenarios."

"Yeah, that doesn't quite fit together. Hey, I have a brilliant idea. Let's go ask her."

"No." He paused. "Not yet. It's clear she's involved. She doesn't yet know we're on to her. We need to be cautious, maybe—"

Even in the darkness, Declan could see the growing impatience in Julia's face.

"Come on, Declan. You make this dramatic appearance, want to talk to me alone, you think she doesn't suspect something's up? I'm gonna confront her now."

"No, you can't just—"

"Yes, I can, and you can come with me or not." Then she softened. "Look, you just drove a long way to warn me. I appreciate that. But I still think we should confront her now. Tell her what we know. Demand the truth."

Declan nodded slowly. "Maybe, but I say we call the cops."

"Declan, she's just a pathetic old woman. She knows something about the canister, yes. Maybe she had it. Maybe it was in that pharmacy bag. I want to find out."

"What I'm saying is, we're getting in over our heads here."

Julia rubbed her chin again. "There was something kind of odd today. We stopped at that bombing memorial in Oklahoma City. It was weird how much Elizabeth knew about it; how much she apparently knows about terrorism. Maybe she is more than some helpless homeless person, that's true. But, still, I don't think …"

"She could be dangerous, Julia."

Julia threw her hands into the air. "Come on, Declan, I'm going to talk with her. Now. And you can join me or not." With that she started back toward the campsite. Declan followed her, unsure of any other option he had.

They'd only made it halfway back when a bright flash, illuminating the sky above the scrub brush, stopped them in their tracks. They exchanged panicked glances, then broke into a sprint to the campsite, but they didn't get far before the heat stopped them. Declan's Corolla was in flames, and Elizabeth was nowhere in sight.

Chapter 19

Julia gasped for air. Even well back from the inferno, the heat singed her face. She couldn't move her eyes from the ghostly silhouette of Declan's car in the white-hot flames, as Declan's hand gripped her shoulder, maybe to restrain her, maybe to steady her, as a million urgent questions exploded in her mind. Nivvie pulled hard on his leash away from the fire, maybe trying to rescue Julia from the danger.

Where's Elizabeth? Did she do this, then run away? She'd figured out that we were on to her, so she—no that's just not right. Dear God, could she have been in the car? Or maybe she'd sought refuge in the RV. "I'm gonna check out the RV," she said to Declan, as she made a wide circle around the fire to the Minnie Winnie. "Maybe Elizabeth's in there."

Declan nodded but said nothing, his eyes still locked onto his incinerating car.

Still on the entry step, Julia poked her head in through the door and stopped. The place had been trashed. Her heart in her throat, she surveyed the ransacked interior. Papers and clothing strewn everywhere, books pulled off the shelves. Her laptop lay in a corner, screen open, perched upside down like an A-frame. A stab of terror mixed with rage filled her like a slurp of molten metal. Could the intruder still be inside? Shaking, she backed down off the entry step and took a deep breath. "Declan!" she cried out. "They've been in the RV."

Declan was quickly at her side. "Don't go in," he barked. "Someone may still be in there."

"Elizabeth! Are you in there?" Julia cried out. Silence. Now there were sirens in the distance, growing louder. In moments, a fire engine with whirling red lights roared into the campsite. Two people in protective gear quickly uncoiled a heavy hose from the truck, and water gushed onto the flames, as flood lights illuminated the site. One fireman hurried toward them. "Is there anyone inside?"

"I … I'm not sure," said Julia.

Within a minute, the fire was extinguished, leaving a black, smoldering mess. One of the firemen turned to Julia. "There's no one inside."

A police cruiser pulled in, and two people climbed out. The noise of radio traffic from the emergency vehicles and their disorienting flashing red lights now filled the site. All Julia could do was watch, shaking. Nivvie pressed close to her.

The cops, one tall and lanky, the other short, moved toward them, visible only in silhouette from the blinding lights. One cop already had a notebook open, as he said, "Good evening, folks. Officer Wade Purkle. Is anybody hurt?"

"No," said Julia.

"This is Reverend Pam. She's a police chaplain. Sometimes rides with us when there might be people needing extra support. Mind telling me what happened?"

Julia spoke up, her voice shaking. "Not sure. Uh, this is Declan Lewis, I'm Julia Evans. We just took the dog for a short walk, then we saw a flash. We ran back, and the car was in flames. We have no idea what happened."

Officer Purkle and Reverend Pam circled around to the other side of the steaming carcass of the Corolla, and Julia could now see their faces in the bright light. They both wore yellow, high-visibility police jackets crisscrossed with strips of silver reflective tape. Purkle was a young, pale-faced guy with a faint mustache that looked like it'd been a struggle to grow. Reverend Pam was darker skinned, with black hair pulled tight behind her head. Young, probably early thirties. She wore a white clergy collar.

"So, either the car caught fire accidentally, which the evidence seems to indicate," said the cop.

What evidence? wondered Julia.

"Or someone started the fire. I lean toward the accident explanation. What model was this thing?" He looked from face to face.

"Ninety-two Corolla," said Declan. "It was my car."

"Ninety-two? Hell, that baby was older than me. Those old cars have all kinds of wiring problems, maybe a leaky gas tank. And folks, I see your campfire is still going. You left that while you went on your walk? You know I could cite you for that. In fact, your negligence may have caused damage to public property. I could book you both on that."

What public property? thought Julia. A patch of weeds?

"Anyway," Purkle continued, "it doesn't take a genius to conclude that maybe a spark from the fire, combined with a leaky gas tank, and poof. There you go." He looked from face to face, like this should be obvious.

Julia grimaced. It was a good thing that this conclusion didn't take a genius, so maybe this guy was qualified. Hell, the campfire was clearly a safe distance from the car. She said nothing.

A small crowd of gawkers had gathered, a line of silhouettes just beyond the lights—probably the few other campers in the campground. No doubt one of them had reported the fire. Were the people who had started it among them?

Now Purkle asked, "But just to do due diligence, do you have any reason to think someone might have started this fire?"

Julia shook her head, but Declan spoke up. "Actually, maybe," he said. He glanced at Julia, as if acknowledging that what he was about to say would piss her off but then plowed ahead. "A couple days ago, up in Wisconsin, we found a small metal canister with a flash drive inside. It was from an Army base, marked top secret. We were on our way down to Arizona to return it. It's possible someone followed us. Also, you should know that someone vandalized the RV while we were on our walk. We haven't really been inside—weren't sure that someone might still be in there."

Now, Officer Purkle looked down, rubbed his chin with the back of his hand and was quiet for a moment. Then, with his hand resting on the handle of his gun, he walked over to the RV, Reverend Pam following behind. He was in there just a few seconds. When he stepped back out, Julia gave a soft sigh of relief. She didn't like strangers poking around inside her home. "Nobody inside," he said. "So, they just messed things up, didn't do any physical damage. Do you still have this top-secret thing? I'd like to see it."

Julia shot Declan daggers, then retreated to the RV. Softening her anger at Declan was the relief that the canister was still there in its hiding place. In a moment, she returned and handed it to Purkle.

He held the canister up inches from his face and illuminated it with his flashlight. "Where'd you say you got this?"

"We found it in a campground in Wisconsin," said Declan.

"A campground? Seriously, folks, that's not a likely place to be looking for top-secret things." Purkle removed the cap and pulled out the flash drive. "And what's on this?" he asked.

"Don't know. We couldn't open it," said Declan.

"With all due respect, I can buy crap like this over at that tourist trap next door," he said, nodding in the direction of the Cherokee Trading Post.

Reverend Pam spoke for the first time. "Mind if I take a look?" Purkle held his flashlight up while she studied the canister. "What does **USANETC** mean?" she asked.

"**US** Army Network Enterprise Technology Command," said Julia. "The internet says it's responsible for cyberspace security."

Reverend Pam looked up at Purkle. "I've gotta say, Wade, this thing looks pretty authentic to me."

Purkle took the canister back from her. "Well, that's why you do the churchy stuff, and I take care of the forensic things." He illuminated the canister again with his flashlight. "It probably says *Made in China* on it somewhere." He pulled a plastic baggie from his pocket and placed the canister in it. "Anyway, I'll hold onto this as evidence, just in case."

Julia bristled. "Sorry, officer. I didn't say you could take that." She extended a hand toward the officer, wiggling her fingers in a gimme gesture.

"You can put in a claim down at the station, but I better hold onto this for now. Anyway, don't worry, lady, we'll get to the bottom of this. Right now, we've got bigger problems. Like getting what's left of your vehicle hauled away." As if on cue, a wrecker pulled into the campsite.

Julia was ready to explode, but she knew that would be useless. She knew what would happen to the canister. Good ol'

Wade would pass it around to his buddies back at the station, and they'd get a good laugh. Then he'd toss it in a corner.

"We'll get this mess over to a junk yard. You'll need to show proof of insurance or make a deposit or something to the wrecker guy. They ain't gonna let you just walk away from this without some collateral. Let's get your contact info, folks." Julia and Declan showed the cop and the tow-truck guy their driver's licenses, neither mentioning that the addresses were no longer valid. These dudes didn't need to know that neither of them had addresses.

"And insurance and registration, I'm guessing, were in the car?"

"That's right," said Declan.

"The junk yard guys will sort that out with you. As far as your RV getting trashed out, I won't lie, okay, we got some vandalism around here, and we're workin' on rounding these jerks up. But they're just local punks—I doubt we've got any KCB agents sneaking around here."

Julia suspected he meant *KGB*.

The officer did a perfunctory three-sixty, like he was reassessing the situation. "Nope, I sure don't see any spies lurking in the bushes." He gave an insincere laugh, then turned grim. "A more serious problem is the fire on public property caused by your negligence. That's a serious crime, folks. You should have known that. Maybe a felony. I'm still trying to decide if I should go easy and just cite you, which would probably carry a hefty fine"—he smacked his lips like he was weighing a decision—"or haul you both in. I'm leaning toward the latter, gotta say."

Reverend Pam spoke up. "What I see here, Wade, are two campers, out trying to enjoy one of our beautiful parks, and they've had a terrible thing happen to them, and they're shaken up, scared, uncertain. They're looking for help, not condemnation, needing a helping hand, not an iron fist. If we're public servants, Wade, then this is a chance to serve. I know I've overstepped my authority here, but I hope you'll consider what I say."

Julia was surprised that Reverend Pam would confront the deputy so boldly in their presence.

Wade, clearly flustered, snapped back. "That's right, you have overstepped." He shot Julia and Declan a nervous glance. "You're just a volunteer here, not the professional. You know one word from me and your days as a chaplain will be over."

"I know that, Wade, but I'd hope you'd be interested in listening to what other concerned people think."

Wade grunted, then looked down at his notebook. Finally, he said, trying to reclaim some control, "So this is a county campground. We'll notify the bureaucrats about this, give them your contact info. I'm sure they'll need to assess any possible damage to county property." Then he put the notebook away. Julia hadn't seen him write anything in it. "Looks like we've got this about wrapped up. Anything else you need to tell me?"

Declan, seemingly determined to royally screw things up even more, blurted, "There was another person traveling with us, an old—"

Julia cut him off. "Yes, but we dropped her off in Oklahoma City, just some hitchhiker."

Declan started to say more but stayed quiet.

"Officer Purkle," Julia said, leaning in toward the cop to project confidence, "I expect you to take that canister to the FBI. It's clearly a federal matter."

"You can count on us to do what needs to be done, ma'am."

"Sure," said Julia. She shot Declan another menacing glare, then glanced at Reverend Pam, who shrugged. "So, we're free to leave?"

Purkle seemed to ponder this. "I don't see why not. It's only because you've been through a lot that I'm not going to ticket you for not tending your campfire." He shot Pam a hope-your-happy-now glance.

Purkle started for the car, when Reverend Pam said, "Might I get a moment?" She came close to Julia and Declan, then leaned down and rubbed Nivvie's head, who Julia still had on leash. "This must have been pretty traumatic for him. Redbone Hound?"

"Yes," said Julia.

"How you doin,' sweet pup?" Pam said to Nivvie in a coochy-coo voice. She straightened but kept one hand stroking Nivvie's head. "That was a pretty crazy thing you just went through. You guys doing okay?" Reverend Pam's intense brown eyes seemed to search them.

"I think we're okay," said Julia, "but thank you." Declan said nothing.

"Would you like me to stay for a while?"

Wade hollered from the car, "Come on chaplain, we don't have all night."

Pam ignored him. "Watch out for your safety, okay? I know it's getting late, but I wouldn't stay here tonight. And keep that thing"—she nodded toward the RV—"locked." She was quiet for a moment, then said, "If you can't find another place to camp at this late hour, you can park over at my place for the night. It's not far from here." Pam pulled out a business card, wrote something on the back, then handed it to Julia. "If you need anything, call me."

Julia glanced at the card, then stuffed it in a pocket. She nodded at Pam.

"I'll mention you in my prayers tonight," said Pam. Then she turned and left. Within minutes the fire truck had also pulled out. The tow-truck driver talked with Declan, made a few notes, took several pictures with his phone, and told them he'd be back tomorrow when things had dried out a bit. Then he also left. Now they were alone.

Julia turned toward Declan, the fire in her belly matching the one that had engulfed Declan's Corolla. "So, thanks, Declan, for blabbing everything to the cops, without running it by me first. You think I have no say in this?"

Declan matched her glare. "What I did was the right thing. You didn't just have somebody torch *your* car. I've had enough of this 'oh-let's-be-detectives' crap. FYI, we've gotten ourselves ass-deep in danger. Surely, you grasp that."

"Let's just find Elizabeth. Okay?"

"It's not okay." He was pissed. "Think about it, Julia. I showed up, needed to talk to you alone. She figured out that I had implicated her, and she had to make her move. Isn't that obvious? She knew the jig was up, so, while we were gone, she desperately went through the RV looking for the canister. She couldn't find it, so she left in a rage. But first, as a parting shot to the guy who outed her, she set my car on fire."

"I don't think so. I have a sense about her. I don't think she'd do that. And look, Declan, how would she go about setting your car on fire anyway?"

"Easy. A twig ignited in the campfire and pushed into my gas tank. It would take her a second."

Julia considered this. "I just don't think she did it."

Declan ignored her. "Then she fled. Maybe she'll reappear later with help to take the canister by force, but we cut off that possibility by turning it over to the cops. It was the right thing to do. I just wish you'd have told the truth to the cops about her."

Everything Declan said made sense. But she trusted her intuition. And her intuition said Elizabeth was innocent. She took a different approach. "Look, Declan, I'm sorry about your car."

Declan gave her a helpless look. "What do I do now? I haven't got anything left."

Julia had had about enough of Declan for now. "Here's what you can do. You can help me straighten up the RV. And then we've got to find Elizabeth. Whether she did this or not, we need to find her. If someone else did this, and they've hurt her, we need to help her." She turned with Nivvie toward the Minnie Winnie, then looked back. "And don't say you have nothing left. You've still got your three-hundred-dollar Patagonia."

He followed her. At the door of the Minnie Winnie, she turned and faced him, preparing another zinger. She leaned in, hands on hips, an aggressive stance. She felt the heat in her face. Declan wasn't backing down. He leaned in, too, their faces now just inches apart.

"Now what, Inspector Know-it-All?" she hissed.

Then he kissed her. Julia flinched and pulled back, but not far.

She couldn't breathe. Their faces were still close. "That was my first kiss in three years," she said, softly and tentatively, surprised by her words and then immediately regretting them. It felt like a confession.

He put his arms around her and pulled her to him. "Well, here's your second." Her arms came up around him, her hands locked behind his neck.

It probably lasted only a second, but it seemed like forever. When they finally pulled away, Declan backed up a step and looked down. "Good God, I'm so sorry."

"Will you just shut up?" She was still breathing hard. Then she smiled. "So, I guess a good car fire gets the juices flowing, eh?"

"I mean, please just forget that happened."

"Like hell," she said, then laughed.

Chapter 20

Sometimes all you're capable of following a traumatic event is to apply yourself to a menial task. In those first days after Emily's death, it was the myriad mindless but necessary details that saved Declan from a complete collapse. Notifying friends and family, dealing with Social Security and credit card companies, handling the paperwork from the hospital, arranging for a funeral service. Things that would normally be a pain in the ass were now a crutch to get him through to the next day.

And so, helping Julia straighten up her trashed-out RV was about all he could handle for the moment. It was something simple to focus on, a diversion from facing the implications of everything they'd just been through. One good thing about a small RV: even when it's trashed out, it doesn't take that long to restore order.

Before setting about the straightening-up task, they'd searched for Elizabeth around the campground, but that hadn't taken long. Probing the darkness with flashlights and calling out her name had yielded nothing. She was gone.

Now, as Declan piled pulled-down bedding back onto the over-the-cab bunk, Julia said, "Okay, I say that's good enough. Let's go find Elizabeth. I don't want to hang around here one minute longer than necessary. They're probably watching us right now."

They hadn't spoken since they'd kissed. Lord, how had that happened? It had been raw instinct, no real thought involved.

One moment he was annoyed as hell at her, the next moment the only thing on his screen was this good-looking woman inches away from him, and he couldn't resist her. Such impulsiveness was uncharacteristic. Maybe it was the car fire. Maybe it signified the final stripping away of an old life, the beginning of something new.

There was no question that Julia was attractive. He'd noticed that the first time he saw her at the campground. Those bright green eyes—interrogating, questioning, exploring. She was so energetic, so alive, like she was ready to charge off on a long trek into the wilderness. And that keen, stinging wit of hers. Face it, Declan, she's a formidable presence. No dozing off when she's around.

But given Julia's toxic mood before the kisses and their awkwardness afterwards, Declan wasn't eager to initiate a chat. If he had a car, this might be a good time to take off and head somewhere far away from here. Yet, he turned toward her. "I still say you should've told the cops the truth about her."

Julia faced him, arms crossed. "Elizabeth's got enough problems—she doesn't need Officer Purkle hunting for her. They probably still burn witches around these parts."

"I'm sticking to my theory that she started the fire, then split when she couldn't find the canister. Or maybe she called in her partners when we left, then left with them. Seems a little too fishy that—"

"Then answer me this, Sherlock: why would Elizabeth have left the canister in the fire pit in the first place? Why wouldn't she just hang onto it and pass it off to her partners?"

"Maybe she didn't. Maybe she was there looking for it."

"That's bullshit." Her voice was raised now. "Like you said earlier, if that's true, she wouldn't have stayed in your car, where you'd find her."

Declan couldn't find an answer.

Julia continued. "I say someone else ransacked the RV and probably your car, too, and when they couldn't find the canister, they torched the car, maybe as a warning to us. Or more likely, because they were frustrated and just lashed out. Maybe they did kidnap Elizabeth, but I think it's more likely she ran off when she saw them approaching. Like you saw at your campsite, she's a good runner."

Declan considered this. "If that's true, then they were obviously nearby, watching and waiting for you and me to leave. Or maybe they followed me to the campground." He stopped and rubbed his chin. "But I'm pretty sure I'd have seen them behind me coming into the campground. You've been here all afternoon. Did you see anyone suspicious lurking around?"

Julia looked like she was deep in thought. "You know, there was a strange guy over at the trading post. He could have been following us. I wasn't sure. I don't think he bought anything. But I didn't see him again after we left."

"What did he look like?"

"Ordinary looking guy. Young … skinny … white guy."

"Nothing distinctive, huh?"

She rubbed a knuckle against her forehead. "Not really. Oh wait, he had a sweatshirt. Said 'UCLA' I think."

Declan put a hand against the wall of the RV to steady himself. "Did he have a shaved head?"

Julia's eyes widened but she said nothing.

Then Declan told her about the man at Perkins yesterday.

"So, they've been following us all along," Julia said.

Declan nodded. "Anyway, I think we're done with this little saga. Elizabeth is gone. Maybe we should just let her be. She wanted to get to a warmer place—you did that for her. She seems to know how to take care of herself. And we no longer have the canister. Better yet, it's likely our shaved-head buddy saw you hand it over. Personally, I'm relieved."

"Yeah, me, too. I made a big show of handing over the canister to the cop. Hopefully, those jerks think the cops now have the flash drive."

Declan felt like he'd been kicked in the gut. "What do you mean 'hopefully'?"

Julia smiled devilishly. She pulled the small flash drive from her pocket and held it up. "Surely, you don't think I'd give that cop the real flash drive, do you?"

Declan felt the blood drain from his face.

"And I took a pic of the canister, just in case we need to show it to somebody at Fort Huachuca. Now, let's go find Elizabeth." There was a lilt in Julia's voice, like she was in her element, whatever that was. "I know you've got to figure out what you're going to do," she said. "But right now, let's get the hell out of here."

Getting the hell out of there was one thing Declan could agree on. It felt weird climbing into the captain's chair of Julia's RV and pulling out, leaving everything he owned—which was now a worthless black pile of crap—behind.

"Let's drive around the area a bit," she said, "see if we can find some trace of Elizabeth, then head on down the road, I say to a roadside rest, where we can see any suspicious vehicles that might be tailing us. Then we can figure out the next steps."

Declan was already figuring out his next steps. "You're the driver," he shrugged. As soon as he got to the next town, he'd catch a Greyhound—at least he still had his wallet—maybe to LA to see Conor and maybe his parents. Not much of a plan, for sure, but it was enough for now. Julia drove slowly out of the campground, hunched forward, straining to see beyond the headlight beams, while Declan gazed blankly into the still night.

As they passed the Cherokee Trading Post, Declan detected motion from the periphery of his vision, at the rear edge of the building. "Over there!" he said. He pushed his glasses tight against his forehead and squinted. "I saw something."

Chapter 21

Dad loved the new place. The upscale continuing care facility was Albuquerque's finest, and it had cost Alana big bucks, but it was a huge upgrade from that county-funded dump. Clean and bright, with a view out toward the gardens, and assistance just the push of a button away. Family photos filled the wall, mostly of her and him together through all the chapters of their lives. It felt like home.

Dad deserved this. He hadn't been the best dad, but he was the only family she had, after mom left when she was ten. He had largely ignored her, never gave her much praise, even when she excelled in high school. A school counselor had said she could get into any Ivy League school, but she never applied, choosing to stay nearby at the state college. Maybe that was because she was risk averse or maybe because dad, an often-unemployed pipefitter, saw little value in higher education. But her grades in math were so high in college that she was able to snag an entry level computer tech job at the Pentagon. Thirty years there, slowly moving up, the last twenty in document security. Alana stood up straighter. She was the best, despite how the idiots like that fool, Dr. Walsh, had fawned over the sexy smiles of the Regina Ketchums of the world.

She turned again to take in the room. Her new project had made this all possible.

She laughed out loud, as she recalled one of her first security training sessions, when she was just starting her new job. The trainer had asked the class a question to demonstrate the importance of personal vigilance: "What's at the center of

SECURITY?" The funny answer was: "U-R." Alana smiled, as she reframed the question: "What's at the center of *DISASTER?"* Out loud she said, "A-S!" Alana Selkirk.

Now she had a new profession, and she would excel here, too, despite the current temporary setback. And steps were being taken to fix that.

She'd been handpicked for this assignment because she knew what few people knew. Fort Huachuca was a piece of cake. She'd never been there, and she couldn't risk going anywhere near it, because Tucker worried that the FBI was still watching her. He was no doubt right—she'd been fired from a top-secret job and escorted out of her workplace by armed guards. But it didn't matter. Whatever security protocols were in place, whatever elaborate systems they employed, Alana was likely familiar with them. That's why she was running this new project, not her zealous subordinates.

She had just turned her attention to the photos on the mantle of the fake fireplace when her phone beeped. She'd been waiting for the call. Good news, she hoped—the parcel had been retrieved. She walked to the corner of the room so her dad wouldn't hear.

"You went through the RV. Did you get it?" She shook her head then made some notes. "And the old woman?" She shook her head again, then started to scream an obscenity, but caught her dad watching her. But it didn't matter now. She exploded. "You freaking idiots. I didn't authorize you to set a fire." She turned toward the wall, as the man on the other end was screaming, too. This was out of control.

She listened for a moment, nodding.

"Oh yes, we will act, but our timing will have to be perfect—no thanks to your screw-ups: first, allowing the package to be taken from right under your noses, and now drawing the cops in with your stupid violence. It's compromised our whole—" She paused. "What do you mean there's one more thing?"

Alana paced as she listened, then stopped and looked at her dad. She felt her knees wobble and had to grab hold of the bookcase. "The cops have it?" She felt faint. "Are you sure?" She waited as the man spoke. She struggled to breathe.

While she felt the panic expanding in her chest, she said, "Don't do anything. I'll call you back in a few minutes." But she had no idea what she was going to tell them. She knew one thing. She needed to get to where the team was, so she could run the operation directly.

But it was over. Her lunatic colleagues had brought her down—God, she would have never selected these amateurs; this was Tucker's doing.

Tucker had set up her team. Dedicated, yes. But they were hotheads, fed by radical online propaganda. Podcasts—hell, she'd never even listened to a podcast. Good God, what was Tucker going to say about this? Her job was to deliver the parcel to Milwaukee. She'd done that. Others, presumably also organized by Mr. Tucker, would take it from there—she didn't know the details. She had not been told anything about the parcel. Classified data, yes, and that's where her expertise was needed. She didn't know where it would go after the drop-off, or who the ultimate customer was. She didn't want to know, either—if she knew, she would be more of a threat to Mr. Tucker than she already was. But she didn't even know Tucker's first name, where he lived, or who he worked for. That was for his safety as well as hers. If the project blew up—as it now had—then the trail would end with her.

Was it time to call Tucker? She had to rest a hand against the wall, as she imagined Mr. Tucker responding in that calm, gentle voice. She had a number to call if there was a crisis, but he'd said to use it only in a dire emergency.

Alana began to shake. Nothing added up. Why would these people voluntarily give the parcel to the cops? And who were they? She knew so little. But this much was clear: the hyper-competent Alana Selkirk was screwed.

She couldn't bring herself to call Tucker yet. He would quickly eradicate all evidence that might link the parcel to him and whoever he worked for. And that would mean eradicating her.

She paced along the bookcase. But was it really over? The cops have the parcel? Why did this not feel right?

She stopped at a photo from long ago. She was twelve. She was with her dad. They were climbing out of the boat from that fishing trip at Elephant Butte. She held up the big largemouth, glowing, and her dad had a hand laid on her shoulder. He was beaming.

"Come here," her dad called out, seeing her tears. She dropped down next to him in the over-sized chair, and he held her. "You know I worry about you, Hon."

"I know, Dad. I'll be okay."

As his arms enfolded her, he said, "You've been hurt, and I hate that. I don't want anyone to hurt you." Then he said, "I feel so helpless here."

Her tears flowed. "I know, Dad."

Chapter 22

Julia cut sharply into the parking lot and pointed the Minnie Winnie into an alley, along the side of the building. "Back here? I don't see anything."

"Just around the corner." Declan leaned forward, craning to see.

As Julia steered the RV toward a narrow space behind the building, the kind of place where garbage cans are kept, Declan spoke up. "Don't go back in there. It could be a trap. We need to leave ourselves an escape route."

"Agreed," said Julia, as she backed into a space in the parking lot where her high beams could illuminate the space behind the building. There in the headlights, Elizabeth crouched in front of a large dumpster, shielding her eyes from the headlights.

Julia left the lights on, as she pushed her door open, preparing to jump out. She felt Declan's hand on her arm. "Wait," he said. "Let's be sure she's alone."

Declan was right. Julia nodded, as she pulled the door closed again, then checked her mirrors. Nothing behind them. She lowered her window and called out, "Elizabeth, are you okay?"

Elizabeth stood and slowly came toward them, still shielding her eyes. Julia whispered to Declan. "No talk about the canister, okay? I'm guessing she doesn't know we have it."

Declan nodded.

Elizabeth approached Julia's window, visibly trembling. "They were here," she said.

"Who was here?" Julia asked.

"The men from Milwaukee. They've followed me."

"Are they still here?"

Elizabeth looked around. "I don't think so."

"You okay now, Elizabeth?"

Elizabeth gave a weak nod.

Julia glanced at Declan, who shrugged, then said, "Okay, I just unlocked the side door. Get in."

When Elizabeth was in the RV and seated at the dinette table, Julia said, "Buckle up. We can't stop here. But we've got some talking to do." Moments later they were on the interstate, headed west.

A few miles down the highway, Julia took the offramp into a rest stop. Declan and Julia scanned the parking area for anything suspicious, then climbed back into the living area and took seats at the dinette, both facing Elizabeth, who was still trembling.

"Okay, Elizabeth," Julia said, "time for the whole story, the true story. We know you are involved with what happened this evening and much more. We want the truth. We want it now, or we will deliver you immediately to the cops. Got it?"

Elizabeth shook her head, like she was trying to rid herself of a terrifying thought. "I didn't have anything to do with it." She looked down.

"That won't cut it, Elizabeth," said Declan.

He looked tired. God, he'd been through a lot today. For a second, the image of him holding her in his arms flashed in her mind, and she caught her breath, but she pushed the thought away.

"Start with telling us why you were in the campground in Wisconsin," Declan said. "Your evasive bullshit won't work any longer. Got it, Elizabeth?"

Julia worked to suppress a smile. Declan was trying to project a tough-guy image, and it wasn't all that convincing.

There was a long period of silence, then Elizabeth began to talk. "Look, I've done nothing wrong." She looked down again, then began to cry. Julia and Declan waited her out. Eventually, she looked up. "I'm so sorry. I'm sorry about your car … Declan." It was the first time she'd said his name.

"Can I have something to drink?" Elizabeth asked.

Julia pulled a plastic jug of iced tea from the fridge and got three glasses from a cabinet. Elizabeth emptied her glass and asked for more. She took a few sips, then set the glass down and folded her hands, like she was preparing to make an important statement. "I often sleep in the back of unlocked cars. I was near Milwaukee, in some town, I don't know which one, but it was a Doubletree parking lot. Hotel parking lots are good places to find unlocked cars. I guess people with rental cars don't care if someone snoops around inside, I don't know. Anyway, I got into the back seat of a car and tried to go to sleep." Then she went silent again.

"Come on," Julia said. "If you really haven't done anything wrong, your best bet is to tell us everything."

Now there was fear in her eyes. "So, I was in this car. I confess, I looked around inside, thinking maybe there's food, a coat or something I could use. I'm really not a—"

"That doesn't matter," Declan interrupted. "We just need to hear what happened." He leaned back, looking skeptical, like a tough interrogator he'd probably seen in a cop show.

"There was nothing in the car, so I stretched out to sleep. But my elbow rubbed against something hard. It was wedged in between the seatbacks. It was a plastic bag, with some kind of pill bottle inside. I didn't have time to look it over carefully, because I saw men coming toward the car, so I just stuffed it into my jacket and fled out the door opposite from where the men were coming. I've done that a hundred times—they never catch me; usually they just shout at me, but don't chase me. But these guys came after me. I'm a really fast runner. I know I'm old, but I've had lots of experience running. But these guys were fast, too." She looked from face to face. "God, I wish I'd left that bag in the car."

"What time was this?" Julia asked.

"I don't know. It was still light. I usually wait until dark, but it was so cold. Anyway, I was scared. I ran for blocks, afraid to look back. Finally, I came to a gas station, and there was an RV there, like I told you before. It was getting ready to leave. I tried the door on the back, and it was unlocked, so I climbed in, just as it pulled out."

"Did the men chasing you see you get in the RV?" Declan asked.

"They must have. They followed me here."

"What did the men look like, Elizabeth?" Julia asked.

"I don't remember. Just men."

"Then what happened?" Julia said.

"We drove a long way. While I was in the back—no one else was in there—I looked at the pill bottle. It was some top-secret thing from the Army. I panicked. I didn't know what to do. I wanted to get rid of it. I was scared." There was a re-lived terror in Elizabeth's eyes, as she recounted this. Elizabeth's hands started shaking, and she put them down into her lap.

Declan asked, "Was there anything else in the bag with the pill bottle? Like a receipt, anything?"

"I don't think so." She pulled the pharmacy bag from her jacket pocket and handed it to Declan.

Declan studied the bag, looked inside. "Nothing," he said. He handed it to Julia.

She studied it. *Sierra Vista Pharmacy*, just as Declan had said. She wondered what a pharmacy might have to do with the theft of secret information. "Then what happened?"

"After a long time, the RV stopped, and the driver got out. I heard him cursing. I climbed out the back of the RV, planning to sneak away, but he saw me and started screaming at me. There were woods all around. I ran into the trees."

It was now coming together for Julia. "I'm guessing the driver was cursing when he saw the sign that said the campground was closing the next day. Do you think anyone else saw you, Elizabeth?"

Elizabeth shook her head. "I didn't think so, but now I'm not so sure."

"So, then you wound up at my campsite," said Declan. When Elizabeth nodded, he said, "What did you do then?"

"First thing I did was throw the pill bottle away. Into a campfire pit. I suspect it's still there. I knew it was important, so I didn't just toss it into the woods. Figured someone would find it and turn it in. But I was freezing, so I got into your car. I knew it was risky, because your tent was right there, and I knew you might catch me, but I was so cold."

Elizabeth's story had the ring of truth. And it was clear to Julia that she didn't suspect the flash drive was just across the table in her pocket. "So, Elizabeth," Julia said, "you said the men tonight were the men from Milwaukee. How do you know that?"

"Because of the car."

"I thought you said you didn't know the model of the car." Julia said.

"I didn't. I do know it was black."

"There are lots of black cars," said Declan, sounding annoyed.

"But this one had a rack, one of those plastic boxes that go on the roof."

"Like a Yakima rack?" Declan said.

"Is that what you call it?"

"Even so, there are a lot of cars with those kinds of racks," said Declan.

"This one had a big decal on it, right above the door I got into."

"What did it say?"

"I didn't notice. But it was white and big, shaped like an oval."

Julia turned to Declan. "Sounds like the national park stickers that tourists put on their cars. They're all over the place out west, so maybe this car came from out west. And that rack says it wasn't a rental car."

"But it was unlocked. I didn't break in."

Julia leaned forward. "Did you see what state it was from?"

"No."

"And you saw this car again?"

"When we stopped to get gas."

Declan looked at Julia. "I remember that," he said. "She paused when we were heading back to the RV." He looked at Elizabeth again. "And you saw that car again tonight?"

"I'm not sure but I think so. It was black, I think, and it had a rack. It came into the campsite as soon as you left. I'm not sure they saw me, but as soon as I saw them, I snuck off into the darkness but kept watching. There were two of them. Men. They were quick. One came in here. The other one went into the car. I bet they were looking for the pill bottle. Looking for me." She shook her head again and resumed her crying. "God, I didn't know what to do. I watched them for a minute, saw them pour something all over the car and set it on fire. That's when I ran away."

Declan leaned toward Elizabeth. "So, how do we know you didn't do all this tonight, ransack the RV, burn my car? Or how do we know you're not in cahoots with these men in the black car?"

"I wouldn't do anything to hurt you."

"Oh yeah? Why's that?" Declan's voice was skeptical.

"Because you are the only ones who've been nice to me … ever since … in a long time."

"Ever since what?" Julia asked.

Elizabeth looked down. "I don't talk about that. It was a long time ago."

Julia and Declan exchanged glances and nodded. Apparently, he bought the story, too. Julia reached over to the nearby counter and pulled the bottle of Oban onto the dinette table. "Maybe we need a little extra libation," she said. Declan nodded, but Elizabeth shook her head. As she poured a dram of the fourteen-year-old Scotch into Declan's and her iced-tea tumblers, she said, "This is how I knew Officer Purkle's theory about local punks ransacking the RV was nonsense. They wouldn't have left this." She held up the bottle. "This sucker's worth a hundred bucks." She manufactured an awkward laugh, then said, "Thank you, Elizabeth, for telling us all that. It must have been hard for you."

"Here's what I don't understand," said Declan. "What would a top-secret canister from some Army base in Arizona be doing in the back seat of a car in a hotel parking lot in Milwaukee? And why would the car door be unlocked?"

Julia took a sip of the Scotch and let the warm fire provide its needed comfort. She shook her head. "Unless that was a drop point, a place where it would be handed off to someone else." Another question troubled her. Elizabeth was apparently telling the truth, but they had not been truthful with her. Should they tell her that they now had the top-secret drive? That the attackers this evening may have seen her retrieving the canister from the fire pit? That they weren't following Elizabeth after all, but perhaps following her? She didn't need to share that yet.

Instead, she said, "So, Elizabeth, when we were at the Oklahoma City memorial today, you seemed to know an awful lot about the bombing. Why was that?" She leaned back, waiting for Elizabeth's answer.

Elizabeth cradled her iced tea glass in both hands and said, "At one time, I taught history." She was silent a moment, then said, "A long time ago."

"So, how'd you wind …" Julia struggled to find the words to the question she wanted to ask, but Elizabeth cut her off.

"Like I said, I can't …."

Julia nodded and let the question drop. She turned her attention to Declan. His eyebrows arched with uncertainty, but he said nothing. A change of subject would be in order. "So, Declan, what are you going to do?"

Declan shrugged. "Maybe I'll catch a bus back to …" He shook his head slowly. "… somewhere." He locked eyes with her for just a second, then looked away, a move that told her that he hadn't forgotten about the kisses, either.

"And then?"

Declan shrugged again, apparently not finding any words.

Julia spoke up. "In any case, we need to figure out where we're going to stay tonight. It's not a good idea to stay here. Might not be legal, and the last thing we need is another visit from Officer Purkle. Anyway, it's way too public here, in case somebody's looking for us."

Declan peered out the window into the darkness. Julia looked out, too. The roadside rest was almost empty tonight—certainly no black cars with Yakima racks pulling in next to them. "It's best we keep moving," he said. "Put some miles between us and here."

Julia nodded. "I agree. Maybe even drive straight through to—" She stopped and glanced at Elizabeth. "Yeah, just keep going. But the truth is, I'm wiped. I need a few hours of sleep before much more driving."

Declan let out a big, fluttering breath. "Me too."

She pulled out her phone and brought up the AllStays app. Shaking her head, she said, "The pickings are thin around here. Good ol' western Oklahoma apparently isn't Yellowstone." They sat in silence, looking at each other. Then Julia fished Reverend Pam's card from her shirt pocket and studied it a moment. *The Rev. Pam Patel, Assisting Priest, Grace Episcopal Church, Bellweather, Oklahoma.* On the back was a scribbled address. "We have an invite to stay at Reverend Pam's." She pulled her phone out, checked for a signal and nodded. "I say, let's give her a call, then go pay her a visit."

Chapter 23

Declan saw the tiny bungalow come into view at the end of a narrow gravel road. Its dimly lit window was the only light on this pitch-black night. Reverend Pam apparently had seen them coming up the road and was waiting for them out front. "Why don't you pull off over there," she hollered, directing them to a large patch of unmowed grass. "It's even close to a fire ring. Sorry, no electric hookups, folks, if you're used to that kind of thing."

"Reverend Pam, thank you for putting us up for the night," said Julia. "Do we need to call Officer Purkle and see if it's okay if we have a fire?"

Pam, now up next to the driver's window, laughed. "I'm pretty sure it's okay, and just Pam is fine." She wore a faded flannel shirt. Her black hair was pulled tight around her brown forehead and hung as two long braids on her shoulders. Her large brown eyes sparkled in the light from the RV's instrument panel.

As the three of them climbed out, Pam's eyes fixed on Elizabeth. "And who is this?" she asked with suspicion.

Elizabeth took a step backward, like she might have to run away again.

"This is Elizabeth," Julia said. Aware she was about to be caught in a lie, she nonetheless offered a blasé answer. "She's the hitchhiker I told you about." Declan stood quietly with arms crossed, enjoying seeing Julia squirm.

Pam's laughter vanished. "I thought you said you dropped her off in Oklahoma City."

Julia looked away, then back at Pam. "I lied about that. Sorry. But I was afraid you guys would track her down, arrest her for starting the fire or something. She didn't start the fire. She ran when she saw two guys drive up. We found her after you left."

Pam looked hard at Julia.

Julia squirmed as Pam stayed silent. Finally, she began to speak, but Pam spoke first. "I guess I could see that happening." A smile replaced her look of suspicion. "Anyway, welcome, Elizabeth. Your witness could be important in resolving this case, you know. What did they look like?"

Elizabeth looked around warily, like she was about to be accused of something. She spoke at a nearly inaudible level. "I couldn't really see in the dark. Men. Young, I think."

Pam nodded but looked like she would have more to say about this. "So, you guys must be exhausted. I'll let you get to bed." She looked from face to face, then turned and headed back to her house.

Getting to bed would be a problem. There were now three adults sharing the RV. The vehicle wasn't all that large, and Declan now understood the "Minnie" in its name.

Apparently, Julia had already been thinking about that. "Declan, do you think you can get by on the front seat? It reclines all the way back. We can hang up a sheet to give us all some privacy."

"Anything that's approximately horizontal sounds good right now," he said.

A half-hour later, after much squirming on the slippery vinyl seat, Declan was still completely awake. Sure, the seat made a terrible bed, but it was the events of the day that wouldn't let him fall asleep. He lay there for another fifteen minutes, staring out through the windshield into the darkness. Finally, he quietly pushed the door open and climbed out. Still fully clothed, he leaned up against the side of the RV and gazed up at the night sky.

Then the side door of the RV slid open, and Julia poked her head out. "You can't sleep either? That seat must be really uncomfortable."

"Oh, the seat's okay," he lied. "I just couldn't doze off. Too much going on in my head."

Julia stepped down and leaned up against the RV next to him. She wore the same clothes she'd had on earlier. "I know what you mean." She walked to the rear of the RV, opened a hatch and pulled out the two folding camp chairs. Now Elizabeth stuck her head out of the RV, too, which caused Julia and Declan to laugh.

"So here we are," laughed Julia. "Now what?"

He looked into Julia's face, bathed in a soft glow of starlight. The memory of those kisses returned, and if Elizabeth hadn't been nearby, he would kiss her again.

For a few minutes the three of them stood in the silence of the night, then a light came on down at the cabin, and soon Pam appeared in her doorway, craning her neck to see what was going on. "You all okay?" she shouted.

"Just can't sleep," Julia shouted back. "Sorry if we bothered you."

Pam disappeared for a moment, then reappeared with two more camp chairs. When she arrived at the RV, she said, "If you all would give me a hand, we could get some firewood over here and get ourselves warm."

They each carried an armload of firewood to the fire pit from the side of the house. Declan said, "I'm pretty good with campfires. Why don't I get it started?"

"Good idea," said Pam. "Julia and Elizabeth, why don't we go back to the house and find some snacks." She was obviously happy to have visitors.

After watching all his possessions go up in flames, at the hand of someone who meant him harm, Declan wondered why it now felt good to start a campfire. In his past six months of camping, he'd had very few fires, because campfires are for reflecting and remembering, things he'd been avoiding. But now, out here—he didn't even know exactly where he was— building a campfire seemed like the right thing to do. Maybe it was the catharsis of Elizabeth's sharing of her ordeal, maybe it was Pam's gentle acceptance, maybe it was kissing Julia— whatever it was, this was something new.

Awhile later they all sat around a roaring fire. David Niven sprawled between Julia and Pam. They'd passed around chips and salsa and sipped hot chocolate. Pam even provided some of those tiny marshmallows that make the cocoa special. Their talk had been light and laughter-filled, which, after the heavy topics they'd already dealt with, seemed appropriate. Julia had everyone laughing, recounting their experience at the Cherokee Trading Post, and Pam got them laughing even harder with some stories of her own about tourist traps along the highway.

Then Julia glanced at Declan, blew out a loud breath, and looked straight at Pam. "I lied about something else, too."

Pam steepled her fingers. "You want to talk about that?"

Julia turned back to Elizabeth. "First, I need to tell you something, Elizabeth. The top-secret thing you found in that car is a computer flash drive. I found it the next morning in the fire ring, where you dropped it. I've had it ever since."

Elizabeth looked hard at Julia but didn't say anything. Then Julia turned back to Pam. "Not sure why I feel the need to be so honest right now, maybe it's because you're a priest, but the truth is…" Julia paused, gathering her words. "I didn't give the real Army flash drive to Officer Purkle. I only gave him the canister it came in. I still have the secret flash drive."

Pam smiled. "I knew you didn't give him the real flash drive."

"What?"

"Maybe some folks would fall for your trick, but I'm a computer geek of sorts. That canister looked official, but I know a cheap commercial flash drive when I see it. You can get that thing at Walmart for five bucks. It had no special markings on it, so I was pretty certain it wasn't some secret data drive."

"Why didn't you say something?"

"For the same reasons you didn't give Wade the real drive. 'Nuff said?"

Julia nodded.

Pam leaned toward Julia and placed a hand on her arm. "One more thing. Thank you for being honest with Elizabeth and me. That was a good thing you just did."

Julia shot Declan a quick, slightly embarrassed look.

Declan returned an approving nod.

"So, I take it you're still going to Fort Huachuca with that thing?"

Julia glanced at Elizabeth. She hadn't mentioned this to her, as far as Declan knew. "Yes."

Elizabeth showed no surprise.

"Why?" asked Pam.

Julia's mouth fell open, like she wasn't prepared to answer that question. She shook her head. Then she started to speak but stopped. There was more silence.

"Wait here a minute," Pam said, then headed back toward the house. Was she going to call Officer Purkle? Declan was certain she wasn't. Soon, Pam reappeared, carrying a piece of polished wood—it looked like a musical instrument.

Pam held the instrument up for them all to see. "This is a Native American flute. Maybe you've seen one before." It was a beautiful carved cylinder of wood, with intricate engravings and embedded pieces of turquoise. Two thin strips of leather encircled the flute.

Declan wanted to ask more about the flute, but this wasn't a time for words.

Pam held the flute to her lips and began to play. At first, the sound was so soft and slow as to be almost inaudible. It could have been an evening breeze. Then a more haunting sound emerged that reminded Declan of the mournful cries of coyotes he'd heard on those long-ago backpacking trips in the Sierras. It had an otherworldly sense of sadness and longing. Then the melody became simpler and repetitive—comforting, like rain drops on the roof of his tent. Healing. Like a calming hand touching a throbbing wound with a soothing salve. Just as he was becoming lulled into an almost hypnotic peace, the pace of the music accelerated, suddenly becoming louder and more lively, almost celebratory. The simple, quiet flow of a brook became the torrent of a waterfall.

Declan, who had always shied away from anything he regarded as overly sentimental, felt like dancing. He didn't know how to process this confluence of emotions. He had been sitting, but now he was standing; he didn't remember getting out of the camp chair. He stepped back from the fire and looked up into the night sky, and his breath was almost taken away by what he saw.

It was like this was the first time he'd ever seen the night sky. The Milky Way, which he knew was just the edge of our own spiral galaxy, was a brilliant swath, backed by an uncountable number of other stars. Declan knew that in fact the total number of stars visible on even a clear night such as this was only about ten thousand, a miniscule fraction of all the stars in the universe. He knew that if stars were grains of sand, that all the stars visible tonight would barely fill a teaspoon. But the number of stars in the universe was more than all the grains of sand in all the deserts and beaches of the earth.

This information about the universe was there in the physics courses he had taken. But those courses never called out the universe for what it was. There were equations and data and numbers, but there were never tears. There should have been tears. The universe is a thing of awe, incomprehensible awe, but also a thing of beauty. Why? Why wasn't it a thing of terror? Against the backdrop of Pam's flute music, he sensed a bigger picture encompassing his life, everything, his joys and sorrows, even Emily's death.

Maybe it was because the universe, maybe life itself, is ultimately not about loss and failure and death but about the almost aching beauty and sublime moments that were everywhere. In the simplicity of strangers huddled around a campfire on a starry night, even a faithful dog lying at their feet, about spontaneous kisses that take you by surprise.

Julia was standing, too, looking straight ahead, eyes closed. Elizabeth still sat in her chair, sobbing.

When Pam put down her flute, there was silence. How long had she been playing? Just a minute or two? Maybe hours?

Julia looked to the sky, as if seeking some inner resolve. Still looking up, she said, "You asked why I wanted to go to Fort Huachuca, and I couldn't answer. But now maybe I can." She looked around at them, laughed, then shook her head. "Geez, I don't know why this is so hard."

After more silence, she said, "I dropped out of college when I got pregnant, never finished my degree. I don't think my mom and dad ever forgave me for that. I had a part-time dead-end job, which had no real purpose. Except it allowed me to make a new best friend that my husband left me for. I think my mother blames me for Gary leaving, too. I do have a beautiful daughter, but she's so busy I almost never get to see her."

Declan thought Julia might be about to cry, but she didn't.

Julia continued. "So, I've been trying to write novels, but I've struggled with that, too. I've been trying to write thrillers, but apparently, I don't have anything thrilling to talk about. It just seemed like here was a chance to complete something important: return this thing to Fort Huachuca, where it belongs, finish the task, instead of just handing it over to some Officer Purkle type."

Again, silence.

"Thank you, Julia, for your honesty." said Pam. "It is difficult to say such personal things. So, how are you feeling right now?"

Julia laughed, as she looked from face to face. "Surprisingly, I feel really good." She looked up at the sky for a moment, like maybe she'd been captivated by all those stars, too, then said, "Reverend Pam, I mean Pam"—she giggled like a shy teenager—"Your music was so beautiful. Thank you."

Declan nodded but said nothing. Elizabeth had stopped crying and was focused on Julia.

Julia continued. "So, I'd love to hear some more about you. Were you raised around here? How did you come to be a priest?"

Pam dipped a large chip into the salsa and chewed, while she apparently pondered where to start. "Well, yes, I was born here in Oklahoma, off to the east. My mom is full Choctaw, and my dad is an Indian—an India Indian—who was an engineer at the Phillips Lab over in Bartlesville. People always laugh about my parents both being Indians, but from two sides of the world." She paused to take a sip of her hot chocolate. "They both still live in Bartlesville. My mom teaches in a preschool there. I get my geeky computer stuff from my dad, I guess, and my more intuitive side from my mom. Anyway, I headed off to Oklahoma State to become an engineer, and while I was doing that, someone invited me to go to church with them. Totally blindsided me."

She laughed and reached for another chip. She started talking again, while still chomping on her chip, then apologized and covered her mouth. Laughing, she said, "Excuse me. Anyway, I got hooked on church. No, what I really got hooked on was God."

Declan looked up at the sky again. What did it mean to get hooked on God? Is God the universe? If so, he could totally relate to Pam's unexpected comment. But he suspected she meant something more.

Pam continued. "My parents aren't religious, so this was all new to me. Changed my life. I finished up my engineering degree at State, but instead of heading off to grad studies at some engineering school, I headed off to seminary. That was a long process, and we don't have enough chips or firewood to get through all that."

Everyone laughed.

"I knew I wanted to serve near my home, so I wound up out here, assisting priest at an Episcopal church. Barely scraping by, barely able to pay the rent on this old shack." She glanced back at her cabin. "I don't have a family, at least not yet." She paused and Declan thought he could make out a mistiness in her eyes. "It gets lonely at times. Maybe I'll get a dog like ol' David Niven there."

"You're an inspiring person," said Julia.

"I'm just a person. I'm not that wise Indian woman romanticized on TV shows. In fact, I had a hard time getting a position after seminary. Guess some places don't think of a thirty-two-year-old, five-foot-tall woman when they envision a priest. I love it here, but sometimes I call out to God, asking why I'm out here in the middle of nowhere. Then I get a call for someone in the hospital and they're scared. And I can go and sit with them. Maybe not with a bunch of wise words from a wise Indian woman, but just the presence of someone who loves God."

Pam stood and placed another log on the fire. "So, what about you guys?" she asked. "Three people out here in the boonies in an RV. Some stories there."

"I'd like to hear those stories, too," said Julia. "We've only been together a couple of days. I don't really know much about these two."

"What about you, Elizabeth?" Pam asked. She poked at the fire with a branch, waiting.

Elizabeth shook her head, as she stared into the fire, but said nothing.

They waited a while in silence, until Pam said, "That's okay, Elizabeth. Nothing is required here."

Everyone's eyes turned toward Declan. Pam settled back into her chair, then leaned forward with her elbows on her knees and her chin cradled in her hands, as if ready to hear a good story.

Declan shifted in his chair. After Julia's emotional testimony and Pam's story, it would be hard to avoid this. He cleared his throat, then said, "So, yeah, I grew up in California. My dad was a physicist at an aerospace company, worked on the space shuttle, so naturally I went to college to study physics. Somehow got into Berkeley for grad school." He laughed shakily. "Got my PhD, although that was a struggle. My dad was proud though. It was during those last years at Berkeley that I met Emily."

He looked over at Julia and was surprised at the warmth in her eyes. "She loved backpacking almost as much as I did, and we'd be camping almost every weekend. So, it took me a long time to finish school, and I barely passed the comprehensive exams." He stood and paced, looking up at the stars again. Come on, Declan, he thought, there are trillions of stars up there that don't give a shit about your sob story. He laughed out loud. "So, I was a pretty good physicist, not great but okay." There was more to say. Much more, but not now. "So, I decided to quit. Went to work, helping my brother, Conor, with the business end of his restaurant." He shrugged. "So, I've been talking long enough. That's all I'm going to say."

"Thank you, Declan," said Pam, with a gentle smile.

But then Declan continued. He wasn't sure why. Pam had given him permission to stop. Again, he cleared his throat.

No one else had said anything, as if they had expected all along that he had more to say. "No. No." Declan shook his head, then turned away. He stepped away into the darkness for a moment, looked up at the stars again, then came back. "Actually, that's not true."

Oddly, those kisses—the first connection he'd had with anyone in so long—made it possible for his confession. Something had opened up in him. Freed him. Like the gate of the corral being opened in the middle of the night and horses escaping into the darkness. He didn't understand it, but he knew he needed to go with it.

"I was a physicist, like I said, at a national lab in California. We worked on new energy concepts for the country. Really important stuff.

"There was a lot of pressure to succeed, and in a lot of ways, I was out of my depth. One day, my division leader called me in and told me he needed me to give a briefing at a funding agency in Washington. A big contract—millions—was on the line. A colleague who was scheduled to go had come down with the flu, and they needed me to go make the presentation. I'd never done anything like that before—I'd never even been to Washington—but my sick colleague had already prepared the PowerPoint presentation, and all I had to do was deliver it. Shouldn't have been that hard, but I had no experience in these kinds of things. I remember the division leader saying something like, 'You've gotta really talk it up. Sell this project. I know this may not be in your nature, but you need to tap into your inner used-car salesman. They'll expect that from you.'

"I should've refused." Declan shook his head. He'd said enough. They didn't need to hear the terrible part. But, after more silence, he continued, and he told them everything. Yes, he should have said no to the division leader. After all, he wasn't good at speaking in front of a group or thinking on his feet. It was only because of the excellent PowerPoint presentation that he agreed. As he stood in silence, gazing into the fire, he relived, for the millionth time, that trip. He'd taken a late flight to DC, got in after all the restaurants were closed, so his dinner was power bars from a vending machine. He got almost no sleep, and the next morning, he showed up at the funding agency jet-lagged, tired and scared. In the waiting room, he saw three of his lab's competitors from Sandia Labs, all reviewing their presentation, which would follow Declan's. "Hey," he remembered one of them laughing, "Don't take all their money. Leave a little for us."

There were only a few people gathered around a long conference table in the stuffy, windowless room. It was so hot, he thought he might pass out. At the head of the table was Gerald Bender, the agency director for Advanced Energy Concepts, who he knew by reputation. An important and intimidating figure, he'd heard.

"Okay, Dr. Lewis." Bender glanced at his watch, then said, without any greeting, "What have you got to tell us?"

Declan began going through the presentation, which should've been straightforward, since it covered material with which he had some familiarity, and all he had to do, really, was repeat what was already displayed on the excellent PowerPoint slides. But it wasn't long before Bender interrupted. "So, Lewis, can we just cut to the chase? The last thing I need right now is to watch another damned PowerPoint presentation. So, just put that crap away and talk to us. We need to know how close you are to demonstrating the VT. Can you talk about that?" He glowered at Declan through thick glasses that magnified his judgmental stare.

The VT—the viability threshold—was an elusive technical goal that several research groups, including the one in which he worked, were pursuing feverishly. He wasn't an expert on the VT experiments—he worked in a different section of the group from the VT researchers—but he knew a little about them, knew his group was close to demonstrating the VT—at least he was almost certain he'd heard that at a seminar last week. Maybe they'd already accomplished it. And he knew this would open an exciting new energy option for the world. His natural tendency would be to say that he didn't fully know the status of the VT work, but what rang through his head was: *tap into your inner used-car salesman.* It was imperative that he brought back good news to the Lab. He would be held accountable.

But now, he was without his crutch, the skillfully prepared visuals that his more-knowledgeable colleague had prepared. He was on his own in front of this intimidating group of people, who probably *did* get enough sleep last night.

Declan mustered everything he had. "Yes, I was just going to get to that." Fortunately, someone had placed a glass of water next to him, which he desperately needed to dissolve the wad of cotton that suddenly filled his mouth. These guys expected a used car salesman, some promotional spin; that's what he needed to give them. He cleared his throat and dug his grave. "I'm pleased to say that we have, in fact, just demonstrated the VT. It's not part of my presentation, but, yes…" Was he hyperventilating? "It'll require some more confirmation, of course, but we've done it, sir." He felt faint and worried for a moment that he might pass out.

Bender jumped to his feet and looked around at the others in the room. "No shit," he bellowed. "I've heard so many of your group's briefings in the past, and always there was little progress. That's extraordinary. How did you do it? That toroidal suspension thing you've spent years on?"

Declan tried desperately to recall what had been said in that seminar last week. That presentation had been, in fact, on the toroidal suspension method, one of the many approaches being used around the world to pursue the VT. And the presentation had been very optimistic. Lord, he wished he'd been paying more attention. "Yes, the toroidal suspension method. It's still tentative, of course, and all very recent," said Declan, suddenly trying to backpedal and trying to buy some time. Like a bucket of ice water had been tossed in his face, he suddenly realized what he had done. The heat. The pressure. The jet lag. The lack of sleep. Oh, my God. He needed to retract his statement. Sure, he was convinced his group was on the path to demonstrating the VT, maybe they'd already done it, but now he wasn't certain about anything, except that he'd just committed professional suicide. "Dr. Bender, I need to—"

"What you need to do, Lewis, is start celebrating." Bender looked around at the others again and said, "I think this merits a round of applause." After the clapping had subsided, Bender said, "So, we can't make this official today, of course, until we see the data, but I think you can tell your folks back home that the check's in the mail." Bender laughed, then stepped forward and shook Declan's hand. "Of course, we'll keep this under wraps until you're ready to announce your results, but I say you can count on that contract being yours. You're going to break the hearts of those Sandia guys out in the waiting room, but that's the way it goes."

Sara Stein, the Assistant Program Director, wore a troubled look and spoke up. "Jerry, maybe we should wait at least until we see some data before we commit."

"You're probably right, Sara, but I'm feeling lucky, and we know that this team has a good track record. I trust them, and I'm convinced we can move ahead with implementation." He put an arm around Declan like they were the best of buddies. "Dr. Lewis, I'd say this has been a very beneficial meeting." Declan needed to speak up, but words wouldn't come out. He managed a weak smile. He knew he was dead.

By the time Declan arrived back at the Lab, the word was already out. Most likely, the Sandia guys had given Bender a dose of reality. So, now Declan had brought humiliation to his group and himself. There was a lot of screaming. Words like lying, fraud, even undermining the Federal government were used. His attempts to explain were futile. He had damaged the reputation of the whole national laboratory.

The Lab gave him a choice: resign or be fired. Firing would engage a lengthy HR process—it would be expensive, humiliating, exhausting. The Lab considered it a humane gesture to let him resign.

Declan had relived that terrible day of bad judgment and failure many times, and he never forgave himself. That day had shaped his life. But that didn't make the recounting of the story to Julia, Pam and Elizabeth any easier. "So, I had to quit," he said. After a few deep breaths, he continued, "I confessed my lie to my father and to Emily. And then later to Conor. Not to anyone else until tonight. Emily was ashamed but tried to support me. It was clearly a catalyst in the disintegration of our marriage. My father disowned me. I haven't seen him in five years. Got a brief, awkward call from him when Emily died. That was it.

"So, I went to work doing accounting in my brother's restaurant. I think I also stopped trying in my marriage sometime in there, too." He ran fingers through his hair. "We'd been going through the motions for so long. I guess, when we both started working so hard and stopped living for our backpacking trips, we just didn't have much in common anymore. I still cared about Emily. I think we loved each other. But we drifted apart."

This wasn't quite right, and he'd come this far in his revelation, he needed to get it right. "Actually, I think it was because I was lazy and self-absorbed. I should have been a better husband." Those last words came out blubbery, as his face felt ready to explode into tears. He swallowed hard. "Then Emily got Covid and died. I never got to tell her I was sorry. Never got an opportunity to give our marriage another chance." His throat tightened up again, and he was uncertain he could continue. His voice shook as he spoke. "So that's my story. Fired for lying. Death by Covid. All my possessions up in flames. Those are final things. Endings. Completions. Here I am, forty-four, and everything is now gone. I have nothing."

Everyone was silent. Geez, he really had droned on too long with his sob story.

Then Pam stood and came toward him. She took his hand in hers and held it tightly. "Declan, you are an amazing man, out here in some stranger's field, being so honest about yourself. Most people I know couldn't have done that." She looked up at him—she was about a foot shorter than him—her eyes like lasers, her smile like the soft music from her flute. She said, "I don't even know you, yet I have a sense that you are on the threshold of something good, something beautiful. Maybe it's true you have nothing. But it's when your hands are empty that you may be ready to take hold of the world."

Declan trembled, and he worried that he might be about to cry in front of these people. But he glanced at Julia anyway. There was no way he could interpret what he saw. The only word that came to his mind was peace.

Maybe it was the flute music, maybe it was the star-filled sky above the campfire, maybe it was the power of Julia's confession or was it her lips pressed to his and his guilty thought during her emotional words that he'd like more of that. Maybe it was a cathartic reaction to his car and all his remaining possessions going up in flames. Maybe they needed to go up in flames. It was like something—he didn't know what—had changed in him. Like something had changed in them all.

He looked down at Pam again. "I really appreciate this," he said.

Then Declan stepped away from Pam and went over to Elizabeth. He peeled off his Patagonia jacket and handed it to her. "I need to say I'm sorry, Elizabeth. This time it's really yours. Yours to keep."

Chapter 24

One of the first rules for writing a novel is to develop consistent writing habits. Write every day. Establish a routine. Today—with a full day of driving ahead—would be Julia's third consecutive day of not writing. Oddly, she hadn't even thought about writing for a while, and, what with everything else going on, that didn't concern her much. Maybe more important than writing a thrilling novel is to live a thrilling life. But maybe even more important than a thrilling life is a meaningful life. Her cathartic confession last night, prompted by Pam's gentle, inviting persona and that calming flute music, gave her visions of peace, even though she'd felt little peace. All that had brought her to a new place this morning. Unsettled yet more secure. A new place that required exploration.

She rolled onto her side and surveyed the brown grassland beyond the bedside window of the Minnie Winnie. A few oaks dotted the landscape, and low gray hills defined the horizon. Smoke rose from the chimney at Pam's cabin.

Julia rolled onto her back again and stared at the ceiling, continuing to reflect on last night. They'd all headed for bed soon after Declan's gut-wrenching story. Julia had slept amazingly well, considering the emotional buzz-saw they'd all been through. She looked toward the front of the RV, where Elizabeth was turned against the wall in the overhead bunk. Declan had been upfront in the reclined passenger seat, but the sheet they'd hung between the cab and the living space prevented her from seeing if he was still there. It was a cozy arrangement, but it was the best they could do. Pam's tiny house, really a cabin, was no more than a studio apartment inside, and there just wasn't space for a guest.

Julia climbed out of bed and pulled on Levi's and a Yellowstone T-shirt. A shower would be great, but a shower in the RV seemed unfeasible this morning, with all the population crammed into her small living space. Washing her face and brushing her teeth might be all she got today.

She clicked on the stovetop and started the water for coffee, as she considered the day ahead. They had talked about driving straight through to Sierra Vista, but that was fourteen hours away. Declan had said he planned to find a bus in the next town, and she'd never be able to make that drive by herself in one day. There was no way she would risk turning over the wheel to Elizabeth. Stopping for another night could invite another unpleasant encounter.

She pulled three coffee mugs down from a cabinet and stared out into the morning, while she waited for the kettle to whistle. A lot more to process from last night, but she needed some caffeine before tackling any of that.

A few minutes later, Julia poked her head around the sheet to check on Declan. She'd worried that the front seat, even reclined, would be uncomfortable, but Declan was snoring softly under one of the wool blankets he'd borrowed just two nights ago. He still wore his clothes from yesterday. She shook her head—those were all the clothes he owned. But then she smiled, as she noticed Nivvie curled up at Declan's feet. Dogs are good judges of character.

Although she'd tried to be quiet, her stirring woke Declan. He looked around with unfocused eyes like he was unsure where he was, which was probably the case, then looked up at her, momentarily startled. He yawned, ran a hand through his shaggy hair, then smiled, "Good morning."

Julia held out a mug of coffee. "Hope you like it black."

Declan raised the seat into an upright position then took the mug. He looked outside again, probably still trying to get his bearings. "Why don't you join me?" he said, gesturing to the driver's seat.

Julia climbed over into the driver's seat, then looked down at the dog. "Sorry ol' Nivvie crashed your pad last night."

"It's okay," said Declan, reaching a cautious hand down to give Nivvie's head a tentative pat. "David Niven is starting to grow on me."

Even though Declan looked like a disheveled guy who'd just awakened, there was a dignity about him. She thought about the kisses again, then quickly chased those thoughts away. A sudden tap on the door made them both jump. They looked at each other, startled, then laughed. Pam was at the door, carrying a platter of food.

"I'd suggest we eat out here in the camp chairs," Pam said, "but I'm afraid they're a little damp from the dew." She wore tailored slacks and a blue shirt with a white clergy collar.

"Come on in," said Julia. "We've got room at the table."

Pam placed the platter on the cozy dinette table—toasted English muffins and slices of ham—while Julia pulled down another coffee mug from the cabinet. She'd never had this many people in the Minnie Winnie.

"I need to head out to the church soon but wanted to say good morning before I go. You have a long drive ahead of you today, if I remember correctly."

"Yeah, fourteen hours to the army base. Sounds a little more challenging this morning than it did last night." Julia shot

Declan a glance, wondering if he was rethinking his plans to catch that bus today.

Elizabeth climbed down from the over-the-cab bunk, still wearing the Patagonia jacket, even though it was quite warm. Pam gave her a nod, as she slid into the dinette booth.

They shared superficial chit chat and laughter, none of them bringing up the heavy topics of last night. Then Pam leaned forward toward Julia, her eyes piercing. "Julia, what you and Elizabeth told me last night about the two men coming into the campground would be very helpful to the police." She let that hang in the air, waiting for a response.

Julia munched on a corner of her muffin, considering her answer. "Look, I lied to you yesterday, and you know I feel bad about that. You went easy on me. But I'm not sure the police would be so easy. I'm driving straight through, so very soon I'll return the flash drive to where it belongs. I'll tell the authorities everything then. Are you okay with that?" Julia leaned back, then added, "Pam, we don't want to put you in an ethical hard place."

Pam appeared ready for this. "I won't reveal this to anyone. I'm pleased that you're going to turn this thing over to the Army soon." She looked from face to face. "But I'm worried that the people who did this awful thing last night are still out there and will return. You must be very careful. If you change your mind about talking with the police, give me a call. Maybe I can help make that conversation a bit easier. Meanwhile, I'll be placing you in God's care, but I'm still gonna be worried."

"I appreciate that. We'll be careful. That's why we're going to keep moving."

"Fourteen hours. That'll be tough."

Julia didn't know what to say. She nodded her acknowledgement.

Declan spoke up. "I'll be helping Julia with the driving today. Shouldn't be so bad with two of us splitting the work."

Julia opened her mouth to speak, as she turned toward him, but she couldn't find words. She wanted to hug him, wanted to ask him why he'd changed his mind, but she took another bite of her muffin instead.

"I have a good friend who lives down in that part of Arizona," Pam said. "Prisca. You'd like her. She's a ranger in the Chiricahuas. Beautiful place to camp. It's got a sad history, though."

"Why is it sad?" Declan asked.

Pam looked at Declan, as if she was considering her response. "I'll let Prisca fill you in on that." There was a catchlight in Pam's eyes that said she could say more, but instead, she stood. "Be back in a minute." Then she left. Soon, she returned carrying a small bundle, bound with a leather band, and took her seat at the table. "Declan, take this. My grandmother made it. I guarantee you won't find this at the Cherokee Trading Post."

Declan looked stunned. "You're giving this to me?" Declan untied the leather strip that bound the bundle and held up a colorful wool blanket. "It's beautiful." He shook his head, then gave out a nervous laugh, like he couldn't believe it. "Oh, I couldn't accept this."

"You came here and lost everything, Declan. I'd like you to leave with something you gained."

Declan's eyes misted up, and his Adam's apple moved, as he struggled for words. Finally, he said, "Pam, you've already given me a lot, more than you can know, actually." He looked at Julia, then Elizabeth, then back at Pam. "I will treasure this."

"I'm not gonna preach you a sermon. You might be expecting a priest would do that." She was quiet for a moment and looked like she might be about to stand, but then she sat back down. "Okay, I am going to say something here. Hope this isn't too heavy to hear before your second cup of coffee." Pam's face beamed, like she was totally in her element now. "Something I've learned, and I see it in you, is that the most important thing in life is love."

Now Pam was silent as she looked from face to face.

"And the first thing I believe we need to learn about love is that we are loveable. So many of us, beaten up by life, have concluded that we're not very loveable." Pam looked at Declan, but he averted her eyes, looking down at the blanket and tracing a finger along an intricate pattern. Elizabeth turned her face toward the window.

Julia closed her eyes and saw herself standing before her mother, telling her that Gary had left.

Pam continued. "I know each of you has been through a lot, and I know there may be more challenges waiting for you on the road today. But don't lose sight of the fact that there is a lot of love and good and kindness in this world." She leaned forward and rested one hand on Julia's arm and the other on Declan's arm. Her eyes moved from Julia to Declan to Elizabeth. "I see those things in each of you. Hang onto them for dear life because they will give you life."

Then Pam stood. "I'm gonna be late," she said. They all exchanged hugs with Pam, even Elizabeth, and then she left. About halfway back to her house, she turned and said, "God be with you."

Chapter 25

What else was Declan supposed to say? It wasn't like he had many other options. Yet, Julia had looked surprised when he'd said he'd help with the drive to the army base. This didn't mean he had come around to thinking this was a good idea. He was still unsettled that Julia had not given the flash drive to Officer Purkle. If she had, the secret drive would be safely in the hands of law enforcement, and they both could be on their way without this burden and possible danger. But after her words at the campfire last night, he understood better why this delivery was important to her, and maybe a part of him just wanted to help her out.

Declan studied Julia in profile as she drove. She'd been at it for an hour, sitting up military-straight, focused on the endless interstate ahead. With a high forehead and hair pulled back, she had a refined look, like a woman who should be doing a poetry reading at the bookstore, not someone who'd been living in campgrounds for the past three years. Her nose was delicate and her lips—those lips he'd kissed just last night—were full. She wore no make-up, as best he could tell, but then she had the kind of smooth skin that required none. Her complexion was fair, and she obviously took measures to protect it from the sun. She dressed simply in a dark T-shirt with a Yellowstone logo— she'd probably been a camp host there—and faded jeans. Yet, he could envision her delicately lifting her China teacup on the veranda of a Boston mansion. Sure, he was projecting onto her, based upon almost no knowledge. But one thing was clear. He was sitting next to a good-looking woman on a long road trip. That prospect alone should be reason enough to help with the driving.

Declan nibbled from a bag of Goldfish from the stash, as Julia called the drawer just behind the driver's seat. Then he passed her the bag and she took a few. He topped off her travel mug from a large Stanley thermos of coffee, nested between the seats.

They'd already agreed that they probably were no longer being followed, but some things still didn't add up. The shaved headed guy following them but not directly confronting them. The car fire. Yes, they had a straight shot to the base, and they would probably be okay. But his physicist's mind was trained to be troubled by things not adding up.

A more pleasant thought—her lips—returned, but he pushed it away. "So, you're a novelist?"

Julia frowned. "Well, I'm trying to be. There's a difference between being a novelist and someone who's trying to write a novel." She gave a soft, self-deprecating laugh.

Declan ignored her negativity. "What kind of novels do you write?"

"I'm trying to write thrillers, but I'm re-evaluating everything right now."

"What have you written so far?"

"Two self-published novels, but frankly they weren't very good, and few people read them. I'm working on a new one now."

"That's impressive. Maybe I could—"

"No, it actually isn't impressive. And it's not ready for prime time yet."

Maybe a good time to change the subject. "So, last night you said you have a daughter."

"Jenny. I'm very proud of her. Starting her senior year at Stanford."

"Sounded like you were worried about her."

"I guess that's what mothers do. She's a wonderful kid, but she's so busy I almost never get to talk to her."

"Guess that's pretty typical."

"She said she'd call yesterday, but …" Julia shrugged and gave Declan a helpless what-can-I-do look. Then she said, "Do you have children?"

"No." But before Declan could say more, his phone beeped. He checked the screen—Conor. He worked to project an upbeat voice. "Hey, Conor, how's it going?"

"Just checking in on my little brother." Declan hadn't seen Conor since that sad day of tears, six months ago, standing outside his newly closed restaurant. But they talked by phone about every two weeks; most of the time, Conor initiated the calls. He always showed an obvious concern for Declan, with good reason. "What are you up to today? Still in Wisconsin?"

"Actually, I'm on the road somewhere out in western Oklahoma."

"Okay, that's new. Hopefully doing something fun, with a pretty girl traveling by your side." Conor was a slap-you-on-the-back, greet-you-with-laughter kind of guy. A total opposite from Declan. His extrovert persona had been a factor in his success as a restauranteur.

"I don't know about the fun part, but—" He shot a glance at Julia, who stared straight ahead but was no doubt listening in—"the other part in the affirmative."

"Woot! Woot! Now, that's what I want to hear!"

"Well, it's not—"

"You're not gonna wimp out on me, are you? You got a pretty girl with you—do I have to come out there and show you what to do?" Conor had never been married, but always had an attractive woman with him, usually a different one every time you saw him.

"Okay, okay," laughed Declan, glancing again at Julia and hoping she couldn't hear Conor's end of the conversation, "you didn't call me to check on my—" He'd started to say "love life" but stopped.

"So, actually, I did call with some good news. I think I found a place." This was good news. Conor had hoped to open a new restaurant in the LA area, but it had been hard. Closing Conor's in Chicago had left him not only crushed emotionally, but also with a fair amount of debt—Declan knew; he kept the books—and he'd struggled to get a start in California because of the high property costs. He'd even gone back to living with their parents for a while.

"Excellent, Conor. I want the details."

"I think I've found a place in Manhattan Beach. Close to the water. Conor's Seaside Bistro, I think I'll call it. What do you think?"

"I love it, Conor."

"Well, Dad did float me a little loan to help me get started, but I expect to pay that back in no time. I'm hoping to sign a lease, maybe as early as today. I just couldn't wait to share the good news with you."

"How are Dad and Mom doing?" Declan's voice had suddenly gone soft and tentative.

"They're okay, I guess. Look, Declan, Dad can be a real jerk sometimes, and I have a hard time understanding the way he's treated you. But I'm still hoping he'll come around at some point. He's got a lot of ego, but, of course, you know that." Conor paused, then said, "But, bro, the main reason I called is that if everything goes as planned, I'm gonna need a good business manager, and I know just the guy. So, I'm officially planting a seed. Declan, I know you like to go slow in making decisions, but I'm gonna need to know soon." Another difference between them. Conor made quick decisions. Declan needed time to ponder and analyze. That inability to think quickly on his feet had sealed his fate as a physicist on that infamous trip to Washington. "Think about it, Declan, you and that hottie out here, frolicking on the beach? It could happen!"

Declan laughed, as he shot Julia a guilty glance. "You always get me going, Conor. Sure, I'll think about it." When he hung up, he said to Julia, "That was my brother, the one who had the restaurant."

Julia nodded, keeping her eyes on the road. "I heard you mention your mom and dad. You said last night that things between you and your dad weren't great."

Declan looked out the window, where some brown formless plains rolled by. Then he looked back at Julia. "Yeah, he's kind of written me off." He felt his throat choking up.

"Because of one mistake you made?"

Declan let out a shaky breath. "Nice of you to say 'one mistake.' My dad sees it as more of a failure of character, and so do a lot of other people." He looked down, as a wave of shame returned.

"You look at me, Declan."

He raised his head and met her steady gaze.

"No, Declan, what you told us about last night was a mistake. Yeah, you screwed up. But that wasn't who you are.

Otherwise, you wouldn't be so burdened by it. Everybody screws up." She raised her eyebrows, inviting a response, then returned her attention to the road.

When Declan didn't respond, Julia continued. "I'm sorry about the way your dad treated you. He's your dad. He needs to get over that, and I'm guessing he will. Don't give up on him."

Declan glanced over his shoulder and noticed Elizabeth, seated in the dinette booth, listening in, which made him even more self-conscious. "Thank you," he said to Julia.

The GPS said they'd just crossed into Texas on I-40, but the landscape remained the same. Dry, brown and flat, stretching to the horizon. He remembered a classmate from somewhere out here once saying that the Texas panhandle was the place where you could look farther and see less than any other place on earth.

They were quiet for a while, as the monotonous terrain rolled by. Finally, Julia said, "Do you ever think about physics?"

Declan let out a heavy sigh. "Yeah, all the time."

She gave him a smile. "Tell a story from your physics days," she said.

Declan had been thinking about one, in fact. He pulled up the rolled blanket that Pam's grandmother had made. "This beautiful blanket," he said, holding it up for them both to admire again. "I still can't believe she gave this to me." The blanket was a rich and complex pattern of vibrant colors, dominated by a bright red zig-zag pattern against a blue background. "Anyway, it got me to thinking about Henry Chee. One of the first Navajo to get a PhD in physics." He spread the blanket across his lap and turned toward Julia. "Henry was a brilliant man, but he never fit in at the national laboratory. Maybe it was his Navajo culture that enabled him to think differently from the other physicists. While we thought in terms of equations, it seemed like Henry was thinking also in terms of images and patterns."

Declan closed his eyes and could see him now, his chiseled brown face and deep-set brown eyes that twinkled with mystery and humor. Henry was soft-spoken, and it was always a problem for him when he presented at a seminar. His voice was more soothing than commanding. "Can you speak up?" someone would invariably yell from the back.

"And you worked with him?"

"For a while. He was brilliant, he worked hard and was a friendly colleague. But, like I said, his problem-solving approach was different."

Julia seemed captivated. "How?"

"Well, he'd often say things in meetings that seemed totally off the wall. Sometimes he seemed to go in a different direction from the mathematical arguments of other physicists. At times it seemed like Henry just didn't follow where the science was leading—it wasn't because he *couldn't* follow, it was like he was following something else."

"Like what?"

Declan shrugged. "Henry wasn't a leader. He was more like a resident philosopher, or a shaman or maybe a priest." Declan let out a big sigh. "I didn't realize at the time what an opportunity it was for me to learn from him. Once Henry invited me to go with him to his home on the reservation out in Arizona and speak to students about science. But I told him I was too busy." He looked at Julia and sagged. "I always regretted that."

"Geez, that would have been cool. But what's the blanket got to do with Henry Chee?"

Declan stroked the blanket and said, "One day we were at some fancy reception for some big muckity muck, and Henry and I were both uncomfortable being there. We hung out on the periphery, admiring the art on the walls. One Navajo rug caught my attention. It was quite mysterious, with a mixture of colors and strange symmetries."

Declan looked down at the blanket in his lap and ran his hand over its surface. "This blanket kind of reminds me of it." He was silent for a moment. "Henry looked up at that rug and said, 'Declan, do you see that pattern in the rug?' Oh, his eyes were twinkling. Then he said, and I'll never forget it, 'That's how a laser works.' At first, I thought he was joking. Lasers work on complicated atomic physics principles, described by elaborate equations that Einstein helped develop." Declan looked at Julia and shook his head. "But as I looked closer at that rug, I noticed something very interesting. There were these linear patterns of different bright colors, maybe like the energy levels in an atom, like the atomic structure that causes a laser to work."

Julia seemed so locked into his story, he worried she might not be paying enough attention to the driving.

"You thought he was joking?"

"Yeah." He shook his head. "My thinking was too limited. But in the years since then, I've thought a lot about what he said, and I think he might have been right."

"So, is the story you just told me about physics or is it about art?"

Declan trailed his fingers along the intricate patterns in the blanket. "Henry Chee might say, 'What's the difference?'"

Just east of Amarillo, Declan took over the driving. The plan was that they'd each take two-hour stints behind the wheel with no stops, except for potty breaks and to switch drivers.

They'd left at eight; hopefully they could make it to Sierra Vista by ten p.m. It would be a long slog. They were making good time, even with a quick stop at a Walmart just off the interstate, where Declan purchased two changes of clothes, some toiletry items, a cheap sleeping bag and an inexpensive tent.

It took a while for Declan to feel comfortable driving the RV; after all, he'd driven a Corolla for the past two years. It didn't help that strong crosswinds had now kicked up, making the steering a challenge. Using the huge mirrors to see behind and to the side of the large vehicle was amazingly helpful. And one thing he was watching for in those mirrors was a black sedan with a Yakima rack. But, within ten miles, Declan felt like a veteran. He even found himself humming "On the Road Again."

He glanced over at Julia, who had been craning her neck to take in as much of the landscape as she could. Apparently, she found something interesting in this endless desert. But now she looked at him, as he hummed, obviously pleased with his driving, if not his musical talent.

He returned his attention to the road just as a car with Florida plates passed them. In its rear window a Miami Heat sticker displayed a basketball bursting into flames. And the memory of last night returned. He squirmed in his seat then checked the rearview mirror again and tightened his grip on the wheel. How did he know the perpetrators weren't right behind them now, ready to run them off the road? He could picture the nervous young man with the shaved head, leering at them and preparing to make his move. He swallowed hard and again glanced at Julia, who had resumed her study of the landscape. His imagination could run wild with this. That imagination that serves a physicist so well was now a source for personal terror.

Good Lord, Declan, get a grip. Exhaling a huge breath, he willed himself to relax.

It happened suddenly, without warning. The RV first began to shimmy, then it fishtailed. Panic surged through him, as the RV was out of control and careening toward the median and into the oncoming traffic.

Chapter 26

Julia was a born traveler, although she'd only discovered this truth about herself three years ago. Being on the road in her Minnie Winnie was life at its best. Her curiosity propelled her down the highway just as surely as the big Ford F350. What awaited her around the next bend? In the next town? At the next park? So, despite their sudden travel emergency today, she was pumped about seeing Tucumcari, New Mexico, an iconic Americana Route-66 town, for the first time. Billboards tantalized her over the last fifty miles, with messages like "Where western hospitality meets the mother road" and "Get your kicks on Route 66." The terrain, as they left Amarillo and approached New Mexico heightened her anticipation and confirmed that they were really in the west. The brown grassy plains had changed into arid desert, with scrubby Chamisa the only vegetation and tumbleweeds blowing across the road.

And so, even though this would be an emergency stop, Julia's spirits were high, as they left the interstate and headed down the historic main street of Tucumcari, US Highway 66, with all the romantic images that those words conjure up. But Tucumcari was no longer the charming slice of American history it may have once been. They passed stores with boarded windows or surrounded by chain link, some looking like they'd been this way for years. Sixties-style diners, where cross-country travelers had laughed over ham and eggs and waited for coffee refills from a brassy waitress who may well have been named Flo, were silent. Motels, where weary travelers would overnight on their way to California, now rested with tumbleweeds piled against their front door. Gas stations, now abandoned, had been taken over by tall weeds growing up through cracks around the pumps. Graffiti covered the walls. It was sad. Maybe the town had been in decline for years, but Covid, which decimated travel, no doubt had something to do with this. A couple old motels, with Route 66 figuring prominently on their signs, one with a vintage Chevy parked out front, were still open, but the abandoned businesses outnumbered the open ones two-to-one.

But Julia and Declan weren't here for a scenic tour. An hour ago, they were on the side of the interstate, after Declan had skillfully muscled the Minnie Winnie to the side of the highway. While huge eighteen wheelers roared by doing seventy-five, rattling the RV, they began a walk-around to find the trouble. It didn't take long. One of the rear dual tires, an inside tire, was nearly flat.

Declan kept glancing back down the interstate, as if expecting someone to pull in behind them. "How do we know this wasn't intentional?"

Julia rubbed her chin. "You mean, like someone fired a shot at our tire?" She studied his face but he didn't respond. She stared down at the tire again. "I can see why you'd ask that, but I'd say that seems unlikely."

Declan nodded like he was trying to buy into her confidence.

"I have a battery-powered inflator," she said. "Let's give that a try."

But the tire wouldn't hold air.

"Should we call someone?" Declan leaned over, looking at the flat. "Do you have roadside coverage for this kind of thing?"

"I do, but I wonder how long it would take someone to get out here." She scratched her head. "I've read that it's possible to drive with one flat tire on a dually. Maybe we should try to limp our way into Tucumcari and find a shop there. It's not that far."

Declan stood, then looked up and down the interstate again, as if help might be arriving, before looking back at Julia. He nodded. "I trust your judgment on this."

That was all it took. Julia pulled his head down to her and gave him a long kiss. His arms came around her, and she could feel his hands on the muscles of her back. She finally pulled away, breathless, but only inches. She laughed. "Now we're even."

His arms still held her, and she briefly considered how this would be a good way to spend the afternoon.

"I'm beginning to like this competition," he said.

After limping along the shoulder, with emergency flashers on, staying under forty for an hour, they made it to Tucumcari. Google Maps had shown a tire place on the main drag, but it was closed. Now they were at a Flying J truck stop, out next to an on-ramp to the interstate, where they were told it would be three hours to get the tire fixed. They'd already lost an hour, crawling along the interstate. It didn't require a Mensa membership to realize that their ETA for Sierra Vista was now 2 am at the earliest.

The three of them sat in the waiting room of the Flying J, Julia drumming her fingers on the edge of her plastic chair. This was not how she wanted to spend her day. Finally, she stood and said to Declan, "Think I'll go give my daughter a call." She was already bringing up the number, as she headed outside, Elizabeth following behind. Jenny was supposed to call yesterday but didn't. It should be okay to call her, without looking like an annoying clingy mother.

Jenny picked up on the first ring. "Oh, God, Mom, I know I said I'd call yesterday. I'm just so busy, I … anyway, I'm walking to class, so I've got a couple of minutes. How are you?"

"Doing okay. On the road. How 'bout you, sweetie?"

"I'm great. What are you up to, Mom?"

Julia recognized this kind of question: the "How are you doing, Mom?" That invariably meant that her daughter was buying time before announcing some important news about herself. But she had no choice but to go along. "I'm fine, traveling in New Mexico right now." She surveyed her depressing environment and shrugged. A huge expanse of blacktop, half-full with big trucks, surrounded her, beyond which a bleak sage-brush-dotted desert extended to the horizon. A big diesel idled nearby, and off in the distance was the endless drone of the interstate.

"Wow. New Mexico. I thought you were still in Wisconsin. What are you doing out there?"

"Heading to Arizona." She couldn't tell Jenny about the flash drive or that dangerous people might be following her.

"Alone?"

Why would Jenny ask this? "Well …." She paused, thinking about her words carefully. "I'm taking an elderly lady with me—"

"Who?"

"Just a woman who needed help."

"A homeless person?"

"Yeah, but she's—"

"It's okay, Mom, you're free to do whatever—"

"There's also a man." Julia had to be honest with her daughter.

"Huh? Another homeless person, or—"

"No." Well, actually, Declan was homeless. "He's a physicist."

"Physicist? Cool. Where'd you meet him?"

Julia squirmed. "At the campground."

"And is there anything going on with this guy you met in the campground?"

"Oh, no. Uh, well, I'm not sure …"

"Good God, Mom, whatever."

Enough of this. "What about you, Sweetie?"

"Well, I've kinda got some news. I think I'm in love."

Julia felt a sudden chill, as her own senior year and the pregnancy flashed in her mind. She had to stuff those old feelings away. "Wow, that *is* news. Tell me about him… I assume it's a him?"

"He's wonderful, Mom. Works here at the university in Admissions."

Another alarm bell went off. "You mean he's not a student?"

"Oh, he was. For a while. Couple years ago, I think. His name is Blake."

"Great," she forced herself to say.

"I'm thinking about taking the spring semester off, maybe next year, too, and travel. May be the last chance I get."

"And not finish your senior year?" Julia leaned up against a wall to steady herself.

"Oh, Mom, I knew you'd react like this. I knew you'd relive your dropping out through me. Well, in case you haven't noticed, I'm not you. I'm a different person." Then her voice calmed a bit. "Anyway, I'll finish my senior year when I get back."

"And Blake will go with you?"

"That's the whole point, Mom. God, you can be so dense sometimes."

Julia crumbled. "I'm sorry, sweetie, I don't mean to be dense. I do trust you. It's just that I love you so much."

"Well, then really trust me. Here you are, traveling across the country with a homeless woman and some new lover boy you met in a campground. Doing your camp-hosting thing, acting like it's some kind of legitimate profession. Mom, campground hosts are old people who don't have anything else to do. Not people who are forty."

"Forty-three," Julia interjected.

"Yeah, anyway, it's hardly something you go get a degree in at Harvard. Maybe I should be giving you a lecture."

"Maybe you should." Julia felt deflated. "It's just that I love you. That's all."

Jenny shrieked, "Will you please stop saying that? If I'm so loved, how come I don't have a home to come home to? Dad's basically disappeared, and you are out—I guess the term is *finding yourself* or some such crap. Anyway, why would I want to hang around, when I don't even have a home to hang around?"

These words were not new. She'd heard them over and over for the last three years. But this time it hit, like a light switched on in a long-dark room and she could suddenly see clearly. Her daughter was calling for help, and she had ignored it for too long. But her brain couldn't keep up with her emotions. Her response was not the one she really wanted: wrap her arms around her child, nurture her, provide that safe and happy space, that homecoming that she understood but lacked herself. But she should give it to her daughter. Her daughter, who'd received that awful tear-filled call from her mom when she was just a freshman at Stanford, still finding her footing in her new environment, that call from her needy mom sobbing the news that she and her dad were getting a divorce. A call that Jenny hadn't needed, with all of her mental and emotional energy being demanded in challenging subjects about literature and history and calculus and making new friends in a place where she knew no one. And here was the one solid thing she could rely on—her parents—suddenly broken.

Julia needed to sit down.

All she could come up with was, "Look, Jenny, we've gone over this before. You know I—"

"Actually, Mom, I'm not sure I do, and I—"

"Now, listen here, Jenny, you don't know—"

Jenny cut her off again. "Yeah, there's a lot I don't know, but I do know this. I'm done with this stupid call." Then she hung up.

Julia, shaking, struggled to catch her breath. God, not only was she a failure, she was a failure in the eyes of her daughter.

Declan emerged from the waiting room and approached her, grinning. "They're saying it'll be at least another hour before they can get to it, but, meanwhile, here we are in scenic Timbuktu."

He stepped close and leaned in, but Julia pushed two hands against his chest. "Go away."

Declan immediately pulled back, looking confused, then turned and left. Julia looked around, disoriented. Dear God, Timbuktu is right, and here she is with her "new lover boy from the campground."

She leaned an arm against the brick façade of the building. A large wasp crawled slowly across the rough surface. She knew it was a yellowjacket, its beautiful body banded in black and gold. It moved slowly. Was it injured? She leaned closer. It wasn't healthy, that was for sure. But it was persisting. What the hell was this wasp doing out here in this lifeless desert? Was there a home it was longing for? Do insects have something more than instinct that keeps them going? Maybe hope?

"It's okay, Miss Yellowjacket, I'm here."

A booming voice said, "Whatcha lookin' at, ma'am?" A big trucker leaned in for a better view.

Before she could respond, his huge fist pounded the wasp flat. "Those things can hurt you," he said, as he turned and headed into the Flying J.

Julia could no longer hold back the sobs, as she collapsed onto a nearby bench and buried her face in her hands. She felt a touch on her shoulder and looked up. It was Elizabeth.

"What's wrong, Julia?"

Julia made no effort to hide her crying from Elizabeth. "It's my daughter. I'm afraid I'm losing her."

She felt Elizabeth's touch become a grip. Elizabeth looked like she was about to cry, too. She said, "I had a daughter once."

Chapter 27

He'd screwed up again. What got him in trouble in Washington had been his inability to respond quickly and correctly in a stressful situation. Here he was again. He'd turned and left when Julia pushed him away, instead of asking her what was wrong, instead of patiently being present until things got sorted out. But she had said, "Go away," and, unable to react in a more assertive way, he had. Now he sat with questions. What happened to Julia? Was it the call to her daughter? Had the immensity of their dangerous situation finally taken hold in her mind? Or had she realized that this relationship between them, whatever it was, was heading in the wrong direction, and she was decisively putting a stop to it? He could get up right now and go back outside and speak with her, but maybe he should give her space. The truth was, he didn't know what to do.

He sat in a molded plastic chair in the service waiting area, amid the strong smell of tires and stale popcorn. The all-white, stark room, illuminated by harsh fluorescents, was as bleak as the eastern New Mexico landscape outside. Two other men, both ruddy looking truckers with beards and logo caps, shared the space with him, gazing vacantly at a TV mounted in the corner, blaring some expert on Fox News.

Declan pulled out his phone and scrolled mindlessly through a sports site, then put the phone away just as a young man sat down next to him. Declan returned his friendly nod.

The man checked something on his phone, then turned toward Declan. "So, what are you in here for?"

"Getting a tire fixed."

"Blowout?"

"Not sure. They should be looking at it soon."

"That Winnebago yours?" the man said, nodding toward the service area.

Declan began to speak, then stopped. Why was this guy interested in his vehicle? He gave a noncommittal nod and pulled out his phone again.

The guy didn't give up easily. "So, where you headed?" He was a decent looking young man, maybe thirty, smooth shaven with short-trimmed hair. Maybe one of the men Elizabeth had seen at the campsite?

"Just traveling." Declan didn't want to give away information but also didn't want to alert this man to his suspicion. "How about you?"

"Heading west. Just seeing the country."

Declan stood, stretched and yawned, doing his best to look like a bored, weary traveler. He walked to the entrance and did a quick scan of the parking lot. Mostly trucks and a couple large RVs. Then his eyes landed on the sedan, black, parked at the far edge of the parking area. There was a black storage box on top. Dear Lord. He considered what to do. Go out and alert Julia and Elizabeth? Go check out the sedan? He licked his dry lips, then turned, doing his best to look nonchalant, and returned to his seat. "What are you in for?"

The young man lowered his phone and smiled. He didn't seem to be feeling the stress that Declan was. "Just getting a couple things checked out."

Declan nodded, doing his best to look uninterested. He realized that what he said next might reveal his suspicion. But maybe that would be a good thing. Maybe this man needed to know that Declan was onto them, wasn't afraid of them, would push back. But then he imagined this clean-cut young man with the smiling face pouring gasoline on his Corolla last night, and he shrunk back. For all he knew, this guy had a gun tucked into his Levi's, beneath his Life-is-Good T-shirt. What would The Rock do? Probably grab one of the plastic chairs, whack this guy good, and beat a confession out of him. But Declan didn't know what to do.

"So, figured out where you're camping tonight?" the man said. He leaned back, looking relaxed, one leg across the other.

Declan shrugged. Maybe he wasn't the best in the spontaneity department, but he was a physicist, after all, a practitioner of analysis and observation. So, he would do everything he could to commit to memory every detail about this dude. From the gold earring in his left ear to his Sperry Topsiders with no socks. Five-ten, one-seventy, he guessed. Thirty. Green eyes, nearly black hair. No visible tattoos. All-American voice, with no hint of a regional accent that might identify his origin.

Elizabeth said there were two men. Where was the other one? Maybe the shaved-headed guy? Outside, grilling Julia? Or, God forbid, in the service area, going through the RV again. Declan stood and slowly made his way over to the service bays. The RV sat in one of the bays, but it didn't look like anyone had started working on it yet. The other bays were filled with truck chassis. He watched the RV for several minutes but saw no indication of suspicious activity. He turned back toward the waiting area. The young man was gone.

Declan raced toward the door. No sign of the man. The black car in the parking lot was gone, also. He stood with hands on hips, fighting off hyperventilation. He was certain now. This man, who looked like a wholesome young dad from suburbia was, in fact, the man who'd torched his car. The man who probably had stolen top-secret property. The man who was a terrorist. An enemy of the country.

Declan hurried out to the front of the building, where Julia had been. She was gone.

Chapter 28

"I used to have a good life," Elizabeth said. "You wouldn't know it, but I've got a master's degree from the University of Chicago. I taught US history at a community college. I loved it. I was good at it." She spoke slowly and carefully, looking straight at Julia. Her eyes showed little emotion, but her hands fidgeted with the glass of Diet Pepsi in front of her.

Julia sat across from Elizabeth in a plastic booth at the small Denny's attached to the Flying J. The tears from her disastrous call had dried, and she was now completely focused on Elizabeth, who at last seemed ready to talk about herself. Apparently, those tears and her confession about Jenny had triggered something in Elizabeth, and the flood gates were opening.

"How long ago was this, Elizabeth?"

"Twelve years." All the years of wandering the streets, sleeping in unlocked cars, stealing food, and running from the authorities had taken a toll: the gray hair hanging in tangled strings around her face, the skin like corrugated leather, the teeth that showed the effects of no dental care in over a decade.

Julia sipped her Sprite and waited for Elizabeth to continue.

"I was a gentle, intellectual person. But I killed someone." Elizabeth pinched her mouth tight, and her eyes bulged, like she was struggling to hold something in, but was about to explode anyway. Julia worried that she might be having a heart attack.

But then she took another sip of her Pepsi and looked away, like she was searching for something in the distance. When she looked back at Julia, she said, "My granddaughter."

Julia could barely breathe. Had Elizabeth really just said that? She wasn't sure how to respond.

"You're the first friend I've had in twelve years," Elizabeth said.

Julia swallowed hard, then ventured, "What do you mean you killed your granddaughter?"

Elizabeth tilted her head, like a dog discerning the words of its master. She looked down and was silent for a long time. Julia waited. Then she looked up and began. "Angie was a beautiful child. Five years old. That beautiful yellow dress…" She closed her eyes for a moment, like she was seeing it. "She and I—"

Declan burst in from out of nowhere, breathless. "They were here. I just talked to one of them."

"The men in the black car?" Julia rose halfway out of her seat. "Are they here now?

Declan told Julia and Elizabeth about his encounter with the man in the waiting room, about seeing the black car with a roof box. "Maybe they're gone, but they know where we are."

"Where were they? I never saw anyone. Did you, Elizabeth?"

Elizabeth shook her head.

"Come, I'll show you." They went to a window just behind their booth that faced the parking lot. "It was over there," he said, pointing toward the far edge of the lot.

"Oh, my God," blurted Julia, "it's still here." A black sedan with a roof rack was now pulled up next to one of the pumps. As they watched, the driver's door opened, and a young woman climbed out. She reached back in and brought out a toddler, then began to fill her tank. "I don't think there's anyone else in the car," said Julia, squinting toward the vehicle. "Did you see the man get into that car?"

"Well, no."

"I'd like to look closer," said Elizabeth. "At the other side."

Declan and Julia followed Elizabeth out around the front of the Denny's to the other side of the pumps. "What are you looking for?" asked Julia.

"The sticker. The white, oval sticker. It's not there. That isn't the car."

Julia turned back toward Declan, who was shaking his head. Her eyes searched him, but she said nothing.

"Okay," said Declan, "maybe I was wrong about the car. But the guy I talked to. He …." His voice trailed off, as his eyes darted between Julia and Elizabeth, like he was convinced they thought he was crazy.

Julia looked out towards the endless desert beyond the blacktop, her mind awash with the chaos of the past hour: Jenny's call, Elizabeth's horrible story and now Declan's report of the mysterious man. She wasn't sure one way or the other about the guy Declan met. She looked into his face and laid a hand on his shoulder. She'd been such a jerk to him earlier. She had a lot to work through, but she didn't need to take it out on him. "I believe you," she said, then stepped close to him and laid her head against his chest for just a moment. To hell with Elizabeth's bizarre story, and Jenny's call, and the canister. Forget Fort Huachuca—one of those run-down motels along Route 66 sounded like a good destination right now. She closed her eyes and relived that moment in his arms out on the interstate. She wanted that again—wanted more, right now—all that "lover boy from the campground" crap be damned.

Chapter 29

A stupid nail. It took three hours before the mechanics could look at their damaged tire, then just fifteen minutes to fix it. Now, they were back on the road, off the interstate and headed out on a desert highway that would take them south to Alamogordo, New Mexico—Declan recalled that some type of nuclear weapons testing happened near there—on to Las Cruces, then west across more desert into Arizona. Sierra Vista was still nearly ten hours away. Even with the hour they'd gained when they crossed into the Mountain Time Zone at the New Mexico border, it was already after three.

He was certain that Julia hadn't bought into his conclusions about the man in the waiting room, and now, after the embarrassing black-sedan fiasco, he wasn't sure either.

But one thing he'd learned as an experimental physicist was to not hastily dismiss evidence, no matter how meager. He knew the story well of how, at the beginning of the twentieth century, many scientists thought physics was a closed subject. They had the classical mechanics of Newton and the electromagnetic theory of Maxwell and Faraday. With these tools, scientists could calculate and explain everything of interest, from the motion of the planets to the behavior of electric circuits. But there were a few small glitches in the great explanations, tiny discrepancies between what the theories predicted and what was measured. Tiny discrepancies that could easily be ignored. And most of the scientific community did just that. But there were a few physicists like Einstein and Planck, who wouldn't overlook the discrepancies. And their closer inspection of these small details exploded into a whole new realm of scientific understanding and brought forth the great theoretical workhorses of the present day: relativity and quantum mechanics.

Declan stared out the window at the empty desert speeding by. He was no Einstein, but he wasn't going to ignore the small details. He would treat this like the scientist he was. He shook his head slowly. Or maybe he was just a paranoid fool.

Julia was focused on burning up the miles. And since she pushed him away out front the Flying J and then his making an ass out of himself over the guy in the Life is Good T-shirt, he was giving her some space. Yes, she had later pressed against him briefly, but that was probably out of pity for his embarrassing behavior.

Julia broke into his hypnotic gazing at the unchanging landscape. "You said you always regretted not going with Henry Chee to teach the kids on the reservation. Why was that?"

He turned toward her, surprised she wanted to talk. For a woman who had been on the road for pushing eight hours and hadn't showered in God-knows-how-long, she looked fresh and—dare he think it?—quite sexy. Her hair that had been neatly pulled behind her head this morning was now a windblown mess that gave her a free and reckless look. Her lips had a slight upturn at the corners, like she knew some juicy secret or more likely was getting ready to lay one of her saucy zingers on you. He cleared his throat. "Guess I was curious to see his home." No, that wasn't right. He rubbed his chin. "Maybe I always wanted to teach children, especially about science."

"Did you ever consider being a teacher?"

"No, I never … " He looked again out the window at the bleak landscape, struggling for an answer to her simple question. Then he turned back toward her. "Truth is, my dad wouldn't have approved. He wanted me to be a researcher." He swallowed. "Guess that makes me look pretty spineless."

This would have been a good time for one of the smartass comments he'd come to expect from Julia, and in fact enjoyed. But, instead, she said, "I don't think that's being spineless. It's normal to want to please your parents. I certainly didn't please my father when I dropped out of college, and when I got divorced, my mother thought it was my fault." She groaned at this, then laughed. "I think I'm just now getting over all that."

Declan laid a hand on her forearm. "I'm sorry. Do you still see them?"

She looked down at his hand on her arm and was silent for a moment. "Not very often."

"But you were just in Wisconsin. Surely, you saw them then."

"Actually, I didn't contact them while I was there." She looked like she was about to say more but didn't.

Declan sensed that she needed some quiet. He tore open a bag of trail mix from the stash and held it out to her.

She peeked into the bag, probing for a moment, as if searching for an M&M among the nuts. "I don't really want to talk about that right now, if that's okay." Quickly moving on, she said, "So, it must have been exciting being a physicist at a big lab. I bet you met some famous scientists."

Declan let his mind wander back to his physics days. "Yeah, I guess I met a few big-time scientists, but physics research is mostly a solitary world. Just you surrounded by a sea of equipment. At least, that's the way it was for me."

"Tell me about that."

It was always pleasant to relive those special moments that only an experimental physicist knows about. Moments that come after months of hard and frustrating work on research equipment that often fails to perform as hoped—after months of pulling your hair out over computer programs that won't run, undiscoverable leaks in a vacuum system, the elusive noise in the recording electronics that you can't eliminate. "Physics experiments can be very frustrating. They are usually so complicated that it's almost impossible to get all the equipment working together at the same time."

Though she was focused on the road, she shot him curious glances every few seconds that said go on.

"There's an old joke about how to identify what kind of research is going on in a laboratory you enter. If it stinks or pops, it's chemistry. If it moves, it's biology. If it doesn't work, it's physics."

Julia bounced in her seat with laughter.

"But then there are those rare moments when it all comes together. Maybe it's two AM, and you're there by yourself, and you're watching the readout on some recorder, and the long-sought data comes rolling in. Data that gives you an exclusive peek into some aspect of reality that no other human has ever seen."

"Wow."

"You want to jump up and down and holler. You want to call someone, but no one's awake at that hour." He recalled those infrequent times, surrounded by purring vacuum pumps, flashing LED displays in racks of electronics, lasers, optical systems of mirrors and lenses and super-high-speed cameras, and the jungle of the electrical cables—all of it suddenly performing as you had hoped. And yet, despite being state of the art, the equipment could not grasp the significance of this moment. They emitted no cheers or laughter, they showed no inclination to jump up and down and holler with you. They did what they were supposed to do, but they were lousy companions. "Yeah," he said, "those were special times." He was quiet for a second. "That was a long time ago."

Then he looked at her, and it almost took his breath away, this beautiful woman and her eyes probing him. The last thing he wanted now was to be back in that lonely lab. Even with his car torched last night and the perpetrators possibly still in pursuit, he wanted to be right where he was. Next to her.

Chapter 30

Julia had made several of these long cross-country slogs over the past three years. Endless miles across the flat, monotonous midsection of the country. No interesting mountains, bodies of water or skylines to hold your attention. But that was okay with her. Usually, she just soaked up the silence, excited about what awaited at her destination. Her world was a self-contained package, just Nivvie, her home and herself, rolling down the highway toward the next adventure.

But today she had Declan next to her, and she couldn't imagine a better traveling companion. He bore a mystery about him—this brilliant man, alone and wounded, carrying regrets that never allowed him to laugh for very long. But then he had grabbed her—yes, grabbed was probably the right word—and kissed her last night. And those kisses at the side of the interstate. Lordy, that could have escalated quickly.

Julia straightened in her seat as she felt his eyes sweeping her body. It was just a brief glance then back to the road, but it caused her to flush. Was she slouching too much? It was an appraising glance, and it was like electricity. Needing a diversion, she leaned toward the dash and punched on the radio. "The USB on this old wreck doesn't work, and I don't have any CDs for the CD player. Wanna find us something to listen to?"

Declan could find only a few AM stations out here. He scrolled past an emotional voice preaching about eternal damnation, then past another guy ranting about all the things wrong with the country. He settled on an oldies station, where

Creedence sang "Who'll Stop the Rain," then leaned back and closed his eyes, apparently satisfied.

It was becoming clear to Julia that they'd never make it to Sierra Vista tonight. It'd be the middle of the night when they got there. And who knew what would await them when they arrived—they'd need to be fresh and at the top of their game. She imagined a guard at an entry gate that they'd need to convince to allow them to speak to a security official. She wasn't going to just hand the drive over to another Purkle type, then drive off to get coffee. She was going to see this thing through.

So, if they weren't going to make it to Sierra Vista tonight, what were they going to do? Considering the options was a more pleasant alternative to replaying the tape of Jenny hanging up on her.

Julia realized she had the steering wheel in a death grip. She exhaled a long cathartic breath. Here she was in her beloved Minnie Winnie driving out across the great American Southwest, with the streaking afternoon sun and mountain shadows creating a slowly swirling palette of golds and grays before her.

Declan had nodded off almost immediately after Creedence had begun, and she could afford a long look at him. She imagined sliding over and snuggling in close, resting her head on his shoulder as he napped. Maybe he would come awake and take her in her arms, and who knows where that might lead. This "lover boy from the campground." Hah. Those words had humiliated her when Jenny had hurled them at her. Now she savored them.

Julia squirmed as she had to refocus on her driving. Her mind turned to the troubling conversation with Elizabeth. She'd killed her granddaughter? What was she supposed to do with that little factoid? Julia shot a troubled glance toward the rear, where Elizabeth napped in the dinette area, her head resting against the window, Nivvie curled up at her feet.

Declan yawned and stretched. He couldn't have slept well in the front seat last night. "Oh my," he groaned. "I didn't mean to nod off. Have I been out long?"

"Just a few minutes."

"Guess I needed that," he said, stretching again. Then with a fake-alert, serious voice, obviously meant to arouse laughter, he said, "So, where were we?"

"So, you said you don't have kids."

He gave her a disinterested shrug, then, as if looking for a distraction, began poking around in the glove compartment, finally pulling out the owner's manual for the F350.

"Trying to be prepared, in case you need to change a taillight bulb?"

He put the book back into the glove compartment, then stared out at the highway that stretched in a straight line toward the horizon. "Frankly, I'm not sure why we never had children. Early in our relationship we talked about it, and we both agreed we'd like to have kids at some point. But then we got busy with careers, and somehow the idea of kids just kept getting pushed off into the future." He gave out a cynical chuckle, then added, "You think you've got all the time in the world, but you don't." Now he looked at her. "Then I got fired and our marriage began to take a nosedive, and we didn't talk about kids after that. Then she got sick, and …" He shook his head. "So, no, I don't have any children."

Well, that sounded depressing. She gave him what she thought was a sympathetic look. She'd been savoring romantic fantasies, and here he was lamenting how his life had been a tragedy.

He was apparently ready to change the subject. "So, how'd you become a campground host?"

She gazed out at the road stretching to infinity, leading to new experiences, to things she'd never seen, perhaps never even dreamed of. To a place where everything was new, where yesterday's regrets did not matter. All that, of course, was the answer to his question.

But how it actually happened was simple. She glanced at him out of the corner of her eye, as she watched a big semi ahead that she'd have to pass soon. "I was just starting out with the Minnie Winnie, and I was a real rookie. Didn't even know how to start a campfire. And I remember meeting these campground hosts, a retired couple, who were so friendly. The way they welcomed me, didn't judge what an amateur I was—I think it was right there I decided I wanted to be a campground host. They gave me a website to look at, and the rest is history."

"You're really good at it. I mean you seem so natural talking to people."

Julia blushed as she recalled her ridiculous invitation to Declan to come in for hot chocolate. She nodded a thank you.

Of course, she now seemed to have a new vocation: managing a mobile homeless shelter.

Jenny's snide comment about no one ever going to Harvard to get a degree in campground hosting popped back into her head, causing her to wince. But she had to admit that was the kind of smart-ass comment she'd have been proud to come up with herself. A smile replaced her grimace, as she reflected on her profession. Okay, profession was a stretch for an activity that is a volunteer position, usually staffed by retired folks. But she was making ends meet. Close to making ends meet. Sure, she had zero salary, but a campground host did receive a free campsite, usually one of the best—lots of million-dollar mansions had worse locations. And it came with free utilities. On top of that, the tips she received—for delivering firewood to people's campsites, providing information, and just being a welcoming presence—covered most of her food costs. So, the basics were covered. Her few other costs—cell phone, gas for the Minnie Winnie, a couple of writing classes a year and maybe a once-in-a-while splurge on a new fleece from LL Bean—came out of her small savings account. She figured she could keep going for ten years at this rate, before she had to get a job. By then she'd no doubt be earning money from her writing. Wouldn't she?

She almost laughed out loud when she recalled the tongue-in-cheek writing advice she'd heard from one novelist at a conference: "The first twelve years are the hardest."

She'd never consulted a financial planner—that would cost too much, and anyway, who could look you in the eye without bursting into laughter when you shared your career goal of being a campground host?

Declan's comment about thinking you have all the time in the world came back to her. She now drew a quick, almost imperceptible breath, as she pulled around the semi. Who was she kidding? She was out here—she again considered the endless wilderness in all directions—heading down the highway like there was no tomorrow. But there is a tomorrow, and it wouldn't be long until Jenny would no longer be in it. She'd be off living in Geneva or Mexico City or New York, and she'd never get to see her. There would be no more pleading for a place to come home to, for a mom to be present. She choked back a sob. What the hell was she doing here? As best as Julia could discern at this moment, she was nothing more than a runaway.

She glanced at Declan with pleading eyes. Come on, she thought, say something that would get her laughing again.

But he came back with, "So your daughter's a senior at Stanford, as I recall. Do you get to see her often? I mean with you traveling and all."

She would have kicked him if she could. But all she said was, "Yeah."

"You must be very proud."

She didn't want to talk about Jenny. "I am."

"That doesn't sound very enthusiastic."

"We're going through a rough patch right now. Communications kind of thing."

"But you talked to her today, right?"

Julia nodded. Reliving that call again wasn't on her bucket list.

"That's good."

Julia gave out a cynical laugh. "Yeah, it'd be good if I didn't think she hated me."

"Oh, come on, Julia. She doesn't hate you."

"She thinks I'm meddling in her life, thinks I don't understand what she's going through. Then, on the other hand, she thinks I'm not there for her. I don't have a home with a cozy bedroom just waiting for her." She blurted out these words quickly in an emotional gush.

"I'm sure it's not that bad."

"Look, I don't want to talk about this right now. I've just got some crap to work through."

"Okay." He turned his attention to the road ahead.

But after a long silence, Julia continued. "She wants to take some time off before finishing her senior year. Wants to see the world with her new boyfriend. Butch or Boffo or ... Blake, that's it. Damn it, that's what I did. And look at me. Forty-three years old and I never finished my last year of college."

"What did you say to her?"

"I gave her some parental-judgment lecture. I didn't mean to. I meant to be a good listener, be understanding." She gave out a growl of disgust. "What do you think I should say to her?"

"Hey, I'm not some expert, you know."

"You're the only expert I've got right now," she said.

"I don't know what you should say. But I do suspect a couple things. I suspect you're a very good mom. And I suspect that down deep Jenny knows it."

Julia shot him a defeated look. "That's a sweet thing to say. But I'm still feeling shitty about this."

He sighed slowly and whispered, "Why do relationships have to be so complicated?"

"I'm working on the answer to that question."

"I'll bet it fuels your novel writing. I mean, that's a topic everyone's interested in, right?"

It should fuel her writing, of course. But there was little about relationships in her novels. Why was that? Why was she writing thrillers when she obviously knew so little about what a thrilling life is? "Not really," she said. "Thrillers, remember?"

Declan nodded, then smiled. "You mean like a campground host finding a top-secret canister?"

Julia had to laugh. "Yeah, something like that."

"I guess I'm surprised you're not writing more about human relationships. I mean, I hear you talking about your daughter, but I also saw how ..." He glanced toward the rear, where Elizabeth still slept … "How you show compassion for other people. You're much better at that than I am."

"Oh, really, Mr. Drive-halfway-across-the-country-do-gooder?"

"What I'm trying to say is that you've got insight about people, and maybe you're including all those things in your novels already, but if you're just trying to produce Jack-Reacher-two-point-oh, then …" He seemed suddenly to be at a loss for words. "Geez, I don't know where I'm going with this. I don't know anything about writing a novel, and I sure don't mean to tell you how to run your life."

But what he had just said hit a nerve, maybe had more impact than all the advice she'd gotten from the pros at those writing conferences. Oddly, she'd never even considered focusing her writing in a new direction, like he'd just suggested. She'd started working on her first manuscript shortly after Gary left. Maybe her foray into writing was a Hail Mary pass to rescue herself from the spiral into despair. Plunging herself into a wild world of assassins and espionage and malevolent criminals prowling in the darkness had provided her with an escape from the dreary reality of her life, even though she had little knowledge about any of these things. *Velveeta.* Maybe she should be grateful to that critic in Madison. Writing about anything personal and emotional would have just been too painful in those first days on her own. But even though she may have launched off into the wrong genre of writing, she had discovered something more valuable than being acclaimed the next David Baldacci. She discovered that she loved writing.

Declan's eyes were still locked on her, as his comment about writing about relationships had gone unanswered. It felt good to have him look at her this way—inquiring, assessing.

The eyes of someone who was interested. Yes, she had stayed away from topics like romance and love and heartbreak and deep longing. But now, as she met Declan's gaze, it seemed clear that writing about those things was what she'd always been called to do.

Since her divorce, she'd been convinced that her survival would be dependent on her tenacity. That had stood her well in those early days of learning how to drive an RV, how to live alone in a campground, how to persist in her writing, how not to be easily intimidated as she once had been. But now she wondered. Maybe courage is to set out in a direction and stay the course, stick to your plans—that had been her credo for the past three years. But maybe courage is something else: to deviate from a set course, to toss away the well-crafted battle plan, and to head off in an entirely new direction. She was already thinking about an opening line of a new novel: *Her daughter didn't call again this week.*

Finally, she said, "Thank you."

Declan continued to study her. "So, what do you imagine is on the flash drive? I mean, maybe it's just the weekly cafeteria menu."

Julia laughed. "What if it's a list of secret agents?"

He nodded agreement. "Or some kind of code encryption? I mean, that place works on computer security stuff, right?"

"Or blueprints for the latest tactical weapon."

"Or the cafeteria menu," he said. Their shared laughter felt good.

"You know what?" she said. "It's kinda nice having someone like you to talk to out here in the middle of nowhere." She would move into his arms if they weren't strapped into seat belts and heading down the highway at sixty miles an hour.

Chapter 31

For mile after mile, short vegetation dotted the otherwise barren landscape. Only an occasional distant windmill and, in one place, a wind farm, gave any evidence of human existence in this harsh land. So, an hour later, when they arrived in Alamogordo, New Mexico, which the city limits sign said was home to thirty-thousand people, it felt like they'd arrived in Manhattan.

Elizabeth was now alert. "People have been living around here for over ten thousand years," she said. "The Clovis culture was one of the earliest signs of human existence in North America. They were hunter gatherers."

"Sorta like us," quipped Julia.

They all laughed, then Declan said, "Elizabeth, how do you know that kind of stuff?"

Elizabeth shrugged, then Julia nodded back at Elizabeth, "She's got a master's in history from the University of Chicago."

Elizabeth continued, "And the first test of a nuclear weapon was at Trinity Site, not far from here. It's odd to think that this is one of the places where human culture began in North America and one of the places where mankind set in motion the ability to end it."

Julia and Declan looked at each other with raised eyebrows.

Steep rocky mountains loomed behind the dozen blocks of downtown Alamogordo. The weathered old storefronts were a mishmash of motifs, no doubt reflecting the city's diverse heritage: part dusty cowboy town, part adobe Mexican pueblo, part old-brick Midwest Main Street—all of it having seen better days. The sad reality of many storefronts with faded *For Lease* signs in their windows was a clear reminder of the pandemic and those last days at Conor's.

But Conor had ultimately prevailed. Today's call proved that. What was Declan going to do about Conor's offer to join him in California? He glanced over at Julia, craning her neck to take in as much of Alamogordo as she could. Maybe he was beginning to prevail, too. "How about a coffee?" he said, gesturing toward Piñon Coffee Roasters, which had that look of a good place.

Julia laughed. "I was just thinking the same thing. We've still got a way to go."

Piñon Coffee Roasters bustled. People of all ages gathered around mismatched, antique wooden tables—from laughing elderly couples to young students hunched over laptops. Two baristas were busy behind expensive-looking brass and stainless brewing equipment, backed by a huge chalkboard listing a tantalizing array of coffees and snacks. Old wallpaper that looked like it was from a Wild-West bordello, and ceilings of hundred-year-old hammered metal made you think that Butch Cassidy might stroll in at any moment.

They took seats around a rickety old table that could have been a museum piece, next to a window that allowed them to keep an eye on the RV. As Julia checked out the big chalkboard, she said, "This is way beyond my budget, but screw it, I'm having a latte. Sometimes you've got to live it up a little."

Declan ordered a small black coffee. Elizabeth didn't want anything, even though they offered to treat her.

"I love these old places," Julia said.

"I do, too. Out in LA, where I grew up, there aren't many places like this. That's one of the things I love about Wisconsin."

"Yeah, but you had the ocean. So, were you a surfer dude?"

Declan hadn't sat in a coffee shop with friends for years. "Me a surfer dude?" He laughed. "Of course."

"Funny, you don't look like a surfer dude."

"Looks can be deceiving."

She cocked her head, like she was studying him closer. "I'd say you really do look like a physicist."

"Uh oh. That nerdy? Ouch."

"No, no. Not nerdy at all. Well, maybe a little nerdy." She pressed a forefinger against her chin. "What I mean is that you look thoughtful, serious, intelligent—like you're evaluating solutions to global warming."

Right now, he was evaluating her face, her inquisitive green eyes and those lovely lips and fair skin he wanted to touch.

She giggled after he'd been quiet too long. "What?"

"Nothing." He felt like laughing, too. "It's just that … I'm really enjoying this."

"Me, too."

Even Elizabeth, who had sat quietly with them at the table, was smiling.

"Hey, why don't I get a selfie? We are kind of on vacation." Julia already had her phone held out at arm's length.

Declan straightened. "I'll try not to look too nerdy."

"Here, squeeze in," she said.

Declan scootched his chair closer.

"You, too, Elizabeth. You're a part of the gang."

Elizabeth shook her head but moved her chair closer.

From behind them came a woman's voice. "Want me to take your picture?"

They all turned to face a smiling, middle-aged woman at the next table, her hand extended toward them.

"Uh, sure," said Julia, handing her phone to the woman.

The woman leaned back, trying to frame a perfect family shot. She took one, checked it and shook her head. "Let me try this again." She took several more, then scrolled through them. "That's better, I think." She tapped in a few commands. "Just a sec, I can't resist editing a bit." Apparently becoming irritated, Julia extended her hand, and the woman quickly passed the camera back to her. "I'm sorry, don't mean to be snoopy. I just love looking at people's pictures."

Julia took the phone with a bit of a tug that showed she didn't appreciate the woman's nosy behavior.

"I'm travelling. Always looking for ideas of things to see. I'm Evelyn." Probably mid-fifties. Her light brown hair, heavily streaked with gray, cut in a no-nonsense bob. Somebody's grandma.

Declan thought how impressive it was that women like Julia and Evelyn travelled alone out into places far from civilization.

Julia seemed to relax. "No problem," she said. She looked at the photos, then passed the phone to Declan and Elizabeth.

They all turned back to their table, but then Evelyn said, "I love this place. I know it looks old, but it really hasn't been here that long."

Declan wasn't in the mood for a visit.

Julia said, "You live around here?" Channeling her inner camp host, no doubt, making people feel comfortable.

"No, but I come through once in a while." Evelyn wore a thick flannel shirt, unbuttoned over a gray T shirt. "How 'bout you?"

"Oh, no," said Julia. "We're traveling."

"Where to?"

Julia glanced at Declan, took a sip of her latte, then said, "Just seeing the country." Good work, Julia, thought Declan.

"I'm headed out to San Diego to see my sister. Guessing you're heading west, too." She fiddled with a lock of her hair, then took a sip of her coffee. "Probably have to stop for the night pretty soon. Maybe Las Cruces." She waited for them to respond.

Julia glanced at Declan again, then nodded at Evelyn but didn't say anything.

Declan remembered Mr. Life-is-Good asking where they would be staying tonight. Geez, Declan, you really are paranoid. He offered a friendly see-you-later smile, but Evelyn leaned forward on her elbows. "What do you all do?"

Julia was clearly more skilled at making small talk. "We work remotely." Declan was certain that Julia was proud of her evasive answer. "Well, nice meeting you," Julia said, as she turned back toward Declan. "Guess we should be hitting it, huh?" she said to Declan, signifying the visit was over.

But Evelyn apparently wasn't through chatting. "I love seeing a couple out traveling with their mom." She wrapped a strand of hair around her finger again.

Julia glanced at Elizabeth. She started to speak but then just nodded.

Evelyn looked hard at Elizabeth for a moment, then said, "I forgot where you said you were heading."

"We're just making it up as we go along."

Evelyn nodded, perhaps unsatisfied with Julia's evasive answer. "Where in Wisconsin are you from?" She must have noticed Julia's surprised look. "Oh, sorry, I saw you get out of your RV out there. The Wisconsin plates. Don't mean to be nosy."

Declan's paranoia kicked into gear again, and he hoped Julia would be careful with her answer. Evelyn looked about as harmless see as they came. Come on, Declan, dial it down.

"That's okay," said Julia, not answering Evelyn's question. She glanced at Declan, as if sensing his unwarranted concern.

For just an instant, it seemed like a mood shift flashed in Evelyn's eyes. Anger? But then it vanished, and Declan questioned his observation. Anyone might be annoyed by Julia's evasive answers.

"Well, you all have a great time," Evelyn said. With that, she turned back toward her coffee.

They were all laughing, even Elizabeth, as they climbed back into the RV. Declan wondered what it would be like to be on a real vacation with Julia, like Evelyn had suggested. His imagination could run wild with that. He felt his body tingle, and he almost laughed when he remembered a physics demonstration in high school. Students would touch the electrically charged globe of a Van der Graaf generator, and their bodies would buzz and their hair stand on end. That's what it felt like being near her.

Maybe it was the coffee. Maybe it was sheer exhaustion. Without verbalizing it, they seemed to have had enough of the emergency drill. There seemed to be a relaxation settling in.

At a Conoco station, where they topped off the tank of the gas-guzzling RV and took David Niven out to do his business, Julia pointed toward the busy parking lot next door. A tall sign advertised Blanche's Pistachio Orchards. "Hey, we need to go there. I love pistachios. I mean, we're not going to make it to Sierra Vista tonight anyway. May as well see the sights a little. Right?"

They'd already seen several pistachio stores on the way into town and one sign that boasted Alamogordo as the pistachio capital of the world, a claim Declan doubted. Julia was in a good mood after their coffee break. Even with the car fire, it was almost like they were on vacation, like Evelyn had wondered.

The amazing Blanche's tested Declan's ability to imagine so many ways to market, of all things, pistachios. While he scanned the assortment of pistachio flavors—salty, green chile, lemon-lime, candied, and more—Julia selected several bags for the stash in the RV. Meanwhile, Elizabeth couldn't pull herself away from the big table of free samples. It was the first time Delcan had observed her having fun. And he acknowledged to himself that he was having fun, too, which he had not experienced in a long time.

He watched Julia deliberating over her pistachio selections. She made him think about fun. Even after his car and possessions had just been destroyed, even with the possibility—though faint, they had now concluded—that they were still being followed. Maybe it was foolish, but maybe it was time for this rational steady man to enjoy a little foolishness.

Julia turned to Declan. "You need to try this—green chile," she said, as she held a nut between her forefinger and thumb up to his mouth, with a naughty temptress smile. As she fed him the pistachio, she trailed the fingers of her other hand along his cheek. Declan closed his lips on her thumb and forefinger and held them for a second, like maybe he wouldn't let go. Julia's eyes widened in surprise. Good God, did he just do that?

The store was busy today and for good reason. Tourists seemed to be searching for the perfect pistachio gift for grandma back in Ohio. Laughter and energy were everywhere.

A man across the store caught Declan's attention. He was about the right height, maybe five-ten. There are lots of guys that height, he chided himself, so why had this man caught his attention? Before Declan could study the man's face, he disappeared into another aisle. But in the fraction of a second that he saw the side of the man, he noticed distinctly the gold earring in his left ear. He stepped close to Julia. "There's a man over there," he whispered. "Not sure, but he could be the guy I saw at the Flying J. I'm going to check him out."

Julia's laughter stopped. "Be careful."

Declan nodded, then followed the man, pausing along the way to briefly examine labels. Near the checkout he saw the man leave without purchasing anything. From behind a pillar, he watched him climb into a black pickup truck at the far edge of the lot. The truck didn't leave. Maybe he was waiting for them. It was a big Chevy with a topper on the truck bed. Declan couldn't identify the model from this distance, but it had a large black grille guard over the front bumper. He could see the plate—it was a dark maroon—but couldn't make out the lettering on it. Dark-tinted windows prevented him from seeing if there were other passengers inside.

Julia had followed and was beside Declan now. "He got into that black truck? Not a sedan with a Yakima box."

"Yeah, but they could've switched vehicles. This one is from … he scrolled through his phone looking at images of license plates. There was only one dark maroon plate—Arizona. He held the image up for Julia to study. "That guy had an earring in his left ear, just like the guy at the Flying J. And he left without buying anything."

"Maybe he doesn't like pistachios," she shot back, in her usual smartass way, but then added, "Okay, to play the devil's advocate here—not saying you're wrong—there are going to be lots of Arizona plates around here—it's New Mexico. And I'll bet there are a lot of guys with earrings." She had her hands on her hips and a worried look on her face. "Having said all that, good work, Declan. Maybe it's him, maybe it isn't."

Of course she was right. There's a balance between being reckless and being paranoid. And he'd usually veered toward paranoia. And if you're paranoid, then everyone you meet looks like a threat. Truth is, if he hadn't been so shaken by the fire, then none of the people they'd seen today would stir any suspicion.

He turned back toward the interior of the store and tried to recapture the upbeat mood. "So, what are we going to do now? I don't see us making it all the way to Sierra Vista tonight. Just too far."

"I agree. I say we go as far as Las Cruces; it's not that far from here."

"Fine. But let's not camp out in the boonies again. We need the safety of people around us."

"I found a KOA just west of Las Cruces. Hopefully, we'd be surrounded by big rigs, but that doesn't sound too bad right now. Then tomorrow, it's a four-hour drive to the base. Here, check this out." She held up the map displayed on her phone.

Declan nodded. "So, we're going right past White Sands National Park. Sorry to miss that."

Julia studied the phone, as she rubbed a knuckle under her chin. "A national park … If we're only going to Las Cruces, we'd have time for a short visit. But maybe that's too risky?"

Probably not the prudent thing to do, he thought. He looked into her eyes. But do prudent people ever have fun? The image of her fingers between his lips was too fresh. "I say, let's stop at White Sands." He stared out at the black truck. "And if anyone is watching us, a side trip might be a good diversion. Maybe convince them we really are tourists."

"Geez. A freaking national park. Let's do it."

It was clear she wasn't ready for the fun to end. He brushed the side of Julia's face with two fingers. "You're something else. You know that?"

Julia giggled shyly.

Then he added, "Yeah, let's go. Even for an hour."

Chapter 32

Julia wasn't a big fan of cities, even small ones, so it felt good to be leaving Alamogordo. Sure, she'd driven right into the heart of a large one yesterday, but that was to see the bombing memorial—it was a focused goal; she could drive in, then drive out. Maybe the last few years had changed her. She had, after all, been raised in Milwaukee, gone to college at an urban campus there, got married there and settled down for almost twenty years in the burbs. But nowadays, she'd much rather be writing on her laptop from her campsite looking up at the Grand Teton or out across Morro Bay or into the thick of the Northwoods. She attributed that change to finding her true self. So, a short visit to a national park couldn't be passed up, even when you're delivering a top-secret package.

The entrance to White Sands National Park, a twenty-minute drive from the pistachio place, was just off US Highway 70, the route to Las Cruces. The high dunes came into view almost as soon as they left Alamogordo—snow white hills of sand on the horizon. Julia read aloud from her phone about the park, as Declan drove. "Okay," she laughed, "when we get closer, I'm putting this damned thing away. I'd rather actually experience White Sands than read about it." But the White Sands literature got her heart pounding, with the heading: *Like No Place Else on Earth*. "Listen to this, guys. It's the largest gypsum dune field in the world, spread out over nearly three-hundred square miles."

He cut in. "Can you say that again? I love it when you say, 'gypsum dune field.'" They laughed.

She skimmed a bit, then added, "Turns out gypsum is rarely found in the form of sand, which makes this place unique."

She skimmed some more, then said, "Geez, several hundred million years ago, this area was the bed of a huge sea, which extended all the way to the Pacific Ocean."

Declan and Elizabeth were taking it all in.

"Ooh, and the best news of all is that Nivvie is allowed on the trails. Very unusual for a national park."

The literature about White Sands wasn't the only thing Julia was paying attention to. She'd kept an eye out for the black pickup, ever since they'd left Blanche's. The pickup had remained in the parking lot, as Declan maneuvered the Minnie Winnie out into traffic, and so far, she hadn't seen it again. She soon realized that there are a million black pickups on the road, but so far, she hadn't spotted one with a grille guard.

At the edge of the dunes, a low-slung complex of hacienda-like buildings housed the visitor center, which the sign said contained a museum, gift shop, and information kiosks. But there would be no time to stop, except to pick up a park map. And to scan the parking area for vehicles—black trucks with grille guards, sedans with Yak racks, or anything else suspicious.

It was already near sunset, and they'd been on the road nearly twelve hours today, including the unplanned stop in Tucumcari. Their visit to the dunes would be a short one, before they headed to the KOA in Las Cruces.

A narrow road led west into the park from the visitor center, following the north flank of the dunes. About a mile in, the road turned directly into the dunes and after another two miles ended at the Alkali Flats trailhead.

Declan pulled the RV into the small parking area.

"Time for a short hike?" Declan asked. He was glowing. The prospect of a hike obviously put him in a good mood and likely dispelled, at least temporarily, thoughts about anyone who might be following them.

The trail from Alkali Flats was more of a route than a trail, a narrow path of sand, compacted by the feet of many hikers. Red metal posts, spaced every hundred yards or so, kept you from getting lost in this vast, featureless sea of sand. The trail was steep, ascending one dune, then down the other side, which was more like sliding than walking. Although the three of them struggled with the sand hills, Nivvie loved it. He'd lead the way up one hill then bound down the other side, leaping as he slid his way down. Julia couldn't remember seeing him this energetic.

They arrived at the top of a high dune just before sunset, where they sat side by side, with Nivvie between Julia and Declan, and watched in silence. There is something about a sunset that quiets any crowd.

"Being out here kind of makes you think about big things," Julia said.

"I was thinking about our conversation with Reverend Pam this morning. She said something like we need to learn that we are loveable. I think she was talking to me."

Julia poked him. "You kidding? She was definitely talking to me."

He laughed. "Yeah, I really liked her. What do you think makes her tick? I mean, look where she lives. Doesn't she get lonely?" He looked out toward the horizon. "I wish I could've spent more time with her."

"Me too." Pam would love this view, she thought. "When she left, she said, 'God be with you.'"

"Yes."

"I think that was more than just some churchy kind of goodbye. It felt like she was saying something more serious, like maybe a prayer."

Declan looked like he was considering something important. They were quiet again. The sun was now about halfway down behind the mountains. The thin lines of clouds were now picking up more color.

Julia asked, "What do you think about God?"

Declan looked at her, rubbed his chin with a forefinger, then said, "My mom was raised Catholic, but my dad made fun of religion, thought it was irrational, that it was for people who were too weak to face life. He liked to mock religious people—said they believe in some invisible guy in the sky who watches out over things." He let out a soft grunt. "My mom never said much about it, but I wonder if down deep she wanted to go to church but was afraid to challenge my dad." He drew his finger through the sand between them, then shook his head.

"But what about you?" She watched him intently now, waiting for his response.

"You know it's funny. Maybe a scientist isn't supposed to think about things they can't prove. But I think the best scientists do. I think maybe I'm open to religion—I just don't know how to approach it. How about you?"

"My mom and dad went to church occasionally. It seemed like it was their duty—I don't remember them wanting to go. Yet, when I got married, my mom was adamant about my wedding being in a church, but we had no church. She found one, though, that would do the wedding. So, I was married in a church in Milwaukee—you know I was so focused on the wedding, I really didn't pay much attention to anything about that church." She watched a long strand of cloud light up orange in the sunset, as a momentary stab of sadness caused her to gasp, and she waited until it had passed, which she noted with a sigh. "Gary wasn't interested in religion—he didn't seem curious about things like that—so it wasn't on our screen." She laid her hand atop his for just a moment, then pulled it away. "Sometimes when it's quiet out in the woods, I think about God. I'd like to go deeper. I saw it in Pam. She seemed to have something I'd like more of."

"Me, too."

Now the sun was gone, and a sudden light breeze brought a chill. But the colors were at their peak, like the crescendo of some cosmic symphony. The sky seemed to be in conflict with the earth: a chaotic swirl of colors, like one of those modern paintings where the artist flings buckets of paint at the canvas. Reds, yellows, golds, blues. A wild feast of color, compared to the dark jagged mountains on the horizon—still and foreboding. And the dunes that stretched out before them displayed a seeming infinity of subtle gradations of white to black. This foreground, in contrast to the sky that looked like the moment of creation and the bleak mountains that hinted of danger, was peaceful. Like different realities. Somewhere in all this was the question for her: What is the reality that I am in?

The dark feelings took her by surprise and almost overwhelmed her. She lay back on the sand, still warm from the sunny day, and closed her eyes. What is my reality? Is it daughters and husbands who suddenly leave you? Is it being broke and alone, with no future beyond the next camp-hosting gig? She glanced up at Declan, who was still transfixed with the view. Was reality the sadness this man has experienced? A wife disappearing for good behind the door of the ER? A career suddenly lost because of a momentary lapse in judgment? A car and all your possessions suddenly engulfed in flames? Is reality a place where people steal government secrets with the intent of doing great harm? A place where secrets are necessary in the first place?

And there was Elizabeth, who sat with her eyes closed. Alone, with no direction, burdened by a terrifying past. How was Elizabeth, whose past was somehow so terrible that she couldn't talk about it, that different from Declan or her? Maybe just a few years older.

She needed to pull herself out of this. She sat up and turned to Declan. "What thoughts are stirring in you, Declan?"

Without looking at her, he said, "Thinking about those patterns in the sand." The sand displayed beautiful ripples, patterns no doubt caused by the wind. "I remember my mother making buttermilk pancakes, and the ripples on the sand remind me of the buttermilk pattern in the emptied measuring cup." He laughed. "I hate buttermilk, but I was entranced by those ripples."

She wasn't interested in the damn ripples right now, no matter how beautiful they were, but she'd go along with him. "So, what causes them?"

Declan explained the physics, as Julia quickly tuned out. He said something about wind speed, the size of the sand particles and their density, not that different in principle, he said, from the way water waves are formed.

Julia nodded with fake fascination. Unable to hold back any longer, unable to avoid the reality that another day was ending, another day of her daughter being—let's face it, she thought—

an orphan. She closed her eyes and the tears began. She didn't want this to happen, but the tears came anyway. She felt Declan's hand on her shoulder. She felt Nivvie's nose pushing against her thigh—he understood such things. She heard Elizabeth saying softly, "There, there, Julia."

Now, Declan's arm came around her.

"I'm okay," she said. "I'm okay." But she wasn't. She recognized these feelings, and she dreaded them, feelings she had not experienced since those first days of utter hopelessness after Gary left. But she had pulled herself up out of that. She had triumphed over the darkness. She had broken free and taken risks. Bought the Minnie Winnie. Hit the road. Became a writer. More than that. She had become a victor.

Or had she?

It was like the interrogation room in a TV cop show, where the bright light comes on and almost blinds the guilty perpetrator. Exposing her. Condemning her. Not just her latest crime but her whole broken life. Her thoughts turned to her mother, as she knew they would, and she was pulled into that dreaded scene, just inside the door of her parents' home.

Even after a week, she hadn't told anyone, even Jenny. She'd tried to call her mom several times but hung up. She longed to be held in her mother's arms but just couldn't face her yet.

Finally, she went over to their house, a simple Craftsman in Waukesha, just three miles away. It was the same house she'd grown up in, and the familiar sight of it comforted her.

Just inside the door, she said, "Mom and dad, I need to tell you something." Her voice shook, and she had to place a hand against the big hutch that had been in the family forever.

Dad stayed seated in his lounger chair, looking straight ahead. Expressionless, as he often was when important topics were being introduced. He only came alive during Packer games on TV. Mom stood and came halfway across the room and stood before Julia, sensing something important. "What is it, Julia?"

Julia was determined to hold back the tears, suppress the shaking. "Mom and dad …" She stopped and closed her eyes and drew a deep breath. "Gary left me. Last week." She looked down at the blue carpet that had always been there, worn and needing to be replaced. She couldn't make eye contact. "For Marylin Shubert, my friend from work. They'd been having an affair for several years."

Her mom took a step toward Julia, maybe to give her a hug, but then stepped back. "Is he coming back?"

She was surprised at these first words from her mom. "No. I'm pretty sure not."

Mom turned abruptly and left the room without speaking. Dad remained in his chair, not saying anything, not making eye contact. But he gripped the arms of his chair tighter than when she'd entered. She imagined him saying he's not surprised— he'd never forgiven her for dropping out of college. Her dad was a high school graduate, who was so proud that his only child was headed off to college, the first member of the family to do so. Getting pregnant was enough of a shock for her conservative family, but when she decided to drop out to raise her child, some door between them had closed.

He remained silent.

Julia shuffled, dying inside.

Then her mother returned. Now would be a good time for that hug. But that's not what she got.

Her mother looked into Julia's face with such intensity she had to avert her eyes. "Dear, you've always been such a perfectionist. Gary's no saint. Lord, we've always known that. But it takes two to tango and two to screw things up. Sure, what he's done is difficult to understand, but we can't always know what's going on inside our men."

Julia felt faint, questioning if she was hearing correctly.

"They're carrying stuff around that I don't think a woman can easily understand. Maybe, hon, you've set your standards too high. It's hard to be around a perfectionist all the time."

Julia was stunned. She desperately needed hugs, but all she got was judgment from her mother and no response from her father.

She stood looking at her mom and dad through the ensuing silence, hoping there would be more. It had been just a year ago that Jenny announced she was selecting Stanford. Julia was proud—no, it was more like dancing-on-the-ceiling—her daughter getting a full scholarship to an elite school. When she'd announced it to her parents, there'd been a hollow, "Wonderful, dear," kind of response. "I guess congratulations are in order." Then some quiet, as her mom waited before adding, "I guess I can understand her wanting to get away from here."

Julia remembered looking at the photo on the wall of her in her high school cap and gown. Maybe the last thing she hadn't screwed up.

Now she looked down at her hands, gripping handfuls of sand. She shook her head to rid herself of that awful memory, then turned to Declan. He'd asked why she hadn't contacted her parents during her last month in Wisconsin, but she couldn't tell him.

Now Jenny's comments today came flooding back again, exposing her camp-hosting vocation for what it was. Running away. And Declan's words about writing about relationships… of course she had chosen thrillers—they were pure escapism— because they helped her avoid pulling the scabs off wounds that had never healed.

In the swirls of evening light, so colorful but already fading, she could see it now. She'd taken no risks at all. She was unable to take a real risk. All her delusions about a new life were now being revealed. She was the same old pathetic mess she'd always been.

Declan now cradled her, and his eyes bathed her. She didn't want this. She sniffled, wishing she had a Kleenex. She met his gaze, but only for a moment. Then she looked back out onto the great sea of sand before her.

Less than ten feet away, a large beetle made its way slowly across the dune. She'd read in the park literature that they were native to these dunes. Darkling beetles, they were called. Julia couldn't speak but pointed toward the animal, shiny black against the sea of white sand. It was an awkward looking thing, moving slowly on long spindly legs. How did it survive in this harsh environment, with little water and little food to sustain it? Its shiny blackness stood out against the white sand, making it easy prey for any predator. And yet, here it was, apparently unconcerned about all these things, out here on this beautiful evening, living its life and taking one step after another.

Chapter 33

KOA—Kampgrounds of America—was the largest commercial chain of campgrounds in the country. Usually located near interstates, they were convenient overnight stays for long-distance travelers. What they lacked in scenic ambiance, KOAs made up for in amenities like clean bathrooms and showers, sometimes a simple meal service, and a reliable uniformity. They were the McDonalds of campgrounds. Declan, in all his camping days, had never stayed at a KOA. He'd rather be in the wilderness.

The Las Cruces KOA was set on a high hill west of the city, near I-10, with a commanding view toward the Organ Mountains, and indeed these jagged peaks looked like organ pipes. But most campers would not be happy with the campsite Julia and Declan had selected: high walls of huge Class-A motor homes surrounded them on three sides. It was like being in a sheet-metal canyon. The Minnie Winnie looked like a mouse sleeping between hippos. In front of the RV kids tossed a frisbee under the garish illumination from a streetlamp, while a large group at one of the nearby motorhomes rocked with laughter, obviously well into their evening drinking. The site was claustrophobic, noisy and devoid of vegetation. In other words, it was perfect. It would be very unlikely that anyone with malicious intent would bother them here.

Declan turned back toward the RV, where Julia was plugging the electric cable into the shore-power post. She seemed to be doing better after that emotional experience at

White Sands. The beauty of a sunset can certainly mess with your emotions. Maybe that was it. She'd had a long, hard day. She'd projected an air of confidence about the men who might be following them, but Declan knew she had to be worried. He'd been so wrapped up in his own crap about the fire and the loss of his possessions, but this had impacted her, too. She'd had her home broken into and her possessions trashed out. He'd been too insensitive to that. And today's troublesome talk with her daughter obviously weighed heavily on her.

"Can I help you get set up?" he said.

"I think I've got it. Not much to do. But we do need to fix something to eat."

"Man, I think I'm too tired to eat."

She laughed. It was a relief to see her laugh. "Me, too."

"Do you smell that?" Elizabeth said, with her nose in the air like a bloodhound. She sat at the small picnic table next to the RV.

"Somebody's got something grilling," Declan said.

Elizabeth said, "Maybe it's the cookout."

Declan remembered. At the office where they'd checked in, a whiteboard announced a cookout and country music for all campers tonight.

"I say, let's go check it out," Julia said. "Tomorrow, we make the big drop off. Maybe it's time for a little pre-drop-off celebration." The familiar mischievous twinkle in her eyes was back.

Fifteen minutes later, the three of them sat at a picnic table with burgers in front of them. A dozen such tables, about half occupied, formed a semi-circle around a small grassy area in front of a raised wooden platform, where a band played.

It was getting late. The woman running the Weber grill was about to shut things down. "You folks are lucky, getting the last burgers of the night." The three of them had added their own condiments from a folding table next to the grill and filled Dixie cups with lemonade from an insulated jug. Five bucks each. Not a bad deal, thought Declan.

The band was a female singer, with blonde hair hanging around her shoulders from beneath a sequined cowboy hat, backed by a guitar and fiddler. She was singing a familiar song about standing by your man, and Declan was pleased he could identify it—he knew almost nothing about country music. Two couples danced in the grassy area. The band wasn't very good, but listening to them now, while eating burgers with Julia and Elizabeth on a warm October night in New Mexico—there was no place he'd rather be.

Julia nodded toward the grassy dance area, "So, are you willing to try this?" She seemed hesitant, apparently not completely sold on the idea herself.

"No, no. I'm no good at dancing."

"So, you're not going to try it because you're no good at it?"

He shrugged.

"Or are you no good at it because you never tried it? This is hardly Dancing with the Stars."

Elizabeth chimed in: "You'll regret it if you don't. Life is too short. I've learned that."

Declan looked around, contemplating a way to escape. Maybe a sudden upset stomach would be a successful excuse. No way he wanted to dance. He could pitch a tent in a hailstorm, write down the Schrödinger wave equation and balance a spreadsheet. But he hadn't danced since the eighth grade, and this wasn't like riding a bike. This couldn't turn out well.

But then he made a mistake. He looked into Julia's eyes, and his resolve melted. When he saw the vulnerability, uncertainty, and acceptance, he knew there was no way he could do anything that would disappoint this woman.

She really was a beautiful woman. She made her LL Bean fleece, which she'd put on over the Yellowstone T-shirt and jeans, look sexy. And even with windblown hair and no makeup, she was stunning. There was a natural wholesomeness about her that made it difficult to breathe. What was happening to him? Was he having a stroke? He'd been around Julia almost continually for the past three days, and he had certainly noticed and appreciated her good looks, but it was like at this moment a new light had flashed on, and he was seeing her anew. He felt his knees grow weak, and he wasn't sure he could stand up without falling over himself. Suddenly he didn't know what to do with his hands. He needed to look away, even for a moment, to regain his composure. But he couldn't take his eyes off her. Oh God, was he gawking? He was suddenly aware that his mouth was open—Lord, he could hardly breathe. Was he drooling?

He stood and extended a hand to her, hoping she didn't notice that it was trembling. They stepped out into the dance area. She came into his arms. His left hand enfolded her right hand— he'd kissed her several times before, but he'd never held her hand. Somehow this was more intimate. His right hand was around her waist, his fingers pressed against her back through the soft, fleecy fabric.

A solo fiddle began to play a slow intro to the next song. Then a guitar joined in with a sinuous sexy rhythm. Then the singer, who Declan wouldn't remember later because he couldn't take his eyes off Julia, began. "Take the ribbon from my hair …"

As they started to move, slowly and tentatively, she laid her head against his chest and said, "Do you like country music?"

"I'm kinda liking it right now."

"Me too."

Chapter 34

They walked back to the Minnie Winnie in silence. Julia realized—Declan probably did, too—that any words now would be unwanted noise spoiling a sublime experience. They were close but not holding hands. She would have liked that.

Julia felt crushed between two worlds. The world that Jenny had exposed with her phone call today, the harsh reality of her sham of a life. The truth of her neglect of her daughter's needs. She had lived in denial of that reality for three years, but Jenny had exposed today what she'd known down deep all along and culminated in her sunset meltdown at White Sands. But now, walking next to Declan, she wasn't going to let that world ruin this evening. She could worry about Jenny later.

She heard herself softly humming that old Kris Kristofferson love song, *Help Me Make It Through the Night,* and those sexy words of invitation, "Take the ribbon from my hair …." She felt her cheeks redden, and she was glad it was dark.

She'd been like a teenager at the prom. Terrified but exhilarated. Worried about how she looked, yet feeling like a princess. Anxious about whether she could dance (she hadn't since high school), but she wouldn't be anywhere else. Here she was in the middle of nowhere, in a crowded campground, not a place where the cool people gathered. With a guy dressed in the cheapest duds you can buy at Walmart. But it was more romantic than any trendy nightclub in New York—not that she'd ever been to a trendy nightclub in New York.

Declan wasn't as bad a dancer as he'd claimed. Even so, there'd been numerous missteps, even a couple of fairly painful toe mashings, which prompted, 'I'm sorry,' followed by laughter. None of that mattered. As they danced around the edge of the small grassy area, Julia wondered if she was at the edge of a new life.

He had held her like she was something delicate, valuable. For most of the dance she had her head on his shoulder, looking past him. But there was that one moment when she pulled her head back to look at him. There was vulnerability, depth, sensitivity and complexity, like it would take a long time to really get to know this guy. There was that touch of gray at his temples that gave him a mature look, not just aging but growth, as if he'd learned some important things.

As soon as they reached the Minnie Winnie, Elizabeth thoughtfully announced that she was ready to turn in. Julia followed her in to get the Scotch and two glasses.

They sat at the picnic table in the streetlight's night shadow of the mammoth big rigs. Their talk was superficial and awkward at first, until Julia said, "So, what are you going to do after tomorrow? Go work with Conor out west?"

Declan scratched his chin. "Probably. I mean, maybe. Truth is, I don't have anything else to do right now." He took a sip of the Scotch. "How about you? You've still got a few weeks before that assignment down in the Keys, right?"

"Yeah, maybe I'll do that. But Jenny's call this morning got me thinking. Maybe I need to settle down somewhere, get a real place to live, get a real job, be there for her. I guess——" She stopped herself midsentence. She had promised herself not to go there tonight. She looked down at her glass and trailed a finger slowly around the rim.

Declan seemed to ponder her words. "I'm not hearing you say that with a lot of enthusiasm."

Julia looked over at the Minnie Winnie and shook her head. "I'd have to sell my RV, I suppose." *Dammit, Julia, just shut up.*

"What about your writing if you have to get a job?"

Julia felt a stab of panic. "I don't know. Maybe I'll have to give that up, too." *Lord, did she just say that?*

Declan leaned toward her. "I'm sure your daughter wants you to be happy."

"I'm sure she does," she said without conviction. "In any case, being a good mother comes first."

Declan leaned even closer now. "But, Julia, isn't your daughter a senior? And she's just now bringing this up?" His face was full of concern.

Obviously, Jenny's feelings had been bubbling for years, but it seemed like today was the first time Julia had really heard her. Her answer to Declan was a shrug. Then she said, "Look, I don't mean to get all gloomy here." She hoisted her glass. "I mean, this was really fun tonight."

Then she set her glass down and placed her palms flat on the table, preparing to stand. He laid a hand atop hers—just for a moment—and looked like he was about to speak, but he just nodded, then leaned back.

Julia stood. "We probably should get some sleep. Big day tomorrow." Declan stood, too. They turned toward the RV, then stopped.

Suddenly, she was in his arms.

After several long kisses, Julia pulled away. She looked up at the yellow streetlamp just a few yards away. *Not here. Not now.* She turned toward the RV, grasped the handrail and put one foot up on the step, then stopped. She rushed back into his arms. Then she was under him on the picnic table, as the kissing continued. His hands ran through her hair, then down her back and up under her fleece onto her bare skin. They were strong and gentle, and she was helpless not to follow wherever they led. Then they were on the ground, rolling on the concrete pad. Hard concrete be damned, this was the best mattress she'd ever been on. They rolled over up against a big wheel of the RV. The smell of rubber mixed with the smell of him, his sweat—she didn't know the names of such things, his manliness. Pressed against a tire, she looked up at the large black raised letters: *Goodyear.* Maybe, she thought, just maybe.

Julia finally pulled away, and they sat on the concrete, breathing hard. Declan looked desperate, still reaching toward her, not wanting to stop. But then he nodded and stood, extending his hand to her. Without words, they climbed into the RV. He disappeared into the cab area, drawing the sheet they'd hung to separate his sleeping area from hers.

Julia lay on her back, still breathing hard, forcing her mind toward what tomorrow would hold. She saw them arriving at Fort Huachuca and finally placing the drive into the hand of a security official, knowing she had faithfully completed her mission. But as exciting as this image was, another fantasy kept encroaching on it, a thought she tried to push away unsuccessfully: Declan ripping open the sheet that closed off the cab area and coming to her.

Maybe she should go forward and rip the damned thing off herself. Before she could get very far with this appealing fantasy, her phone beeped, causing her to jump. As she fished the phone from her fleece next to the bed, she figured it was Jenny. Geez, she wasn't ready for this now. What would she say? Don't blow it again, she thought as she took a deep breath and looked at the screen. It was Reverend Pam. She checked her watch. 11:30. Oh, God, this is important.

"Julia, sorry to call this late, but I didn't want to wait. First, did you make it to Fort Huachuca tonight?"

"Long story. No. We're in Las Cruces, about four hours from the base."

"I was afraid you'd say that. Is Declan there? You might want to get him, put the call on speaker."

"Declan," Julia called out. Elizabeth was also awake now and raised up on an elbow to listen. Declan poked his head through the sheet with a sleepy look. "It's Pam. She wants to talk to both of us."

Declan hurried to the rear of the van and sat on the edge of her bed. This wasn't what she'd had in mind when she'd fantasized about his coming to her earlier. Julia said, "He's here, Pam. Go ahead."

"So, Wade called me this evening. I wish he'd called me earlier—I called you right away. Anyway, Wade's police car was "attacked"—that's the word he used—last night, and the canister was taken."

Julia straightened as the adrenalin surged through her. "What?" She exchanged concerned glances with Declan.

"He was pretty upset and embarrassed. I tried to get him calmed down. Then I found out what really happened. After he dropped me at my car last night, he stopped by the Seven-Eleven for cigarettes. The canister was in a plastic bag on the front seat. He was only in there a couple of minutes, but when he came out, it was gone."

She felt like someone had kicked her. "Don't police cars have alarm systems?"

"They probably do but the car was unlocked. It took a bit for Wade to admit that to me, and like I said, I think he was really embarrassed. Should've been embarrassed if he wasn't.

"He asked about you guys, thinking maybe you followed him and took it. After all, you made a big deal about that canister being yours. But he concluded he'd have noticed your RV out front. Anyway, I told him you came by my place almost immediately.

"I thought about telling him you still had the flash drive. Tell him about Elizabeth. But you told me those things in confidence, so I just kept quiet about that."

Declan spoke. "What'd he do then? Did he call the FBI?"

They could hear Pam exhale a big breath of frustration. "He said he planned to contact the FBI—but honestly, it didn't sound like he planned to do that any time soon. Anyway, I think he's now taking this seriously. Sorry to upset you guys, but it does mean you have to double up on being careful out there."

Julia pondered what all this meant. While this news validated her decision not to give Purkle the real drive, that was little consolation at this moment. More importantly, it meant that someone had been watching at the campground, after all— maybe the guy with the shaved head, probably part of that group of gawkers—and saw her give the canister to Purkle. It also meant that they now knew the real drive wasn't inside. And it meant they knew Julia had it and that they were no doubt searching for them now.

She looked at Declan and Elizabeth. Their troubled faces told her that they understood this, too.

Chapter 35

The gravel road through the campground was dark once you got a few campsites away from the yellow glare of the streetlamp in front of Julia's RV. The other RVs, mostly big rigs, were dark, too—it was now nearly midnight. With campground quiet hours starting at ten, all the Frisbee-tossing kids and loud conversations had long stilled. It was deathly quiet. The nearby interstate—quiet at this hour—stretched west to southern California and east to Houston and beyond, so most folks had probably turned in early, with a long day's drive ahead of them tomorrow.

Declan strolled quietly along the road with David Niven, doing his best to look like a camper taking his dog out for a late-night walk, but his mission was to check out each campsite for signs of anyone following them.

After the call from Pam, they'd discussed their options. They could call the FBI, call the local police, or they could wait in the relative safety of the crowded campground for another hour or two, until it was clear to anyone watching that they were staying for the night. Then they could leave the campground quietly with lights off, until they reached the highway, and beeline it to Fort Huachuca, less than four hours away. What Declan found on his recon around the campground would help them decide.

They had discussed other urgent questions, too. If the men were following them, then how had they tracked them? Most of the time they hadn't seen any suspicious vehicles. Had a tracking device been planted on their vehicle? Or was it possible that the men were somehow tracking one of their phones? Or were they keeping visual contact with the RV?

The tall Minnie Winnie was easy to spot on the highway. Maybe that's why they torched the Corolla after quickly searching it—the generic-looking subcompact would be difficult to follow visually. And if they'd been watching in the campground last night, which they now knew they had been, they'd seen Julia go into the RV to retrieve the canister for Purkle.

Another question bothered Declan. If the men had somehow followed them, why hadn't they attacked yet? Declan stopped and studied a huge motorhome as he considered this. His best explanation was that there were three of them, and, for the most part, they had been in populated areas, where an attack would be difficult. And the men couldn't be certain they weren't armed. An attack would be risky. But it seemed clear that the closer they got to the base, the more desperate the men would become, and it was unlikely they would allow them to reach the base without an attack

Declan was also bothered by the question of whether there really were two vehicles tracking them—the sedan with the roof rack and the black pickup—or maybe this just proved that their suspicions about being followed were wrong. Or perhaps there were many vehicles in the group that was pursuing them.

But one thought caused Declan to smile, as he walked through the campground, reviewing these questions: Julia. The way she'd felt in his arms, as he was fantasizing about helping her make it through the night, filled him with an anticipation that he'd not experienced in a long time. And a new determination, which he had just begun to process, that he would not allow the creeps who torched his car to harm this amazing woman.

He turned and did a slow scan around him. He should feel safe in a KOA. Why didn't he? How could a place so full of humanity feel so spooky? The tall, dark hulks of the mammoth RVs, lining the road, were like midnight at Stonehenge. It was easy to imagine someone sinister lurking behind any of them.

He'd made it around most of the loop their site was in, and he'd seen nothing suspicious. But then, just three sites away from Julia's RV, he stopped in his tracks. The black grille guard. The Arizona plates. It was the black pickup he'd seen at Blanche's pistachio store.

Declan forced himself to continue walking, not making any sudden movements that might indicate his suspicion about the truck. He and Nivvie walked around to the next loop of the campground, which would take him past the rear of the vehicle.

He stopped next to a huge RV the size of a Greyhound and turned his attention to David Niven. The innocent scene of a guy waiting for his dog to do his business. But then he peered around the corner of the RV toward the truck and committed the truck's plate number to memory, noted that it was a Chevy Silverado with an extended cab. Definitely the truck they'd seen at Blanche's. A chill went down his spine.

Declan pulled out his phone and braced it against the edge of the big RV to steady it for the low-light photo, just as a voice from behind jolted him. "Can I help you find something?"

Declan spun around to see the man from the Flying J. Same clothes. The earring. It was him. "Oh, it's you." That was all he could say, as he struggled to catch his breath.

Where had the man come from? The shower room? Maybe—but he carried no toiletry kit one might take to the shower. More likely, he'd been on a little stroll, too. Right past Julia's RV.

The man had a fake, too-friendly smile pasted on his face. "Oh, hey, you're the guy from Tucumcari. Guess you got your tire fixed, huh?"

Declan glanced from side to side, half expecting to see others closing in on him. "Yeah," he said softly. David Niven pulled on the leash, emitting a low growl. He obviously shared Declan's suspicion.

The man stepped closer to Declan. "So, why are you out here at this late hour checking out my vehicle?"

Declan tried to play dumb. "What vehicle?"

"Oh, come on, you're looking at my truck. You were even getting ready to take a photo of it."

"Yeah, it's a beauty. I'd love to get something like that …" He trailed off, realizing his lame words weren't going anywhere.

The man took another step toward Declan. "Have you been following me?"

Declan sized him up; not a big guy. Declan wasn't much of a fighter—he hadn't been in a fight since the sixth grade—but he could probably take him, if it came to that. But this guy could be carrying a weapon. Not to mention that he probably had partners lurking nearby. He should be shaking, but images of his car in flames and Elizabeth and Julia in danger produced something else. He felt his hands clench into fists but then realized that it was best not to betray his suspicion. "No way," he said.

For just a second the fake smile vaporized and was replaced with a menacing glower and eyes that radiated pure hatred. This told Declan everything he needed to know about this man. Then the man seemed to regain his composure. He even produced a laugh. "Guess, when you're traveling out here in the Wild West, you're naturally gonna be a little paranoid about safety." He stepped back a foot or so. "No harm, no foul, eh?" He extended a hand to shake. "I'm Justin."

Declan shook his hand—a soft hand, not the hand of a guy who did much physical labor—but didn't give his name, then backed away. He said nothing.

Justin, or whoever the hell he was, turned toward his truck. "So, I'm headed off for the sack." He even produced a yawn.

Declan nodded as he backed away.

Back at the RV, Julia and Elizabeth were waiting with expectant looks.

Declan shook his head slowly. "They're here," he said.

Chapter 36

They had seemed so innocent, like the deadliest viper lying quiet, hidden beneath the foliage, waiting for its prey. And that made her seethe. She clutched the steering wheel like she was strangling that hideous snake.

Alana still didn't know who they were, other than the names her team had gathered at the campground in Oklahoma. But now she had seen them face to face. The old woman who stole their prized possession, the younger woman who'd made a big show of handing the drive over to the cops, the guy who'd led them on a diversion in the other direction. So innocent, but inwardly gloating, no doubt.

But there was still so much she didn't know, and that frightened her. Who did they work for? How had they sabotaged her perfect plan? Why were they apparently headed back to Fort Huachuca? Were they armed? She had to assume they were. That had held her back from direct confrontation up to now.

She had ordered her team to pursue in stealth, to learn more and capitalize on opportunity. She was a strategist after all, not a thug. But the opportunities had been slim, and her young punk associates had bristled at her caution. They seemed ready for a Wild West shootout, ready to finish business soon. These idiots wanted to go in with guns blazing tonight in this well-lit location with a population density of a city. Good thing she was here.

She leaned back in the car and stretched her legs. Damn, she was too old for this. She'd driven all day from Albuquerque for that cup of coffee in Alamogordo. Now she was in this Godforsaken campground, just steps away from the thieves. More importantly, she was with the team, where she should have been all along. She was exhausted, but she was ready to direct her team through the final steps. To hell with Tucker's caution.

The parcel was nearby, and the thieves no doubt felt safe here. She could see them laughing at her now. First stealing her prize, then making a clean getaway while she faced the terrifying future that Mr. Tucker would have planned for her.

She hadn't called that number for "dire emergencies only," and her delivery was now overdue. But if they retrieved the parcel soon, she could quickly get the operation back on track.

She felt the familiar rage return as she again pictured the three of them there in that coffee shop. The perfect couple and their mom, wanting to get their family photo taken. She could have almost been sucked in by their façade. But then she'd seen the precious canister right there in Julia's camera roll, next to the family photos she had taken. They'd be getting much more than a photo from her very soon.

The sudden memory of her father holding her threatened to quench the building rage. His words, "I don't want anyone to hurt you," brought a mistiness to her eyes.

She shook her head and pushed the image away. She couldn't let sentimentality threaten her mission. A Wild West shootout was what the team wanted, and that might be what it would take. She'd be ready for it. But it wouldn't be here. Soon the thieves would have to leave, with nothing but empty desert ahead of them. That's where the attack would occur. Soon.

It would be quick. It would be bloody. And it would be successful. She felt a sense of peace for the first time in days.

Chapter 37

Over the past three years, Julia had known fear only a few times. It usually was related to some drunk camper who propositioned her or rudely complained about some aspect of the campground. A quick phone call to a ranger would take care of it. But with the RV doors locked at night and her big pipe wrench next to the bed just in case, she felt safe. She'd met many single women traveling alone in RVs, and they had shared stories. All of them had scary tales to relate, but they'd all agreed that these scary times were rare, probably no more common than in your old neighborhood back home. Most campers are thoughtful and polite—Declan was a good example—and ready to help out in an emergency. Overall, camping for a single woman is quite safe.

But this was different. Now Declan and Elizabeth sat across from her in the dinette, the three of them trying to process all the information and figure out what to do next. It felt good having them with her—she was not facing this alone. But, damn, she was responsible for this mess, and now all three of them were in danger.

Earlier they had felt a sense of safety between the neighboring big rigs. But now those RVs were dark, and what was keeping the guy in the black pickup from knocking on their door with a loaded pistol in hand? They were sitting ducks here.

"This is all my fault," said Julia. "My impulsive behavior has put you both in a lot of danger."

Elizabeth shook her head in disagreement.

Declan shook his head, too. "I went along with this; you can't blame yourself. We are here now. What do we do?"

Julia said, "There are still three options. Call 911 and get some local cops out here. Or call the FBI. Or maybe make a run for it. We're only four hours from the base."

They began to assess the three options. Sure, they could call the police—they were near Las Cruces, after all, a good-sized city which would probably send out cops that would be a definite professional upgrade over Wade Purkle. But what would they tell them? That a suspicious guy is camping nearby, and he said hello when one of us walked by? That we've got this top-secret flash drive that we've been carrying all the way from Wisconsin and we're afraid they might take it? Scratch that option. Or they could call the FBI, but, while Declan was on his walk, Julia had discovered online that the nearest FBI offices were in Albuquerque and Phoenix, hundreds of miles away. It would probably take hours for them to respond. And, they were just a few hours from Fort Huachuca.

"I'm leaning toward leaving in a couple hours," she said, "when everyone's asleep."

Declan looked deep in thought. "I think that's the best plan. Only problem is: if they have a tracking device on our vehicle, they'll know we left. Middle of the night on an empty highway doesn't sound very safe if they know where we are."

"So, can we find the tracking device?"

Declan rubbed his palms nervously across the Formica top of the dinette table. "We should look, but it might be difficult to find."

"Especially at night," added Julia.

"Most likely it's outside, up high, where they could get a good signal—I'm just guessing about that, since we have no idea what kind of device they might use."

"Makes sense, though. But they have been inside here, so they had an opportunity to plant something." She was already scanning the interior from where she sat. "So, how would a tracking device work? You're the experimental physicist. Surely you must know what it would look like."

"Right, like I've seen so many of them in my life," he said with a cynically raised eyebrow. "Bottom line: I have no idea. But I suspect it would work off a cell signal. Could be nothing more than a phone taped onto the RV somewhere. I'm sure big-time spies have miniature devices designed in special laboratories, but these guys don't strike me as that sophisticated. I have a hard time seeing James Bond starting a car fire in rural Oklahoma, but what do I know?"

Julia managed a smile but then turned serious again. "Could they be following the GPS on one of our phones?"

"Hmm, maybe. But if the phone's turned off, I think the *Find My* feature on any iPhone will only record the last location when it was online." Declan pulled out his phone and scrolled for a minute. "Yes, that's right. So, when we leave, we should power down our phones, if we can't find the tracker."

"So, I say let's start looking." She stood and pulled a small flashlight from a drawer and handed it to Declan. "Why don't you take the outside—there's a ladder on the back that'll get you up on the roof. I'll take the inside. Elizabeth, you can help me."

After an hour, they'd found nothing. Declan seemed discouraged. He reported that he had been all over the exterior, on top and underneath. But the exterior surfaces of an RV are complicated, with many vents and tanks, as well as electrical, air and water connections. He could have easily missed a tracking device tucked into the corner of a fan vent.

Nonetheless, it seemed that leaving soon, in the middle of the night, made the most sense. They quietly set about their work. Julia disconnected the Minnie Winnie from water and electricity. They turned off their phones. Then Julia piloted the Minnie Winnie slowly out of the site—lights off—toward the park entrance, while Declan walked behind at a distance, watching for any suspicious observers. At the junction with the highway, Declan climbed in. "I didn't see anyone. I say let's go." Julia switched the lights on, pulled into traffic and headed west toward Sierra Vista.

I-10 was nearly empty at 3 am. For the first ten miles, no one spoke. Julia was still processing everything from the past couple of hours. It was possible, perhaps even likely, that the men would not be able to track them now, with their phones off-line and their middle of the night stealth departure. And they had found no evidence of a tracking device. She knew this didn't mean they were in the clear.

They had discussed the possibility that they were simply tracking them visually. After all, the men knew by now that they were headed toward Fort Huachuca, and they knew the route they'd take. If they had enough resources, they could have observers along the highway watching for the tall, hard-to-miss Minnie Winnie. So, it was comforting that they had seen little traffic.

But just east of Willcox, Arizona, only two hours from Sierra Vista, Declan spotted a vehicle parked on an on-ramp, as they passed. Lights off. He'd kept watch in the rearview mirror, and a quarter mile down the interstate, he saw lights appear. It was far behind them and wasn't gaining on them. He was certain it was the vehicle from the on-ramp.

"What should we do?" asked Julia.

"We could just keep going to the base, but I'm worried they won't let us get that far. They'll do something desperate, maybe force us off the road, probably before it gets light."

"See that gas station up ahead? Let's pull in there and see if they follow us. What do you think?"

"Good idea," he said.

"If they do, then we call the FBI."

Julia took the off-ramp and headed for a brightly lit Marathon station, surrounded by pitch darkness, while Declan's eyes stayed glued to the rearview mirror. "They're getting off, too," he said, anxiety in his voice.

As Julia pulled up to a pump, under bright fluorescents, Declan said, "I can't see them. I think they've cut their lights and are back there in the darkness."

They both climbed out of the RV, both peering into the darkness as Declan filled the tank. It was deathly still, the only sound coming from the click-click as the gas flowed into the tank. There was only one attendant on duty, far away in a small office, hunched over his phone. He probably didn't even know they were here.

Julia turned to Declan. "I think it's time." She powered on her phone and quickly found the number of the Phoenix FBI office. She put the phone on speaker, so Declan and Elizabeth could hear.

A soft voice said, "Federal Bureau of Investigation. Can I help you?"

Julia had been uncertain if someone would answer in the middle of the night, but, of course, this wasn't any ordinary office she was calling. She glanced at Declan for moral support, licked her lips, and said, "Uh, yes, I found a top-secret object that I believe may have been stolen." She should say more, she thought, but bit her lip and waited instead for a response.

"May I get your name and phone number, so I can reach you if we're cut off?"

They must get a fair number of crank calls, maybe even malicious calls, thought Julia. She gave her the info.

"Please hold," the voice said, "I'm connecting you with someone who can help."

The new voice was a woman, a more authoritative voice than the one that answered the phone. "This is Agent Halverson. Can I get your name and contact number?"

She had just done that, but she did it again.

"You said you've found a secret item that you think may have been stolen. Tell me more."

Julia told her everything, beginning with finding the canister at the campsite at Perch Lake. She included all—well, most—of the details, including how Elizabeth originally found the canister, even the detail of the Sierra Vista Pharmacy bag it had been in, but she left out the car fire and handing over the canister and fake drive to Officer Purkle. Those details, she rationalized, would only confuse the story.

"Can I put you on hold for a minute?"

It was more like fifteen minutes. While they waited, Declan never took his eyes away from the dark offramp behind them, where the vehicle waited.

When Agent Halverson came back on, she said, "How long ago did you find this?"

"Three days. Has Fort Huachuca reported anything missing?"

"I'm sorry Ms. Evans, we can't give out that information. Can you tell me exactly what it says on the canister and on the contents?"

Julia checked the photo she'd taken of the canister and relayed the printing on it. Then she examined the drive again and for the first time noticed some small print along one edge. She moved the drive closer to the light, then read off a ten-digit string. "Do you think that's important?"

"I don't know, but we'll relay that to the folks at the base. Can you text me photos of the canister and its contents?"

Julia did.

"Okay, so you've told me where you found the drive. Where are you now?"

"Willcox."

"Here in Arizona?"

"Yes."

"That's a long way from Wisconsin."

"We're returning it to the base."

"Really? Why didn't you contact one of the FBI offices back in the Midwest?"

"I decided to return it in person." Then, feeling she needed to add some justification, she said, "I thought that would be the safest thing to do."

After some silence, Halverson said, "Probably not the smartest move."

Julia felt a sudden tightness in her throat and shot Declan a wary glance, expecting an 'I-told-you-so' look. But he seemed focused on the conversation, not passing judgment. "Maybe," she said.

"At least this item would have been in safe hands, and—"

"I didn't break any laws. I'm taking it back to the base."

"I didn't say you did." There was an edge in the agent's voice, but of course, there'd been an edge in her own voice. After a pause, Halverson said, "Have you talked to anyone else about this?"

Julia told her about Declan and Elizabeth. Then she mentioned Pam. Again, she didn't mention Purkle. If he had in fact reported the loss of the canister, Halverson might say something, but she didn't.

"Okay, so this Declan and Elizabeth are your traveling companions. Do you have contact info for this Pam Patel?"

Julia gave her Pam's contact info.

"Are you safe now?"

Julia chewed on this. "It's possible we're being followed." Then she added, "I'm not a hundred percent certain."

"I suggest calling 911 now. Or do you need me to——"

"I can take care of that."

"Can you describe who may be following you?"

"Not sure. There may be more than one vehicle. But I do have a license plate number of one of them." She gave Agent Halverson the number of the black Silverado.

"Okay, Ms. Evans, here's what I want you to do, after you've called 911. Follow the instructions from the local law enforcement. There's no way we can get to you before tomorrow. So, as soon as you can——unless the local police advise otherwise after evaluating your current situation——I need you to drive to our satellite office in Sierra Vista. I'm looking at the map. It's very close to the base. You're just a couple of hours away. They'll be open at nine."

"Why don't I just go to the base?"

"No, I want you to take it to our office. We'll handle the interface with Fort Huachuca. That's our job."

After the call, Julia turned to Declan, shaking her head. "Well, that's done." She slumped behind the wheel.

"How do you feel about it?"

Like a colossal fool, she thought. "I don't know if that was the right thing to do. Damn, I'm not sure that any of the things I've done recently are the right things to do. Look, Declan, if we're in trouble, I'm so sorry I got you messed up with this."

Declan laid a hand on her shoulder. "I know. But don't blame yourself, Julia. I'm a big boy. I went along with every decision. We did the best we could."

"I think we should call Pam. I gave her name to the FBI. I don't want them upsetting her."

"It's almost four." He drew in a deep breath and let it out slowly, then said, "But I think you're right."

Pam picked up on the first ring. Julia said, "Pam, I'm sorry to call you at this hour."

"No problem," Pam said, "I've been tossing anyway, worried about you guys. Julia, are you okay?"

"I'm not sure. There may be a car following us."

"Where are you?"

"Willcox. At a gas station. Just a couple of hours from the base."

"Is the car there now?"

"Maybe. There's a vehicle off in the darkness that pulled in when we did." She peered into the rearview mirror again but could see nothing beyond the brightly illuminated area of the gas station. "I called the FBI office in Phoenix."

"Good. What'd they say?"

"They said to call 911."

"You should do that."

"I can't believe we're going to get much help out here in the boonies. Plus, we don't really know for sure that there's a car following us."

"You should do it anyway. Now. Your safety is most important."

"We'll do that."

"Okay, I'm thinking you may need a plan B, just in case the 911 call doesn't help."

"You have something in mind?"

"Couple of ideas. First, you could just wait at the station until dawn. Only a couple hours from now, right?"

Julia pondered this. She and Declan looked toward the station office again, where the sleepy looking attendant still hunched over his phone. If they stayed here much longer, it seemed likely the men would risk an attack right here before dawn. That attendant might not even notice. "Not sure that would work," Julia said to Pam.

"So, here's the second idea, and you may think it's crazy. It seems to me if someone is following you, they're going to take some kind of action, probably violent action if they need to, before you reach the base. They know the route you'll take to the base. Sounds like they know where you are. And your vehicle is easy to spot."

"And?"

"I say, take a little side trip. I'm looking at my map. You say you're in Willcox. There's a road that heads south about forty miles to Chiricahua National Monument. There's a campground there; I've been there several times. That's where my friend Prisca is. She's a ranger, so she'll be easy to find. Do you think you can lose that vehicle behind you?"

Julia looked back into the darkness again and swallowed hard. "I can try."

"If you can lose them, then take that road to Chiricahua. They won't be expecting that. Stay there for a couple of days. They'll think they've lost you. Then there's a back way into Sierra Vista; they won't be expecting to see you arriving on that road. What do you think?"

Pam was quite the risk taker, thought Julia, and she liked it. "Do you know if there's cell service there?"

"I know for a fact that there isn't, except for WiFi right at the visitor center."

"That's probably good. We think one way they may have followed us is by some tracking device, maybe a cell phone, they planted on our vehicle."

"Hmm. So, they'd lose their signal from you. Good thinking."

Julia looked again at Declan, who was nodding. "So, I guess that's our plan."

"It's kinda funny, really," Pam said. "The Chiricahuas were a hideout for bandits long ago. Maybe they'll be a good hideout for you, too. Look, you guys, if I can do anything, call me—Prisca's got a satellite link in her cabin that you can use."

When she was off the phone, Julia looked at Declan and Elizabeth. Pam was right. *Your safety is most important.* But how would they explain that they'd been carrying a top-secret item all the way from Wisconsin? This whole trip had been such a foolish idea. It was likely they'd be arrested. In possession of stolen top secret government property—jail time for sure. But … *Your safety is most important.* "Let's call 911."

"Are you sure?" Declan said.

His response surprised her. "I'm sure."

A man answered. "Cochise County emergency dispatch. Can you tell me your location?"

"We're at the Marathon station outside Willcox, off I-10."

"What's happening?"

Julia explained about the car following them, realizing how silly it sounded.

"Has anyone been injured?"

"No."

"Are you in immediate danger?"

"I don't know."

"Where is the car now?"

"Not sure. I can't see it."

"How do you know they were following you?"

"They entered the interstate behind us and got off when we exited."

"What kind of vehicle is it?"

"I don't know. Can't see it."

"Has anyone made any threats toward you?"

"No."

"Is there a reason someone may be following you?"

Julia looked at Declan, who nodded, then drew in a deep breath. "Yes." After a moment struggling to find the right words, she said, "We're carrying a top-secret computer drive to be delivered to Fort Huachuca tomorrow."

After a few seconds of silence, the dispatcher said, "Let me get this straight. You have a top-secret data drive? And you're calling from a gas station on I-10?"

"The FBI knows about this."

"Okay." A few seconds passed, then the dispatcher said, "What did they tell you?"

"They said to call 911."

More silence. Then, with a hint of exasperation, the man said, "Okay, I'll report this. They'll probably send somebody over to check on you. Do you need me to stay on the line with you?"

"I don't think so."

"Okay. I think this concludes our call. You may hang up now."

Julia turned toward Declan and Elizabeth, shaking her head. "Honestly, if I were that guy, I'd think this was a crank call. So, now what?"

Declan was still turned toward the dark offramp behind them. "Guess we can wait until the cops get here. But I'm wondering what they'll do. Or maybe if they'll even come."

Julia also stared back toward the offramp where the car waited in the darkness. She was quiet for a while. Then she turned to Declan, "So do you think you and Google Maps can get us to that road to the Chiricahuas?"

"I've got it right here. It's just west of town." He held up his phone, as she checked out the route.

Julia nodded, "Well, we're gonna take a little detour first. Okay, boys and girls, ready for a wild ride? Let's see what this baby'll do."

Without switching on the headlights, Julia took a deep breath and shifted into drive. She floored the gas pedal and sped to an exit on the far side of the station, cut so hard into a dark side street it felt like she was going to roll the Minnie Winnie. At the next turn, with the pedal still floored, she cut left. After several more such turns, Julia slowed, as she spotted the sign pointing toward the national monument. She didn't switch on the lights for another mile.

"Geez," she hollered into the predawn, wriggling her body like she was doing a victory dance. "That was fun."

Chapter 38

They left Willcox in the dark on the two-lane headed south toward the Mexican border. By the time they entered the narrow canyon at the entrance to Chiricahua National Monument, a hint of pink washed the eastern sky behind rugged mountains. A sign cautioning, "Narrow road—No vehicles over 25 feet," told them there'd be no big rigs back here. A few miles past the entrance, past a closed visitor center, they entered Bonita Canyon Campground, which straddled a creek bed in a steep narrow canyon, lush with trees of many species. Rocky walls loomed a thousand feet above both sides of the creek, and sunlight already bathed the high walls in orange.

Nearly every site was occupied with a camper van, tent camper or tiny pop-up trailer. The Minnie Winnie would be one of the larger vehicles here.

Julia pulled the RV into one of the few unoccupied sites and killed the engine. They stood together in the predawn stillness of the campground, the only sound the gurgling of a nearby creek. They hadn't seen another vehicle since they left Willcox.

Declan said, "Pam is a genius."

Julia stretched and yawned. They climbed back into the RV, and within fifteen minutes, everyone was asleep.

Declan jumped at the sound of the knock on the window, where his head rested. He looked around, uncertain for a moment where he was. It was now light outside. A woman wearing the pale green uniform and flat-brimmed hat of a National Park Service ranger stared at him through the glass. He rubbed his eyes, ran a hand through his hair, and fumbled for the ignition key that would allow him to lower the window.

"Good morning, Declan," the ranger said, smiling. Declan was suddenly alert—how'd she know his name? "I'm Prisca. Pam said you might be stopping by." She had a serious look about her, but there was the hint of a smile, and her green eyes were warm. Declan instantly liked her. "Didn't mean to startle you. I recognized your RV from Pam's description. Welcome to Chiricahua."

Now, Julia was beside him in the cab. "Sorry, we didn't register for a site," she said. "We got in kinda late. Hope this one's not reserved."

"No problem. We'll get the details worked out later. Understand you guys have had a long drive."

"That's an understatement," said Declan, fishing for his glasses on the dash and still trying to come fully awake.

"So, just wanted to say hello." There's something about a park ranger that is reassuring. "When you're up and about, stop by the visitor center; it's just a short walk from here. Meanwhile, here's a park brochure to get you oriented. This is a beautiful place." She waved a goodbye over her shoulder as she headed down the campground road.

While Julia was getting the coffee ready, Declan stepped down out of the RV into a crisp morning to take David Niven for his morning duties. He shook his head, as he considered how improbable it was that he was warming up to this large dog that just four days ago had struck terror in him.

Sunlight filtered through the many trees surrounding their site. He checked the park brochure Prisca had given them to see if the wonderful diversity of trees was mentioned. He was able to pick out an Arizona sycamore, the Mexican pine and its amazingly long needles, and the weird looking alligator juniper with its distinctive bark resembling an alligator hide. He raised his eyes to take in the high cliffs, a brilliant sun-washed orange, rising high above the trees.

Around him, the normal bustle of morning campground life unfolded. A young couple emerged from a two-man tent next to their Outback. An elderly woman tied out her big Golden next to her truck camper. A couple in a camper van next to the Minnie Winnie sipped coffee in their camp chairs. Two elderly men with trekking poles were in animated conversation as they hiked by. The enticing aroma of frying bacon completed this iconic campground scene. Best of all, there was no sign of a black truck or sedan with a Yak rack.

The park brochure emphasized that the real high point of the park was the wilderness of spectacular rock formations, another eight miles up the road. But for now, this was enough: a place of peace, after the last two days of terror and exhaustion.

Ten minutes later, he cradled his coffee mug at the small dining booth of the RV, which was starting to feel like home. Julia and even Elizabeth seemed to be in good spirits, too.

"Gotta say," Julia said, "I didn't get many hours last night, but that's the best I've slept in a few days."

"No kidding," said Declan. "It's beautiful here. How long do you think we should stay?"

Julia shrugged. She took a sip of coffee as she pondered. "First priority is to get the canister to Fort Huachuca and be done with it."

"Amen to that."

"On the other hand, maybe Pam was right that if we lay low a couple days, then we can safely head to the base by a back way."

Julia turned toward Elizabeth. "You okay staying here a couple days, Elizabeth?"

"I've never been to Arizona," she said. Apparently, that was a yes.

"Guess that settles it," said Julia, looking from face to face, like she was a CEO who'd just closed a big deal. "Let's get our butts over to the visitor center and find out what we should see. I'd say let's walk—it's not far, but I'm not comfortable leaving the RV here. We all remember what happened last time we did that."

The visitor center was an old stone building that looked like a vintage CCC project from the Great Depression years. Inside, Prisca stood behind an information counter, going through some papers. Another park employee sat at a desk behind her. Beyond her was a small gift shop, where a few visitors browsed. A sign pointed to a museum in an adjoining room.

Prisca looked up when they entered. "Good morning, you guys," she beamed, then glanced at her watch. "Oops, I should say, good afternoon, almost." Prisca was tall and slender, had the lanky look of a long-distance runner. She no longer wore the flat-brimmed ranger hat, and her long red hair was gathered into a ponytail. With a tanned face and chiseled features, she looked like someone who spent a lot of time outdoors, which she no doubt did. Her green eyes radiated hospitality. She was just the kind of person you hope to meet when you step into a national park visitor center. "Let's see if I got this right. Julia, Declan, Elizabeth."

Julia nodded. "You're a friend of Reverend Pam's?"

"That's right. We're close, but I haven't talked to her in a bit, so it was good to hear from her last night."

Declan wondered what was exchanged in that conversation. "We enjoyed meeting her."

Prisca nodded like she knew that already.

What else did she know about them?

"So, I guess we need to pay for our site," Julia said.

"Sure, we can get you set up right now. Then the fun part. Telling you guys about this beautiful park."

Declan shelled out the cash for the campsite, and Prisca gave them a tag to hang on the post at their site. Then she directed their eyes to a large map, under glass, on the counter. Declan said, "We're interested in hiking." After what they'd been through the past two days, a beautiful hike seemed like a magic elixir.

Prisca was ready. "Lots of great hikes in the park, some good ones starting right here at the office, but I suggest you head up to Massai Point, where the best trailheads are, in my opinion." She pointed out several routes on the map. "All of these are described in the brochure I gave you. The rock formations are amazing, some seeming to defy gravity. I think Echo Canyon and the Grottos is a must for a short hike, but if you're up to it, head on back into Heart of Rocks. It's in the most remote part of the park. Isolated and magical. I think it's the crown jewel of the park."

Declan noted the twinkle in Prisca's eyes and the energy in her voice. She obviously loved this place.

Then, Julia said, "Reverend Pam said that this is a sad place. Why is that?"

Prisca let out a soft laugh, then was silent for a moment, seeming to gather words. "Most visitors don't want to hear about this, but it's an important part of the Chiricahua story."

She waited. When they all nodded their interest, she continued. "The Chiricahua Apaches settled this area a long time ago. They were a small segment of a larger, more widespread Apache culture. The Chiricahua raised their families here. Hunted here. Knew where all the springs were. For hundreds of years, these mountains were their home. Then in the 1850s settlers began to trickle in from the east. The trouble began when a rancher mistakenly believed that the Chiricahuas had raided his property, and he demanded that the military step in to restore order. Soldiers were brought in, and that began a few decades of war."

Elizabeth was now engaged. "That was Cochise, right? And later, Geronimo." She looked at Declan then Julia. "Great military warriors."

"That's right," Prisca continued. "A fort was built just a few miles from here—you can still visit its ruins today. Well, you can guess how that conflict ended. After thirty years of fighting, what was left of the Chiricahua Apaches was relocated to reservations in Florida and Alabama. Geronimo died as a prisoner of war."

"That's awful," said Declan. "How come we haven't heard more about that?"

Prisca shrugged. "You mean other than a few old John Wayne movies?" She shook her head. "But there's more to our local history. These mountains were once a hideout for gunslingers and criminals on the run from the law. Ever hear of Johnny Ringo?"

Elizabeth said, "Yes, of course. Famous gunfighter. Part of the old west story with Wyatt Earp and Doc Holliday."

"Very good," said Prisca. "So, Johnny Ringo was a ruthless, impulsive killer with a bad temper and a fast gun. He had a hideout in these mountains. And it was here where he was gunned down." She looked from face to face. "I don't have to go on, if you don't want me to. Like I said, most folks don't inquire about these things."

"No, we want to hear it all," said Julia.

"The history of violence has even touched the park. Back in the early eighties, one of our park rangers mysteriously disappeared. He was last seen slumped over in the front seat of a car with two men, speeding away from the park. Probably smugglers he had the misfortune to run into. We're just thirty miles from the border."

"I hope those days are gone," said Declan.

"I wish they were," breathed Prisca. "This is wild country. Today, the Chiricahuas are still used by human traffickers and drug cartels, who place lookouts on the peaks to spot Border Patrol activities. Yes, it's all very sad."

Declan thought about the men following them. Might they be the latest chapter?

Prisca glanced at her watch. "Oh my, my shift is up. Gotta head over to the hut. Wanna join me before you head up to the rocks?"

"The hut?" said Declan.

"Well, that's what we call it. It's really a … why don't I just show you? Just take a few minutes. Pam said she hoped I'd show it to you."

Declan shifted uncomfortably. He was ready to get up to Massai Point. Visiting something called the hut was the last thing he needed now. "Thanks, Prisca, but maybe we should just hit the trail. It's already after noon."

"Understood," smiled Prisca. "You're gonna love it up there."

But Julia said, "What do you do at this hut? I thought you were a ranger."

"That's right. I've got the best of both worlds. Half-time ranger and then I volunteer over at the hut. It's really a—"

Declan nodded. "Maybe we can go visit after our hike." He was already halfway to the door.

Chapter 39

As Julia turned the Minnie Winnie up the road to Massai Point, she said to Declan, "Let's stop and hang out the card at our campsite." She shot him a concerned look. "And maybe take another look around the campground."

"Just thinking the same thing," Declan said.

As they pulled into their campsite, they saw two new vehicles. One right next to them, another just across the road from them. Sure, new campers came into campgrounds every day, but two at the same time, both next to their campsite? "Maybe I'm just jumpy," she said, "but that's a bit strange."

Declan leaned forward to watch the new campers through the windshield. "Why don't you go and work some of your camp-host magic? I'll keep watch from here."

The gentleness in his face brought back memories of last night. She wanted to reach out and touch him. Instead, she climbed down from the cab and hung their reservation card on the post in front of their site. Then, casually, she waved at the guy next door, who was pulling a folding camp chair out from a pickup camper. "Nice setup you've got there." One thing Julia had learned is that every camper loves to talk about their equipment. Truth was, Julia loved talking about equipment, too. But mostly, she loved talking to the people. A favorite part of being a camp host was walking the campground and greeting people. She was in her element.

The man set the chair down and turned toward Julia. He was a friendly-looking guy, probably in his fifties, with silver gray hair. He wore an old sweatshirt with an AC/DC logo, over faded blue jeans and roughed up boots. An authentic looking camper. He took a couple steps toward her. "Tell you the truth, this is my first time out with it. I've always been a tent camper, but time seems to be catching up with me." He looked back at his rig. "I like it so far. Kinda wonder, though, if I shouldn't have gotten something a little bigger, like that Winnebago of yours."

A hallmark of all campers thought Julia: always worrying that they'd bought the wrong equipment. "Yeah, I like the Minnie Winnie. Just about the right size for me. I'm Julia," she said. "We just got in last night. Where you from?" She watched for any sign of anxiety or suspicion on the man's part.

"Just moved to Phoenix from Albuquerque. I've been hearing folks talk about this place. I'm Eric, by the way."

Julia nodded and gave Eric a see-ya-later wave, then stepped across the road to where the other new camper, a woman, was having trouble setting up a pop-up trailer. "Can I give you a hand?" Julia asked.

The woman looked frustrated. She turned toward Julia, wiping sweat from her forehead with the back of her hand. "Hey, that would be nice. You ever set one of these things up?"

"Sure." Actually, she'd never set up a pop-up trailer, but she'd seen many other campers do it. She stepped up and pitched in. Funny, she thought: two new campers, checking in at the same time, both rookies.

It took just a few minutes to get the woman's rig ready to go. Then, Julia introduced herself. The woman, about thirty-five, with blond hair and a handsome-but-serious face, said, "I'm Carol," then extended a hand to shake.

"We're from Wisconsin." Of course, the woman could read that on her license plate, so this was hardly divulging anything important. "Feels like a long way from home." She gazed up to the high cliffs to emphasize her amazement at this place. She waited for Carol to respond.

"I'm from Phoenix. Guess that's not too surprising, huh? Must be a lot of us down here, just a few hours away."

Julia nodded and smiled, backing away. "If you need anything, just holler."

Back at the Minnie Winnie, Declan was waiting. "Well?"

"Eric and Carol. Seemed nice. Funny, though, they're both from Phoenix and neither one of them has used their equipment before."

Declan gazed at her intently, and Julia thought he might be about to kiss her. She'd like that. Instead, he said, with a grin, "Next stop Massai Point?"

Massai Point, yes. Time to get pumped about their hike.

The drive from Bonita Campground up to Massai Point would be a scenic piece of cake for someone driving a Rav4, but piloting the twenty-five-foot Minnie Winnie up the eight miles of steep, winding road felt like walking a tightrope in galoshes. Their RV was right at the posted length limit for the road, but on some of the tight hairpin turns it felt like it might, in fact, be too long. When the road finally leveled out at the top of a long ridge, she let out a shaky sigh of relief, feeling like she'd just landed the Starship Enterprise.

A half mile farther, in the parking lot at the end of the road, they stepped out into a crisp blue-sky day at Massai Point. Off to the east, desert-mountain wilderness stretched to the horizon. She could imagine those smugglers that Prisca mentioned looking back at them from one of the peaks. To the west lay a rugged expanse of pinnacles, spires, and balanced rocks. It was breathtaking. "What's the altitude here?" asked Julia.

Declan pulled the brochure from a pocket. "Seven thousand feet. That was quite a climb." He continued to read. "Chiricahua is an Apache word meaning 'land of standing-up rocks.'" He looked up from the brochure to take in the panorama. "Well named if you ask me. It says these rocks were formed twenty-seven million years ago by a massive volcanic eruption." He looked at Julia with warmth in his eyes. "I'm really glad we came here."

"Me, too." She gestured toward a sign at a trailhead that apparently led to multiple destinations. "Everybody up for a hike?"

The three of them looked around the parking area. Only a few cars—no black pickups or cars with Yak racks—and all of them had already been here when they arrived. No one had followed them up the road. "I think we're safe here," Declan said.

Julia looked down at Elizabeth's shoes, sizing them up for hiking. Pretty new looking tennies. She'd probably lifted them from the back of some unlocked car. They looked fine for an easy hike. "Prisca recommended the hike to Echo Canyon. Fairly short trail, which is great. Nivvie's not allowed on the trails here, and I don't want to leave him in the RV alone too long." She was already adding a water bottles to her daypack.

The trail, an engineering wonder chiseled into the rock, descended from the parking area into a forest of spires, pinnacles and huge boulders balanced precariously atop tall rocky shafts. Some looked like they were stacked one on another. The scene reminded Julia of a childhood game she played with her dad—Jenga—where you build a tall tower of wooden blocks, and then each player carefully removes a block until the whole thing topples over.

Declan estimated that some of the huge topmost boulders might weigh as much as a thousand tons.

After about a mile, the trail descended into the Grottos, a labyrinth of caves and narrow passages through the rocks, like a hidden garden, a sacred space. It reminded Julia of monastic catacombs she'd only seen in photos. She half expected to see hooded monks, processing silently with candles. The feeling here was … she tried to put words to it. Solemn seemed like the best word, mysterious yet comforting. Holy. A place where words should be said only in hushed tones.

Julia stopped and handed Declan and Elizabeth water bottles. Elizabeth was doing amazingly well. She certainly didn't have any excess fat, and she'd no doubt gotten plenty of exercise fleeing from rental cars she'd taken up residence in.

She recalled how the swirling sunset hues at White Sands, with their seeming impermanence, had caused her tears. It was different here. The quiet feeling of eternity comforted her. Fear had no toehold here. She could stay in the grottos the rest of the day. "It feels like we should talk about holy things here," she said.

Declan had been looking up at a tall spire, but now he turned to Julia, nodding. "Maybe the last place you'd expect to find someone who stole government secrets."

"It almost feels like if they were here, we could just talk this whole thing through," she said.

Elizabeth now stepped closer. "Doctor King once said, 'Hate seeks to live in monologue. Love seeks to live in dialogue.'" She looked down. "But I'm not sure I really believe that anymore."

"I've got to say, Elizabeth," Declan said, "I wish I'd taken a history course from you."

"I wish you had, too," she said with a rare smile.

Julia caught Declan looking down at his feet, deep in thought. "What's on your mind, Declan?"

"Just remembering a special time. I was at a physics conference in Berkeley and one afternoon the attendees had to travel to a distant location for part of the conference. I ended up sitting in the back of a bus next to Serg Gorkov, a Russian scientist who helped develop the Soviet nuclear arsenal. Talk about an unlikely person to talk to. Some would consider him my enemy."

Julia and Elizabeth gathered closer.

Declan began to pace back and forth like a professor in front of a class. "Well, we had a couple of hours to kill, and everybody was tired of talking about physics, so our conversations turned to our families. I remember Gorkov telling me about his three-year-old daughter. And there was this absolute love and a mistiness in his eyes."

Declan shook his head like he still couldn't believe it. "All the while I was edgy, aware that this man was designing thermonuclear weapons that could kill everyone I loved." He gave out a little grunt. "I wondered what he was thinking about us. If ever there was a person who was my enemy, it was Serg Gorkov."

Julia saw how Declan wasn't just telling this story. He was reliving it. A surge of sadness filled her—he missed physics.

"Yet, in the back of that bus," Declan continued, "I saw him not as some Dr. Evil caricature, but as a father who loved his little daughter, as a fellow human being, maybe almost a friend." He stopped and ran a hand through his hair. "You know, I wonder if talking about our families and trusting each other might have helped edge us toward global peace in some way I'll never know."

"Love your enemies," breathed Julia, moved by Declan's story. "That's from the bible, right?"

"Yes," said Elizabeth. "Doctor King's favorite passage."

Julia watched a shaft of the afternoon sunlight slice through a narrow opening between two rocky pillars. "Maybe it is possible." She raised her eyes toward a huge boulder perched precariously atop a slender spire of rock. Every intuition she had about how things were supposed to work was crumbling here. "I think it may not only be possible, but maybe it's necessary."

Julia looked down, hands on hips. "All this talk about loving people you're struggling with—I can't help but think about my mom."

Declan stepped closer and rested a hand on her shoulder.

"I've been avoiding her for so long, because when I talk with her, it seems like I get hurt."

Declan's hand made a slow stroking motion on her shoulder.

She glanced up at Declan, her eyes wide with determination. "I think I need to talk to her more and hang in there with it ..." Her voice trailed off.

Declan shuffled his feet. Was he thinking about his father? They were all silent.

Then, Elizabeth, who had been quietly looking up at a rock formation, spoke up. "I need to tell you about me," she said.

Julia and Declan turned toward Elizabeth, as she continued to stare up into the rocks.

"You know I used to be a teacher. US history. I loved it. I was good at it. Even won a few awards for my teaching."

She continued to look at one of the tall spires and was silent for a moment. Then she looked back at them with wide eyes and a hesitation like she might not be able to continue. But then she said, "I had been divorced for a long time, but I lived near my daughter, so I got to see her almost every day. She was—I mean, is—my only child. She had a daughter, too, her only child. Angie." A small smile appeared on Elizabeth's lips as she said the name. "Two days a week I got to take care of Angie for a couple hours after school, while my daughter had to work. That was the highlight of my week." She turned toward them, bit her lip, as she searched their eyes.

Elizabeth had seldom made eye contact before. "You two." She was silent again for a while. "You two have been kind to me. It's been such a long time since anyone was kind to me."

Julia fought back tears.

"Angie and I used to walk down to the main street, just a couple blocks from my house, where we'd get ice cream. It was such a special treat. She'd run down the street ahead of me. I'd taught her how to be careful. Look before crossing a driveway. Stop at intersections and wait for me. She was very good. Oh, God, we had such fun.

"Then there was a day. That day."

Julia dug her fingernails into the rock next to her, as she anticipated what was coming.

Elizabeth put her hands over her face.

Julia could hardly breathe. "You don't have to go on, Elizabeth," she said, and Declan nodded.

Elizabeth shook her head, then continued. "We were headed to the ice cream shop. She was skipping, almost dancing. She was so pretty, wearing that yellow dress—she was five." Her next words came out as a sob. "Oh, God, I loved her so much." She looked down now and softly pounded the rock with her fist.

Julia reached out a hand and rested it on Elizabeth's shoulder.

"My phone beeped. I should have just ignored it. But I didn't. I had to fish it from my pocket. Then I dropped it. I bent over to pick it up. Just as…" Now there was more silence. "Just as Angie came to the intersection. She always stopped and waited for me. Always. She had learned that. She always waited." She turned to face first Declan, then Julia. "But that day she didn't."

Now she was quiet again. Her eyes were closed as she continued. "I looked up just as a car …" She couldn't finish the sentence. Her mouth fell open, like she was struggling to breathe. "That's when my life ended, too."

"Oh, Elizabeth," Julia breathed, gripping her shoulder. She felt like something in her chest might explode. Declan looked like he might cry.

After more silence, Elizabeth said, "My daughter was destroyed by it." She gasped like she was reliving that day all over again. "She couldn't forgive me. She wouldn't even speak to me. When she did, she'd scream that I had murdered her daughter. I pleaded with her … just to talk with me … but she cut me off. So, that day, I lost my daughter, too.

"This went on for a month, with no change. She wouldn't take my calls. She wouldn't open the door when I went to her house. I couldn't take it anymore. I tried to kill myself, but I couldn't even do that right. I didn't show up to work and didn't return the college's calls when they tried to contact me. Then one day, I just walked away. Just left. Didn't even lock the door behind me. I took nothing. Figured I'd walk until I died." She sagged. "But I didn't die. That was twelve years ago. I never told another soul about this until now."

Julia wanted to choose her words carefully. "Is there any hope that your daughter might want to reconnect with you?"

Elizabeth shook her head vigorously. "No way. That door is closed."

Declan took both of Elizabeth's hands in his. "Elizabeth, I'm so sorry. For what it's worth, I'd be proud to have you as my mother. I am proud to have you as my friend." Julia nodded, touched by Declan's beautiful words. Elizabeth looked at Declan, unable to speak.

In silence, they watched the afternoon shadows crawl across the rocks. Elizabeth was between them now, each with an arm around her. It wasn't clear if they were holding Elizabeth because she needed to be held or because they all needed to be held.

Declan finally said, "I guess we should head back up, huh? Don't want to keep David Niven waiting."

At the top, the few other vehicles in the parking lot were now gone. In the stillness, they all looked back at the beauty of the rocks in silence. No words were needed.

Julia opened the door of the Minnie Winnie and Nivvie was right there, happy to see them all. Even after Elizabeth's sad testimony and the terror of their escape last night—or maybe because of these things—Julia felt a hopefulness, almost a euphoric confidence that all would be well. She had the leash in her hand, and as she reached for her dog, she said to Declan, "What a great hike. I can't believe—"

Before she could finish her thought, Nivvie bolted out the door and straight toward the trail they'd just come up.

"Nivvie," Julia called, "Come here." But Nivvie didn't respond to her. In a moment he had disappeared into the wilderness of rocks. "Nivvie!" Julia screamed. In shock, the three of them raced toward the edge of the parking area, called into the rocks. "Nivvie!" Instinctively, they hurried back down the trail, calling out his name, but there was no sign of him. "Nivvie," Julia cried, her voice now cracking.

He was gone. At dark, they stopped looking, but they stayed in the parking area for another hour, in case he returned. Julia collapsed against the side of the RV, exhausted. Declan and Elizabeth extended their hands out to comfort her, but she pushed them away. Finally, she stepped out into the middle of the parking area and looked up into the night sky, her hands raised high, her fists clenched. In pure fury, she wailed, "My Jenny. My Nivvie. The things that depend on me. I've let them all down."

Chapter 40

Declan wanted to cry, too. First, the awful story of Elizabeth's tragedy, then almost immediately the loss of David Niven. That dog meant a lot to Julia. She'd lived alone in campgrounds for three years with him as her only companion. He was her best friend. Just four days ago he'd viewed this dog as a drooling savage, but now he'd come to see him as a living being that was gentle and loyal. He had grown accustomed to David Niven lying near his feet.

Julia didn't need this. She was already struggling with her relationship with Jenny, whether she should move to a place where she could provide her daughter with a home. He understood this but hadn't bought into it. Yes, a mother needs to be there for her child, but Julia had flourished in her new, albeit unconventional, life, and what would happen to her if she had to give up her adventures and go back to a small home in the burbs? He remembered her sad glance toward the RV, as she pondered the need to sell it. This just might suck the spirited, spunky, smart-ass—dare he say, irresistible?—life right out of her. He sensed that Julia, a survivor, rarely cried, but those tears at the White Sands sunset indicated how much emotional burden she was carrying. The concern for her daughter against the backdrop of the secret canister and the people who wanted it back, and now David Niven, might just be too much. He sighed. What the hell did he know about any of this stuff? What he did know was that Julia Evans was a special woman, and he'd do anything he could to help her.

They'd gone straight to the visitor center to report David Niven missing, realizing there wasn't much anyone could do, but it was closed.

They tried an after-hours number posted on the door, and fortunately Prisca picked up.

"Oh, Lord, Julia," Prisca cried. "I'm over at the hut. Why don't you come over? It's just five minutes away."

"The hut?" Julia said.

"That's the place I told you about. Here's how to get here."

Just a mile from the visitor center, a dirt road led a few hundred yards through the dark into a stand of cottonwood trees. Prisca stood outside an old Quonset hut, a corrugated-sheet-metal building that looked like it had been a storage shed at one time, maybe a leftover from some military installation many years ago. A single dim lamp over the door was the only light on this dark night. A Jeep, apparently Prisca's, was the only other vehicle here.

"What did you say you call this place?" Declan asked.

"We just call it the hut. Guess we probably should have a better name, huh?" Prisca laughed. "It's really a kind of school."

Declan did a slow three-sixty at the wilderness around them. "So, how does anyone know this place is here?"

"People tell them." Prisca said, like it should be obvious. She held the door open for them to enter.

Just inside, Prisca turned to Julia. "I'm so sorry about your dog. I've already put out an alert. Maybe someone will see him." She flipped a switch, and the place was filled with light from a half-dozen old fixtures hanging from the ceiling. It had the feel of a high-school gym.

At the far end of the room, about fifty mismatched folding chairs were arranged in a semi-circle around an unpainted plywood stage. Around the periphery of the room were cabinets and what appeared to be work benches. Near the rear, where they stood, a dozen or so folding tables were piled with all manner of things: clothing, pieces of lumber, tools, books and cardboard boxes containing God knows what.

Julia was still shaking, but calmer, no doubt in shock, as she described to Prisca their search for David Niven. Declan remembered how calm he'd been in those first days after Emily's death. He had been remarkably poised and gracious at the funeral, even laughing at funny stories friends told about her at the eulogy and greeting and thanking the great number of people who had come. Then, a week later he fell apart. Julia seemed similarly calm now.

"There are a lot of small animals up there that could have attracted him," said Prisca.

"That's why I always kept him leashed. These hounds get a whiff of an animal and off they go. When they come to their senses, they may be ten miles from home and can't find their way back." Julia spoke almost clinically, but Declan sensed that she could crash at any moment.

Declan surveyed the interior of the hut. "So, you have classes here?"

"Yes, but not like you might imagine. There is teaching, but there's also a lot of learning by doing."

"Doing what?" Julia asked.

"Helping people." Prisca stepped closer to Julia and laid a hand on her shoulder.

Julia's eye widened. "I'm afraid to ask, but will he be okay up there overnight? Are there mountain lions up there?"

"David Niven's chances of encountering a mountain lion are very small. But I've got to be honest. There is a sizeable coyote population."

"Oh, God," breathed Julia. "He's such a gentle thing." She began to sob.

They let her cry.

Julia looked up at Prisca. "Did Pam tell you about our situation?"

Declan thought it odd that Julia would ask that now, but then her emotions were bouncing all over the place.

Prisca shook her head. "Pam respects the confidentiality of what people tell her. She just said you had quite a story, but any more information would come from you."

Julia rolled her tongue against the inside of her cheek, as if contemplating what to say. Finally, she said, "I feel like I need to tell you about us, about why we're here. I feel like I need to tell you everything." She looked at Declan, then Elizabeth, as if seeking their permission to continue. They nodded.

Julia steepled her fingers, took a deep breath and told Prisca about finding the canister, her commitment to returning it, her wanting to follow through on something thrilling—which she now called silly—the car fire and the encounter with Officer Purkle and Reverend Pam, calling the FBI, and the likelihood that they were being followed. She talked fast, most of the time with her head down. When she was finished, she looked at Prisca, as if expecting an alarmed reaction.

But Prisca showed no alarm. There was sympathy in her face, as she listened. She said, calmly, like it was no big deal, "Thank you. It's good for me to know about this, so I can keep my eyes open."

Julia looked around, like she was just now seeing the place. "Seems like a strange place to start a school," she said. "I mean out here in the middle of nowhere."

"I can't think of a better place for a school that helps people. A place of such beauty that's been tarnished by violence and hostility and dare I say it, evil." She looked from face to face.

Declan nodded. "But are there any people around here?"

"Absolutely," said Prisca. "They come from Willcox and other little towns, from ranches—the people who own them and the people who work on them. Some people come from collapsing hovels, where they're struggling to get by. Then there are aging hippies, who fled civilization years ago."

"I'm still not sure what you actually do here," he said.

"Whatever needs to be done. We're trying to live out our faith by helping others. I could rattle through a list of things we do, but you may not want to hear it all."

"Yes, please," Julia said.

"Well, we collect food and other goods for the needy. We do construction projects for people in substandard housing. We visit people who are sick or lonely or perhaps society has abandoned. Cook meals for the homeless and tutor poor children after school. We make crafts, which we sell at fairs all over southern Arizona to raise money for our outreach projects. And we're learning to speak up in the community about equality and justice and love."

Prisca's eyes lit up as she talked about all this.

"That's a lot," said Julia. "But where are the people?"

"Oh, they'll be here. Not much going on this evening, but there'll be quite a few here tomorrow."

The door opened suddenly behind them. Declan spun toward the motion, startled and expecting to see their pursuers.

A tall man with long black hair stepped in. "Good evening, Madre," he said in a soft voice. "Mind if I practice a little?" He nodded at the three of them.

"Of course. Navarro, these are our new friends."

Navarro nodded again and continued toward the far end of the hut, where he moved some of the folding chairs near the stage. He wore a black T shirt, with some logo that Delcan couldn't make out, over faded jeans.

Prisca returned her attention to Julia.

"He called you *madre*," Julia said. "You're a priest?"

"Yeah."

"And that's how you know Pam?"

"We were in seminary together."

Julia placed her hand atop a large stack of hymnals. "So, is this a church?"

"Not really. Like I said, it's a school. We do worship a lot. We sing a lot. We pray a lot. And we learn a lot. Most of the folks here go to church somewhere else, and some don't go to church at all. We've got Catholics and Protestants, even a Buddhist or two—I'm Episcopalian—and some folks still trying to figure out what they believe."

Navarro began noodling on a keyboard next to the stage.

Julia looked down. "I guess I'm one of those folks who doesn't quite fit in anywhere."

Prisca focused her eyes on Julia. "Why do you say that?"

Julia cleared her throat, then shot Declan a glance before continuing. "Look, I basically don't have a home. That RV out front, that's it. I have a daughter, who I'm struggling to communicate with, not very successfully, I might add. I hardly ever see my parents. Other than my dog, and he's gone—" She let out a sob. "These people here, Declan and Elizabeth, they're kinda my only family. Which is a joke, since I've only known them for a few days." Julia stopped for a moment, trying to catch her breath. She'd been talking fast. "I guess, if I ever got my act together, I might go to a church or something like this." Then the tears, just like yesterday at White Sands, began to flow. "Damn it—I'm sorry, I didn't mean to curse. And I didn't want to start crying."

Prisca placed her hands on Julia's shoulders. "Pam told me you are an exceptional person, Julia, and now I'm seeing it with my own eyes."

"But I don't want to be crying. I should be stronger than this."

"Julia, there are sad things that happen in this world, things that are worth crying about. Your crying has nothing to do with not being strong. It has everything to do with being sensitive and loving and caring."

Julia cleared her throat again and wiped her eyes with the back of her hand. She said nothing.

"And as for going to church once you get your act together. Julia, you don't go to church after you've gotten your act together. You go to church *in order* to get your act together."

Julia ran her hand over one of the hymnals. "I don't know what to do."

Now Navarro's noodling on the keyboard turned louder. He tipped his head back and, with eyes closed, began to sing. They all turned to listen. His voice filled the room, reverbing off the high corrugated ceiling. It felt like a concert hall. His voice was powerful, yet like velvet, layered with both yearning and gratitude. The song was like a prayer, pleaded slowly, each syllable elongated …drawn out… like he was meditating on each word.

"Precious … Lord … take my hand.

Lead … me … on … let me stand.

I … am … weak … I am tired … I am worn."

When he finished the final words, "Precious Lord, lead me home," he stood and left quietly.

Prisca let the silence hang in the room for a while, until Julia spoke.

"Those words," she said, "Those words are my words."

Prisca's eyes locked onto Julia. Finally, she said, "Julia, tonight is really hard. Sometimes, it feels like we're just crawling on all fours through the darkness, feeling our way forward. You may feel that way right now."

Julia listened, her breathing heavy.

Prisca continued, "But as we keep watching, we may notice pinpoints of light in the darkness. Those pinpoints are all around us, Julia, and they are gifts from God. They're even here now."

Julia looked at Elizabeth then Declan, like she was seeing them for the first time. Then, she threw herself against Declan and let him hold her.

He nuzzled her hair. "Dear Julia, dear Julia," he said softly, over and over.

Chapter 41

They left the campground for Massai Point before it was light. Declan drove. Julia didn't trust herself on that road in the state she was in. They wanted to be there at dawn and not miss a moment to look for Nivvie. She pictured him waiting there, curled up asleep near where they had parked yesterday. He'd look up as they pulled in, jump to his feet and run to her. He'd be cold, and she'd need to get him inside to warm him up. His big brown trusting eyes would wash her with love, saying silently, "I knew you'd come back for me." There'd be an abundance of treats, and she'd hold him for a long time.

Last night, Julia hardly slept. She'd thrashed in the darkness, alternating between crying over Nivvie then lying still, staring at the vinyl ceiling above her and reviewing what Elizabeth had told them yesterday or imagining what she should have said to Jenny in that phone call. She had considered going up front and staying next to Declan, but that might feel invasive for him. And she would just keep him awake with her despair. One of them needed to be rested tomorrow. It helped to review what Prisca had told her. What did it mean for her to watch for the pinpoints of light in the darkness?

The canister and the purpose of her cross-country journey and the possibility of dangerous people following them were now like cobwebs in a dark corner, barely visible and not worth the investment of her mental energy.

The first pink hints of dawn brushed the eastern sky, as they pulled into the parking area at Massai Point. The Minnie

Winnie was the only vehicle in the lot. There was no sign of Nivvie. They called his name over and over, just in case he was nearby, but there was no response. Julia had to work at pushing away the terrifying images of the gentle Nivvie surrounded by a pack of hungry coyotes.

Julia had had plenty of time during the night to plan how they'd approach the day. She'd used the map in the brochure to lay out a route that would take them on a large loop through the rocks—several square miles—and give them the best chance of finding Nivvie. They'd carry extra water and dog treats for him. If they found him, he'd no doubt be distressed, thirsty and hungry.

There was little conversation as they prepared for the hike. Declan and Elizabeth obviously grasped the gravity of the situation. She looked at each of them: Declan, this wounded man, who just a few days ago had recoiled in fear in the presence of Nivvie, and Elizabeth, carrying her own unbearable grief, both offering themselves this morning to help. Pinpoints of light.

By the time they were on the trail, the sunrise bathed the higher pinnacles in a soft orange warmth, but the beauty held little interest for Julia. Of what value is beauty, when your underlying reality is of loss? The euphoria of yesterday's hike to the Grottos had been replaced with a grim sense of purpose.

Every twenty yards or so, they called out Nivvie's name. And often they stopped to listen carefully and to survey their surroundings for any indication of his presence.

By nine, they'd been at it for over two hours. Now they sat on the trunk of a fallen pine and sipped from their water bottles. Declan and Elizabeth waited for Julia to speak. She ran her fingers across the rough bark of the fallen tree and noticed a small ant emerging from its shelter beneath one of the bark folds. Even death provides the means for life, she noted. But she could see no new life emerging from the bark of her life.

Four miles in, they came to a junction where a rough-hewn sign pointed toward Heart of Rocks, the most remote location in the great forest of rocks. She looked at her companions, probably exhausted yet not complaining from the brisk pace she had set, and said, "I don't see how he could have made it this far."

She was certain she looked pathetic, justifying the sad looks on Declan's and Elizabeth's faces. While Elizabeth nodded, Declan said, "We'll keep going as long as you want."

The trail immediately became steep and rough. According to the map, it was only a mile or so into the Heart of Rocks, but it was a challenging mile. The trail passed through several narrow cracks, where they had to squeeze through sideways, and one pitch that required hand-over-hand scrambling. Finally, they emerged onto a small plateau, which seemed to be the summit of the trail. It was surrounded by irregular spires and balancing rocks on all sides, with signs identifying some of the named formations like Old Maid, Camel Head, and Kissing Rocks. Examining these formations held little interest for Julia now. She called Nivvie's name several times, as she turned slowly, scanning the vast forest of chimney-like rocks, searching for any sign of a brown speck that might be her dog.

Defeated, she leaned against a rock slab and stared blankly out into the park. Finally, she pulled out her phone, then nodded, surprised that there was a cell signal up here——must be the high elevation, she concluded. Time to make that phone call. Stop just speculating about it and finally commit. She tapped the key for Jenny, and she had her speech ready, but she only got voicemail. Sighing, she said, "Jenny, it's your mom. We need to talk. I've got some news." She pushed her phone back into her jeans and turned toward Declan and Elizabeth. "So, Nivvie's not here. I guess that's it. I have to accept it." She looked down at her feet. "Maybe it's a sign that my life is about to change. Maybe that my life needs to change."

She sat on a large boulder. "This is such a beautiful place," she said, looking out again over this bizarre wilderness. "I've been bouncing all over the map about my future the past few days, but now I know what I need to do. I guess down deep I've always known it."

Declan and Elizabeth each found places to sit. They watched Julia in silence.

"I'm going to move back to Milwaukee, near my parents, near where Jenny grew up. Get a job. There must be something I can do. Get a place to live, a real place, probably an apartment will be all I can afford, but it'll be a place that Jenny can come home to. It's what I need to do." There, she'd said it, and hearing it said out loud made it seem official, like she'd decisively set something into motion, something that needed to be done.

"What about your gig in Florida?" Declan asked.

"I'll cancel that. Now that I've decided, I need to get moving ahead as fast as possible."

Declan's eyes drilled into her. "I understand. And I'm not trying to talk you out of it, but are you really sure this is what you want to do?"

Julia couldn't let herself consider his words. She looked away. "Did I say anything about what I *want* to do?"

"I just want you to be happy."

"Happiness is having my daughter be happy."

Declan gave an unconvincing nod, then pulled out his phone and wrote a quick text.

They all sat in silence again. It was easy to be silent up here. In the deathly quiet, there was a lot to hear. The Heart of Rocks seemed to have a voice of its own. What it was saying was uncertain. But there was something eternal and unchanging, yet unpredictable, about this place.

Julia turned at a rustling sound behind them. Three people had stepped up onto the small plateau where they sat. Two of them held guns.

Chapter 42

Declan leapt to his feet, his heart about to explode. Not having a clue about what to do next, he extended his arms in front of Julia and Elizabeth, a ridiculously impulsive gesture, as if somehow he could shield them.

He recognized them immediately. The woman from the coffee shop—Evelyn? The man with the shaved head from Perkins and Justin, the man from the Flying J. The two men pointed pistols at them, while Evelyn stood confidently, smiling. "So, we finally get you alone." She glanced at each of her partners and said, "Congratulations, gentlemen, our patience has finally paid off." Then she glared at Julia. "Nice to see you again. Hope you enjoyed your latte."

Julia was silent, as the three of them, now huddled close, tried to back away, but there was no place to go.

"Don't go getting all panicky, you guys. We just want to have a little talk." Evelyn seemed to be enjoying this.

Shaved Head looked focused and nervous. He stood in a semi-crouch, holding his pistol in a two-handed style, like he might start firing at any second. "Come on, we don't need any talk. Let's do it now."

Justin, looking calm, said, "Cool it, bro. We want to savor this."

"No," Shaved Head barked, "we've already waited too long. Let's kill these assholes now."

Evelyn, who seemed to be in charge, raised a hand to quiet her assistants.

Declan knew he should say something, but his throat felt sealed off.

"We don't have the drive," Julia said.

"Oh, we'll get to that, dear," Evelyn said. "Don't be impatient. We need to have a chat first. Oh, and I might add, whether the three of you live for another minute depends on what you say. Have I made myself clear?"

Declan struggled to fight through his panic and come up with a plan, but so far, the panic reigned.

"You three have done a great injustice to us. And you know, you can't be allowed to get away with that." Her eyes now flashed with rage. "First question: who do you work for?"

"We don't work for anyone," Julia said, her voice shaking. "We just found the canister by acci—"

"—Don't give me that crap," shrieked Evelyn. "We ought to just kill you right now."

Shaved Head took a shaky step closer, raising his pistol in preparation.

Evelyn waved him back again. "My colleagues here are hankering to do it, you know." Then her voice softened again. "Don't insult our intelligence. You stole something very valuable from our car in Milwaukee. Don't tell me you didn't know it was there. Who informed you about it? We need an answer right now."

Elizabeth looked calm. In a steady voice she said, "No one informed me. I was homeless and just happened to get into that car to get out of the cold."

Evelyn considered this for a moment, then said, "What a crock. So, why is a homeless person now in possession of the parcel and on her way to Fort Huachuca?" She turned to Shaved Head. "Shoot the old woman."

The man turned his body toward Elizabeth, but Julia interjected, "No, don't shoot! I can explain it all."

He kept his gun aimed at Elizabeth.

Julia glanced at Declan with terror in her eyes, and said to Evelyn, "She's telling you the truth. She threw the drive away in a campfire ring at a state park where I was the camp host."

"Oh, in a campfire ring? Nice. You found a diamond necklace and a gold watch in there too? Julia, you'd better start telling us the truth, or it's going to get bloody real soon."

"I'm telling you the truth. I found the drive," said Julia, "and I decided to return it to Fort Huachuca. That's all there is to it."

Declan began to realize an opportunity. These people saw them as competitors to be feared, perhaps part of a larger organization that represented a threat to them. How could he use this as an advantage? You need to be a used-car salesman, his division leader had said.

Meanwhile, Evelyn said, "So, you're just a noble citizen trying to do the patriotic thing, right?"

"Yes," Julia said softly. Then she seemed to regain some confidence. "We've called the FBI. They know about this."

"You're pathetic," said Evelyn, manufacturing a phony laugh. She took a step closer, like she might be ready to take a swing at Julia. "So, tell me, why didn't you give the drive to the cops in Oklahoma? Wouldn't that have been the noble thing to do?"

Julia didn't seem to know what to say.

Declan spoke up. "Bottom line is: you want the drive, and you think we have it. And you're afraid of us because you don't know who we might be affiliated with." Even in his terror he was surprised how confident he sounded. "So, if you kill us,

you'll—number one—never find out, and—number two—
you'll never get the drive."

"Smart guy. Maybe we can't kill all three of you. Yet. But,
if you can't tell us what we need to know, we'll just slowly kill
you one by one. Does that get your attention? Shoot the old
lady."

Again, Shaved Head leveled his gun at Elizabeth. "Wait,"
screamed Julia. "It's in the RV."

"Where in the RV?"

"Under the bed in the rear, under the water pump."

"Good to hear. We've got three people going through your
RV right now. So, if it's there we'll find it. It's either there or it's
on one your bodies, and your three corpses will be very
cooperative in helping us find it."

Now, Evelyn paced back and forth slowly, like she was
pondering her next move. "You know, I'm now convinced
we're not going to get any useful information from you. Too
bad you chose not to be more helpful. So, we're going to let
your bodies be our little calling card that we're not to be messed
with." She glanced at the two men. "Boys, kill them all right
now."

Suddenly, Elizabeth pushed her way in front of Julia and
Declan and cried, "No! Just kill me. I'm the one who took the
canister. These two did nothing wrong. Just kill me now."

Evelyn seemed momentarily unnerved. Her face went
blank, like she'd just remembered something, something that
knocked her off balance.

Julia roughly pulled Elizabeth out of the way and stepped
to the front. "No! I'm the one who caused all this. We wouldn't
be here if it weren't for me. They did nothing."

Evelyn looked around like she was struggling to get her bearings. But then suddenly, like she'd been slapped in the face, her lips pursed and her eyes hardened. The hatred that had briefly disappeared was back. A fake grin emerged, as if needed to help eradicate a last shred of useless decency. "Oh, isn't this touching …oh, wait, you're all thieves. Kill them!"

"No, no!" cried Declan, as he stepped in front of both Elizabeth and Julia, again spreading his arms to shield them, then pushed his back hard against them, trying to get them to the ground behind him, just as the two men extended their arms into firing positions.

Shaved Head's eyes widened in anticipation of the killings, but then they darted to his side toward an explosion of motion from behind them, so fast it was hard to grasp what was happening. A furry …something—a bear?—was suddenly all over him. He let out a scream of shock and pain.

Justin spun, redirecting his aim toward the creature, and Declan saw an opening. No doubt a stronger figure was needed in this instant, someone who knew what to do, someone unafraid, someone with a much better track record (and that would be almost anyone), but that person was not here. He launched himself toward Justin, who quickly turned his gun back toward Declan and fired two rounds point blank. But Declan's momentum carried him into Justin, and the two of them fell backward onto the rock. Justin hit with a thud, the gun flying from his grasp. He tried to twist his way from underneath Declan, but Declan would not lose this struggle. Everything was on the line, and Declan, who had struggled his whole life with doubt, had no doubt now that he would prevail. This time love would triumph over hate.

They rolled and struggled, Justin screaming obscenities, thrashing and kicking, but in seconds Declan had him pinned to the rock. Atop him now, he looked into Justin's face. It was a face of hate.

As Justin writhed and screamed at him, Declan risked looking around, and in the midst of the terror, he wanted to laugh. David Niven stood atop the terrified Shaved Head. Elizabeth had Evelyn gripped in a headlock that could make a professional-wrestling highlight reel. Julia had scooped up both guns and stood pointing them in the general direction of the intruders, looking like Annie Oakley in a Wild West show.

But then, two more people stepped onto the small plateau, both with guns drawn.

Chapter 43

Julia felt like her heart had stopped. Her hands shook, and suddenly she didn't know what to do with the pistols she held. Point them toward the new visitors? A gunfight was beyond what she was up for. But she turned toward them, anyway, uncertain there was any other option.

She recognized them immediately. The new campers, Eric and Carol.

Then she saw the vests. Olive colored with bold yellow letters across the front: FBI. "Don't shoot us, Julia," the man shouted. "We're FBI." He flashed a badge. "I'm Eric Sandoval and this is Carol Sheppard."

"Nice to see you again," said Sheppard, apparently the only calm person here.

Julia thought she might faint, as relief flooded her. She kneeled and carefully laid the guns on the ground, where the agents could see them.

Eric looked around and smiled. "My, my, I'd say you guys handled the situation pretty well."

Agent Sheppard was already getting cuffs on Evelyn, as Sandoval said, "Damn, that trail was steep, a little too challenging for an old guy. Sorry we didn't get here sooner." He was breathing hard. "You should know that your RV is okay. Our agents arrested three more people trying to break in."

Julia's brain was a scramble. It was all happening too fast. Dear God, they had almost been killed. If it weren't for the timely and heroic arrival of Nivvie and then the bravery of

Declan charging an armed man, they would have been. The FBI agents would have arrived too late. She felt tears building again, but this time they were tears of gratitude. She would never again say she hadn't done anything thrilling.

But an additional memory troubled her. It was in the moments after Nivvie had appeared and Declan had charged one of the gunmen. Nivvie's attack had caused the man with the shaved head to drop his gun, and it had tumbled between Julia and Evelyn. They both dove for the gun, but Evelyn got there first.

They were both on their knees, facing each other, just a few feet apart. As Evelyn pointed the pistol at Julia's chest, Julia had leaned back, bracing for the shot. She opened her mouth, but no words came out.

Evelyn smiled. "You have nearly ruined my life. So, as I now end yours, I want you to know my name. Alana Selkirk. I want you to know who it was who prevailed. Know who it was who without a blink took your life from you."

Before she could pull the trigger, Elizabeth leapt onto Julia, wrapping her arms around her and screaming desperately, "Please don't hurt her. Please don't hurt her."

Alana opened her mouth like she was also about to scream, but no words came out. Then, her face contorted in distress. She gasped, "Oh, father …," then shook her head and threw the pistol down. She buried her face in her hands.

Julia quickly grabbed the gun and retrieved the other pistol that Justin had dropped, as Elizabeth jumped onto Alana. As she waved the pistols toward their attackers, she couldn't shake the screams of Elizabeth and the tortured response of Alana.

She turned toward Eric. "How did you find us?"

"The same way these losers probably did. You kept hollering 'Nivvie,' every few minutes. We just followed your calls. Who the hell is Nivvie?"

"Here's Nivvie," beamed Julia. She fell to her knees and hugged her dog. "Nivvie and Declan are heroes." She looked over at Declan, who sat on the ground, grinning, after Sheppard had already cuffed Justin. A stab of terror filled her when she saw the blood. "Oh, God, you've been shot!"

She raced to his side, as did Elizabeth. Declan only now looked down at his shirt sleeve, soaked in red. There were two shots fired. Where had the other one gone? She'd heard that a person in shock might feel perfectly normal for a while bearing a mortal wound. "Dear God," she cried. "Help us!"

Julia rolled up the sleeve on Declan's shirt to expose a bloody slash on his arm. "Oh, Declan. Does it hurt?"

Declan was no doubt delusional. "Not with you here next to me," he said.

Sandoval was beside them now. He gently cradled Declan's wounded arm. "It looks minor, thank God. But we heard two shots. Have you been hit anywhere else?"

Declan looked dazed. "Uh, I'm not sure."

"You hold him upright, Julia, while I check him over."

She shifted around behind Declan to support his head and shoulders in her lap, while Sandoval set about checking out the rest of Declan's body. After what seemed like an hour, but was probably no more than a minute, he said, "I can't find any other injuries. I'd say you're a lucky man."

Declan looked up at Julia holding him and smiled. "I'd have to agree." She laid her head down against the top of his head and wrapped her arms around his chest.

"We'll need to get this arm looked at," said Sandoval. "We've got a medical team waiting at the visitor center."

Julia winced. So, the FBI had anticipated violence.

"We'll patch you up enough to get you down the mountain," Sandoval said to Declan. Agent Sheppard had completed the handcuffing and now removed a small first-aid kit from a waist pack and handed it to Sandoval. Sandoval struck Julia as a guy who'd seen a lot of gunshot wounds.

While Sandoval applied some kind of ointment, then wrapped gauze around the wound, Declan looked up at Justin, standing with hands cuffed behind him, head down. "Thank you, Justin," he beamed, "for being such a shitty shot."

Damn, thought Julia, here I am shaking to death, and Declan seems to be enjoying this. She didn't want to let him go. She looked up at Sheppard, and opened her mouth to speak, but nothing came out.

Sheppard, leaning casually against a rock, with a hand resting on her holstered Glock, said, "I guess you never know who you're going to run into at the campground."

"How'd you know to find us out here?"

"Eric called a Reverend Pam in Oklahoma—you gave us her name—she said you might be coming to Chiricahua." She looked around her like she was just now noticing the scenery. "This is a beautiful place."

Julia nodded. "Glad somebody can enjoy the scenery." She looked over at the three assailants, now handcuffed together. "Can you tell us who these people are?"

Carol Sheppard glanced at Sandoval then back at Julia. "We'll tell you what we can when we get back down." She laid a hand on Julia's shoulder and smiled. "This has been a little harder than setting up my trailer, eh?"

Chapter 44

Declan ran his fingers over the new bandage on his arm. They'd had to hike back to Massai Point, and several times along the way the wound started to burn like hell. Everyone was concerned about him. Sandoval explained that he'd ordered a helicopter to airlift Declan out, but the rugged terrain prevented a safe landing, and it was decided a rope lift to a chopper would pose more risk than having him walk out. They'd stopped several times to check on him. Sandoval studied the dressing with concern. "I've got some heavy-duty ibuprofen, but I'm worried it might cause more bleeding, not what you need to make the hike down in one piece."

Declan nodded. He could handle the pain. Julia stayed close by him the whole way, offering a supporting hand under his good arm on the steeper stretches. She didn't say much, but he could read the concern all over her face. What consoled him and enabled him to keep his spirits up was seeing the three assailants, cuffed together, marching ahead of Carol Sheppard's pistol.

At Massai Point, an EMT examined Declan and deemed him ready for the ride back to the visitor center, where the medical team waited. At the visitor center, a doctor changed the dressing and loaded him up with a strong painkiller. She pronounced him very lucky to have incurred such a minor injury.

Now, Declan felt no pain, as they gathered in a back room at the visitor center that looked like a storage area, doubling as a sometimes-meeting room. They sat in folding chairs amidst boxes of tee shirts and other gift shop merchandise, shovels and other work tools leaning against the wall, piles of papers, and even a large stuffed owl.

Eric Sandoval sat in the midst of them—Declan, Julia, Elizabeth, Prisca and David Niven, who was curled up at Declan's feet. Carol Sheppard stood nearby. She struck Declan as the kind of person who couldn't sit still very long. Sandoval had shed the FBI vest but still wore the same hiking clothes he'd had on up in the Heart of Rocks: a down vest over a wool shirt, Levi's and hiking boots. He fit right in as a camper enjoying the outdoors in the Chiricahuas, hardly looking like an FBI agent. He was a slender guy, medium height, with receding gray hair and olive skin and large brown eyes exuding warmth. It was hard to imagine him confronting armed terrorists. He relaxed in his chair, one leg crossed over the other, obviously in a good mood. "This is the kind of happy conclusion that Carol and I dream about. They don't all turn out this well," he said.

He leaned toward Declan and said, "You are a very lucky man, Declan, sitting here after charging into two close-range shots from a Glock 22."

Prisca said, "You guys really gave me a scare. The FBI came into the center this morning and ordered us to close the road into the park. I had no idea what was going on, and they wouldn't tell me, but I was sure it involved you."

Sandoval was clearly enjoying all this. "There are a lot of heroes here."

"Don't forget Nivvie," Declan said. "Everyone thought he was this gentle, sleepy hound, but you should have seen him up there." He shook his head, still not believing it. He reached down and stroked David Niven's head.

Julia said, "What can you tell us about these people?"

Sandoval brushed his chin with a knuckle. "Well, one thing I can tell you is that all six of them, including the three that tried to break into your RV, are on their way to Phoenix in a high-security bus. This is a tremendous accomplishment."

"We've got so many questions," said Declan. "Who are these people? And why had they brought a top-secret item to Milwaukee of all places? And—"

Sandoval held up a hand. "We'll answer what we can," Sandoval said. "First, understand that we cannot tell you everything. Some of these things are highly classified. I have top clearances, and even I'm not privy to some of the facts. Like what's on the drive—I don't have the need to know, they say. But it's important. Huachuca is very concerned about it. I can tell you it contains critical national security information. Losing that to an adversary would have been very costly to our country."

So, not the cafeteria menu, after all, thought Declan. He and Julia exchanged glances.

Sandoval took a deep breath. "But some things I can tell you." He looked from face to face. "These people worked for a larger group that funnels secrets from our country to a range of interests who'll pay very big bucks for them. We think having them in custody will be key to tracking down that larger group. Rounding them up was a major coup.

"Alana Selkirk was a top-secret security specialist at the Pentagon, an expert on classified documents, until she was fired for workplace violence. She's been on our radar, especially for those of us in the Albuquerque office, for a while. But it seemed like she was behaving herself, so we were surprised to encounter her today. Why did she do this? We don't think it was ideological—more likely revenge and money."

"And then there's my buddy, Justin," said Declan.

"That's not his real name, but let's call him Justin for now. He was a key to this operation. Computer tech at Huachuca. He'd been there for several years and had access to classified materials. He's the one who physically removed the drive from a classified safe and got it out. We're still working on how he did that, but no doubt Selkirk orchestrated it. Okay, my knowledge is sketchy here—some of this stuff we've known for just a couple hours. Apparently, he'd become radicalized through online platforms that target disaffected young men. They were closely affiliated with—" Sandoval looked over at Agent Sheppard. "Let's just say folks who are not the best friends of this country."

While Declan appreciated learning these things, he was uncertain why Sandoval was so forthcoming in revealing them.

"Same with the other gunman?" Julia asked.

"That's right. He apparently met Justin in one of those online chat rooms. He was an aide at a pharmacy."

"Sierra Vista Pharmacy," Declan said, softly.

"Would they really have killed us?" Julia asked, leaning forward, elbows on her knees.

"In a heartbeat. They almost did. Like I said, not all our cases end this happily."

Julia spoke up. "I need to tell you something about Alana." She looked at Elizabeth, who nodded. "There was a moment when one of the guns was loose on the ground. Alana Selkirk grabbed it before I could get to it, and she was ready to shoot us. But she didn't. She said something about her father, then dropped the gun. If she hadn't, we'd all be dead." She paused, seemingly choked up as she relived those moments. "I sensed that down deep there was a streak of goodness in her. Maybe it helped save our lives. I hope that will be considered."

Sandoval listened carefully. "Interesting. She's probably looking at a lot of prison time. Would you testify on her behalf? Could make a difference."

Julia looked at Elizabeth again. "Yes."

Declan's phone beeped. He didn't want to be bothered right now but slipped the phone from his pocket and took a quick glance. It was a text from Conor: "You've made my day! Pack your flip flops and your Speedo and grab that little honey and get your ass out here. We got a lot of planning to do."

He looked at Julia again. I don't have any flipflops, he thought, and I don't have a Speedo, and—he looked at Julia— I don't have a little honey. Or do I?

Elizabeth had been quiet until now, taking it all in. She said, "So, why was the drive in the backseat of that car in Milwaukee?"

"Ah, that's very interesting." Sandoval paused, like he was mulling over whether the classification rules would allow him to talk about this. Finally, he nodded. "Sure, I can tell you about that. Imagine your buddy Justin"—he nodded at Declan and smiled—"somehow gets the drive off the base. He needed to get rid of it pronto, since once the base discovered it was missing, he'd be a likely suspect. So he immediately takes the drive to the local pharmacy, where his colleague hides it among a sea of other prescription bags that all look alike. It's apparently about the size of a bottle of meds, so it would arouse no suspicions."

"But how did it get into that car in Milwaukee?" Elizabeth persisted.

Sandoval said, "Yeah, seems very strange, and that's exactly why it was such a clever plan. The problem is how do you go about getting a secret package out of the country. They were smart enough to not head for the nearest airport. Way too risky. Or head to the border, just twenty miles away—if the base had discovered it missing, then the border would be crawling with agents. Getting it out from the west coast would probably be similar— being the direct route to China, it would naturally have greater security. There's a lot of anonymity in driving across the US. Lost in the endless flow of traffic on the interstates. No one checking your ID, no tickets that can be traced, no snoopy TSA agents going through your luggage. You can nap in the rest stops, grab a bite with the big crowds at the fast-food places, where no one is watching you. A good way to travel if you're doing something you shouldn't be doing. Carrying something you shouldn't be carrying. We think they probably used several cars for the trip, most likely made the switches at roadside rests."

Sandoval was a natural storyteller, and he was clearly in his element, obviously euphoric over their successes of the day.

"So, how do you get it out of the country?" he continued. "How about leaving the drive in the backseat of an unlocked car in some hotel parking lot in Milwaukee—tucked between the cushions, where no one would ever look, except the pick-up person, who knew it would be there? In an unlocked car, because the pickup person wouldn't have a key. No human-to-human handoff that could be observed. The pick-up person planned to take it to a commercial vessel docked at the Port of Milwaukee—a sleepy Midwest port: perfect. We now know which vessel, based on the timing of the delivery and the ships currently there. From Milwaukee, it's straight through the St.

Lawrence Seaway out into the Atlantic and then you're home free. Minimal security barriers. These ships go straight from Milwaukee to ports in Asia and Europe." He leaned forward. "But they weren't figuring on you showing up, Elizabeth."

Sandoval sat back with a satisfied look. "No one would look inside that rental car, except maybe a homeless person looking for a warm place on a cold night. Elizabeth, I've got to say, as we begin to piece this story together, your determination to escape those men in Milwaukee, your decision to toss the drive into the fire pit… Hell, you're quite a hero, too." He then leaned forward and said in a soft voice, "On behalf of the United States of America, I say thank you."

Elizabeth, mouth agape, looked first at Julia, then Declan. Was she blushing?

Sandoval leaned back, took a deep breath, and said, "So, that brings us to you, Julia."

Chapter 45

Julia tensed up. She'd known this moment was coming, and she was ready for it. Sandoval had not yet asked for the drive. "You must disapprove of what I've done," she said. "I could have handed the drive over to the FBI in Chicago, and we could have avoided all this."

Declan took her hand. She glanced at him, as he shot her an I'm-with-you-Julia look.

Sandoval nodded. "Well, I've thought about what you did, and at first, I didn't understand it. Turning it in immediately certainly would have been the appropriate thing to do."

Julia looked down, digging for some strength. "I did what I thought was best at the time, and sure, there were risks—I mean, obviously, we know that now—but I needed to follow through."

Sandoval stared hard at Julia like he was trying to see deeper, trying to see something that wasn't apparent on the surface.

She stammered, "I didn't mean to do something illegal. I—"

Sandoval interrupted. "I don't think you did anything illegal. You were trying to return it. It just seemed a little …" He paused. "Irregular."

Declan spoke up. "You need to know, Mr. Sandoval, that Julia is a very courageous person, who has a strong commitment to doing the right thing. I was with her the whole way in this thing, and I've never doubted her for a minute."

Well, that wasn't quite true, she thought—he'd disapproved of her plan from the start—but she appreciated his show of support.

Sandoval put his hands up like stop signs. "I understand, Declan. I admire people who are independent." Now he turned back to Julia. "Truth is, Julia, if we think this through, it was your determination and persistence that drew these criminals out into the open, made it possible for this breakthrough in defeating a terrorist conspiracy. Julia …" He stopped and wagged a finger at her. "Yes, what you did was dangerous, but it was a little like a mackerel swimming across a pool of hungry sharks. We could never have asked you to do this—way too risky—but it got the sharks to come out, where we could catch them. Julia, I'd say you are a real patriot."

Julia wasn't sure what to say next. "I guess you can force me to turn over the drive." In an instant she had a new understanding of things. How naïve she'd been when she first pondered what to do with the canister—finding a thrill for a would-be writer of thrillers. A series of incidents flashed through her mind: the terror of the car fire, driving the Minnie Winnie at breakneck speed through the middle of the night fleeing mysterious followers, holding two pistols pointed at the criminals the FBI had just said would have killed them in a heartbeat, Nivvie leaping out of nowhere to save the day. But above all of this, Declan diving into the line of fire. She would not forget that as long as she lived.

"Julia? Are you okay?" Sandoval said.

Julia shook her head, like she was waking from a dream. She looked around, embarrassed. "Yes, I'm fine. Sorry."

"I understand that after all you've been through, you'd like to hand the drive over to Fort Huachuca yourself. But, yes, I do have the authority to take it from you."

Julia stood, pulled the drive from her pocket and held it out to him. "I'm happy to give it to you. I know it's safe now. Truth is, delivering it to Fort Huachuca doesn't mean as much to me as it did a few days ago." She turned toward Declan. "I've learned some things."

Sandoval pulled on Latex gloves he'd had in a pocket, took the drive, moved closer to a lamp and examined it closely. He looked up and said, "So, this is what all the fuss was about." He then placed it into a locking briefcase he had at his side. It was obvious that he hadn't planned to leave without it. This had been the purpose of the whole evening.

Finally, he looked back at Julia and said, "You've done a great thing for your country."

Julia flushed red. She had just sat back down when the door to the meeting room swung open. Another FBI agent poked her head into the room. "We have a visitor. I cleared her in."

Reverend Pam walked in.

Everyone stood. "Pam!" squealed Prisca, enfolding Pam in a hug. "You certainly have a sense of timing."

Pam stood facing the group, wearing a colorful Native American V-necked tunic over blue jeans and leather sandals over thick wool socks. A daypack was slung over one shoulder. She laughed, as she looked around, checking out Sandoval and Sheppard with raised eyebrows. Now she looked at Julia. "When the FBI called me, asking about you guys, I thought I'd better get my butt down here. I had a couple days of vacay coming. A drive down to Arizona might be a good thing." After a pause, her eyes twinkling, she said, "Have I missed anything?"

Everyone laughed.

After Pam was brought up to speed about the events of the day, the conversation turned to much lighter topics, like camping. The two agents brought more laughter into the room, as they shared stories about their rookie camping foibles. Even the serious Carol Sheppard got everyone laughing with her detailed description of her travails setting up her pop-up trailer.

Finally, Prisca said, "What a glorious time. A day that began with such danger and terror ends like this. Only in a place like Chiricahua could something like this happen." Then she brought out cake, apparently left over from some office event, and put on a pot of coffee.

After more conversation, Prisca turned to Pam. "One more question, my friend. Did you bring your flute?"

Pam smiled. "Of course."

She pulled her flute from the daypack and stood. She was silent for a few moments before she played, as if saying a prayer. When she played, everyone else stood, too, and the haunting sound of the Native American flute was like a healing balm for a broken world. Nivvie's ears perked up. Even the agents looked moved. The sound from Pam's flute was as timeless as the spires of the Heart of Rocks, hopeful as the first hint of dawn, mournful as the separation from the daughter you love, gentle as a lover's head resting on your shoulder.

Later, back at their campsite, Elizabeth excused herself, sensing that Julia and Declan could use some time together. They walked with David Niven to the rear of their campsite, where a narrow trail led through the understory to a small creek. A full moon peeked in and out among the treetops.

As they walked, Julia said, "So, we're never going to see Fort Huachuca and we're never going to learn what's on the drive. Surprisingly, I'm totally fine with that." After a moment, she said, "What will you do now?"

The moonlight danced on his face, as he turned to her. "I told my brother that I'm ready to start as his accountant in California."

"Oh? When was that?"

"This afternoon."

Julia bent down and picked up a fallen leaf, turned it over in her hand, as she studied it. "And when will you start?"

"Right away, I guess."

"Oh?" She stopped and turned toward him.

"Why do you act surprised?"

"Oh, nothing. You said you didn't really enjoy bookkeeping."

"I like helping my brother. And I don't seem to have a lot of other opportunities right now."

"You said something about wanting to teach. You'd be good at—"

"—that was just talk. You don't get to do everything you want to do."

"But …"

"But what?"

"I don't know." It was suddenly difficult to speak. "It just seems so final."

"I guess it is," he said. "As final as you moving back to Milwaukee."

At the creek, they stood in silence, watching the moonlight sparkle on the water. "I'll never go to Fort Huachuca, and that's okay. But I could stay here forever," she said. She took his hand in hers. The way he held her hand tightly said that he could, too. With her.

Nivvie pulled hard on his leash. Terror pulsed through Julia—was there another threat approaching? She saw motion on the far side of the narrow creek. From behind some ground vegetation a strange animal emerged. With thick brown fur, it was twice the size of a raccoon. Declan saw it, too. Soon, several more of these strange creatures joined the first one. They seemed oblivious to Julia and Declan.

"They're coatimundis," said Declan. "I read about them in the brochure."

Julia watched in silence, as the lead coati stopped and looked at them. It had a pointy, white snout and a long brown up-turned tail.

Declan whispered, "It's a native of central America but has found its way up here. The Chiricahuas is one of the few places in the US it is seen."

As the group of coatis moved on and disappeared into the vegetation, Julia said into the darkness, "Why are you so far from home?"

Chapter 46

"Do you think we're suffering from PTSD?" Declan asked. He sat on a bench with Julia and Elizabeth near the trailhead at Massai Point, looking out over the great forest of pinnacles and balanced rocks. Nivvie, on his leash, sat like a sentry next to Declan. They were here for another day of hiking, because that's what you do when you're in a place like this. But they'd only made it as far as this bench, just a few steps from the RV.

Last night, after the moonlight walk to the creek, they'd turned in, mostly in silence. There just didn't seem like much more to say. It had the feel of finality. Then this morning, Declan's arm felt much better, and there was no reason they couldn't head back up to Massai Point for at least a short hike. But their decision lacked much enthusiasm. Sandoval and Sheppard's campsites were already empty when they left the campground, and their conversation on the drive up to the top was subdued.

What was going on with Julia? They'd been through so much the past few days. Had she heard from her daughter yet? Was she planning her return to Milwaukee? Or was she planning anything? Had the chaos of the last twenty-four hours left her numb and scattered like him?

Julia now turned her gaze away from the rocks and looked at him. "I don't know. I guess PTSD wouldn't be surprising. I know Pam and Prisca were worried about us."

Before they'd left for their campsite last night, they'd both expressed concern. Pam had said something like, "Would it be okay with you if we say a prayer? We have a lot to be thankful for tonight." Julia had said yes immediately, Elizabeth nodded, but Declan said nothing.

No one had ever prayed for Declan before. Pam and Prisca spoke comforting words of thanksgiving and made requests to the divine for their peace and wellbeing. It felt right.

Now, as Julia gazed out into the rocks, it seemed like her brain was racing through a million thoughts.

He started to speak, but Julia spoke first. "Okay, this is strange. I mean, here I am in this beautiful place, but right now I kind of want to go back to the hut."

He laid his hand atop hers. "Funny you'd say that. I was thinking the same thing." Elizabeth nodded her agreement.

The hut was hopping when they arrived. At least a dozen cars were parked outside. Inside, Pam worked with a group filling bags with toiletry and hygiene items. She stopped when she saw them. "I'm so glad to see you this morning," she said, bubbling with enthusiasm. "I hope you all slept okay. Not sure I could have."

"We didn't," said Julia, who then laughed for the first time this morning. It was easy to laugh around Pam. "But we wanted to come back, and …" She glanced at Declan. "Actually, I'm not sure why we came back, but here we are."

Pam nodded like she understood. "Well, I'll warn you right up front, if you stand around here very long, somebody's going to put you to work."

Doing work to help someone else sounded appealing to Declan, as he surveyed all the activity. In addition to the people packing bags of toiletry items, others were using woodworking tools, apparently making or repairing furniture—the sound of a whirring power saw filled the room—and others were cooking at a kitchen area they hadn't noticed yesterday. Navarro, the singer they'd seen night before last, stirred a large pot on a stove. Prisca stood next to a table, where people worked on some small intricate items, presumably making crafts. Everyone was busy. "This is an amazing place," he said.

"Isn't it beautiful?" said Pam. "It's all due to a lot of prayer and the hard work of a lot of people, especially Prisca.

"You know when Prisca first came to seminary, she was Priscilla. That's her name. But as everyone got to know her, they started calling her Prisca, because that's what Saint Paul called one of his colleagues, Priscilla. Paul says Prisca actually saved his life and even refers to her as an apostle. A female apostle. A pretty good description of that woman over there."

Prisca looked up from her work and caught their eyes. She said something to her group and came over to them. "So, what kind of nonsense is Pam feeding you now?"

"We've come to work," Declan said. "What should we do?"

Prisca scanned the room. "Declan, I think they could use you over there," she said, pointing to a bench where two people were working with tools. "Julia and Elizabeth, why don't you come with me?"

Two men busied themselves working on small appliances, one on a toaster, the other on a microwave oven. One of them, an old guy, looked up, as Declan approached. "Come to help?"

Declan nodded. "Declan," he said.

"Grab an appliance and see what you can do," the man said. Smiling, he extended his hand. "Ken. This is Greg." Greg nodded. "So, we've got a pile of discarded kitchen appliances that don't work, and we're tryin' to fix them. A lot of folks out there can use these." No one mentioned Declan's adventures of yesterday or his gunshot wound, although he suspected everyone had heard about that.

Ken was a crusty looking guy. Sparse gray hair and ruddy features. He looked like a smoker. "Greg here's the expert, knows what he's doin.' So, we pay attention to what he tells us to do."

Greg looked up. He was a slender, intense looking guy, wearing a grey shirt with a sewed-on name patch. Probably his work shirt. "Grab something and see what you can do. I can help, if you need it. Especially when we get to the electrical stuff." He pointed to a voltmeter, which Declan knew how to use, next to a bank of outlets. "Some of this old crap is beyond repair, but you'd be surprised how much of it can be salvaged."

"Sort of like us," Ken laughed.

Declan had just picked a toaster oven and was examining it when Navarro appeared by his side. He nodded at Greg and Ken, then turned his attention to Declan. "Saw you here the other night," he said. His smooth brown face was encased by a full mane of long black hair. Probably late thirties. "Navarro," he said with an easy grin. "Gotta say, I'm glad my kitchen duties are done for the day. That's hardly my area of giftedness."

"That was really beautiful how you sang the other night."

Navarro studied Declan with large, warm eyes. "Thank you."

"I mean, it really touched me."

Navarro nodded. "I just tried to sing it the way Mahalia would." He leaned over and pulled a blender from the pile of kitchen junk.

"Oh, come on, Navarro," Ken said. He looked at Declan. "Don't let him fool you, this dude's about the best singer around these parts."

Navarro shook his head, seemingly embarrassed.

"So, you're a professional?" Declan asked.

Navarro laughed. "Hardly. I sing here sometimes, but my day job's over at the homeless shelter in Wilcoxx."

"He's the freaking director," Ken added.

Navarro looked embarrassed. "All of us are trying to help," he said. He glanced around the room. "And all of us have something to contribute."

Declan looked around, too. "So, why do you all do this? I mean, this is wonderful, but four guys standing around trying to fix busted kitchen appliances. Why?"

Navarro nodded like he understood. "We're all trying to help because we've been helped."

Declan waited for him to say more.

"Everybody's got a story here," Navarro said. "Me? I don't work at a homeless shelter because that's the major I chose in college. I'm there because ten years ago I was homeless."

Declan swallowed hard.

"I've made a lot of mistakes, done things I regret, things that hurt people. Thought more than once that there was no hope for me, after all I had done." He nodded toward the pile of busted appliances. "About as worthless as those old pieces of junk."

"But we're fixin' those old pieces of junk," said Ken.

Navarro grinned, glancing upward. "Yeah, the same way someone is fixing us."

Declan's brows furrowed in surprise that Navarro would be so candid with a stranger.

Navarro added, "What I've learned here is that it's never too late for a fresh start."

Ken and Greg nodded their affirmations. *Never too late for a fresh start.* He remembered Pam's words: "It's when your hands are empty that you are ready to take hold of the world."

They were interrupted by the ring of a land line on a table in the corner. Prisca answered it, talked for a while, then motioned to Declan. "Declan, why don't you take this?"

"Who is it?"

"It's Eileen."

"Who's Eileen?"

"Well, if you'd take the phone, you could find out." She held the receiver out to him.

Declan looked at Navarro, Ken and Greg, who exchanged knowing smiles. Reluctantly, he took the phone. "Hello?" he said tentatively.

A woman's trembling voice said, "My husband and I have no food."

Declan looked around helplessly. This seemed like something Prisca should take care of. She was the priest. She'd know what to do. He looked for her, but Prisca was already involved in another activity.

He said to the caller, "Why don't you come by the hut— you know where that is?"

"I don't have a car," the woman said.

"Can someone give you a ride?"

"I don't know anyone. Please bring us some food."

Declan wasn't sure what to do. This could be a set up. Someone luring him into a trap. He hemmed and hawed, trying to figure out a way he could let her down easy. While he pondered his strategy, he gazed around the room at the people offering their Saturday to do all this work. He said, "Yes, I'll bring you some food."

The woman—she'd told Prisca her name was Eileen— gave Declan an address. "Please come soon. We're very hungry," she said, then hung up.

After he got off the phone, Declan sought out Prisca, who was busy helping two elderly people preparing to paint a piece of furniture. He had to wait for her to finish their conversation, then he told her about Eileen's request.

She nodded, then said, "What are you going to do?"

Declan let out a nervous laugh. "I was hoping you'd tell me."

Prisca didn't seem to give it much thought. She seemed more interested in getting back to the painting project. "There's food over in that fridge," she said, pointing to an old refrigerator against the wall. "And there are boxes of things and canned goods in that cabinet next to it." Then she turned back to the couple.

Declan's first inclination was to blow it off. There could be a million reasons this wasn't a legit request for help. A million good excuses for him to do nothing and get on with his day. He was, after all, entitled to a day off, after what he'd just been through. Good Lord. An image flashed before him of himself airborne while Justin's pistol flashed twice before him.

He paced back and forth. Then he went to the refrigerator and began packing bags of food.

He'd asked Julia and Elizabeth if they wanted to accompany him. They both said yes, but then Declan had second thoughts. Prisca had asked him, for whatever reason, to take care of this. He said, "Maybe I should go by myself. Mind if I take the RV?"

Julia eyed him closely, apparently realizing that this was important, and handed him the keys. She gave him what felt like an I'm-proud-of-you smile.

An hour later he peered out the windshield at an abandoned motel, set back from the road and surrounded by tall patches of brush. He again checked the address he'd scribbled down. He shook his head and let out a fluttering breath. A narrow weed-infested gravel road led up to the front of the building. No way anyone lived here. Most of the windows had long been smashed out. Many of the doors along the strip of rooms were missing. He pulled the RV up to the front of the building, then turned it to face back up the entrance road, in case he needed to make a quick getaway. He stepped out, worried about rattlesnakes, and left the RV door ajar so he could jump back in quickly. It was deathly still.

He stood there with two bags of groceries in his arms and no clue what to do next. He cleared his throat and called out, "Eileen."

If he'd been smarter, he'd have brought a couple of the huskier volunteers from the hut as backup. Hell, a couple of Marines might be better. He remembered the human traffickers that Prisca had told them about. Might they have lured him out here? But it was just him alone in this silent, lonely, depressing place.

Then a voice called out, "I'm in here."

This was a good time to run, but something kept him there. He wasn't certain what it was. Maybe it was the sorrow he'd seen—Elizabeth and the tragedy of her granddaughter, Julia struggling with her alienated daughter ... Emily's face as she was wheeled down that hallway. Or maybe it was the passion of Prisca and Pam, who seemed to be filled with hope about the world, despite all the evidence to the contrary. Who seemed to be motivated by something bigger, something hidden. They would call it God. He shook his head and walked toward the voice.

At the doorway of one of the rooms with no door, the smell was awful, and the interior was total darkness. "Come in," he heard the voice say. Declan again considered fleeing, but instead he swallowed hard and stepped inside. As his eyes adjusted to the darkness, he saw a woman sitting on the floor. "I knew you'd come," she said. "I'm Eileen." She looked down at a man lying on a dirty mattress beside her. "This is Harold, my husband. He's dying."

Dear God. Declan set the food down and went over to them. Harold apparently couldn't sit up but looked up at him with eyes of sadness. Eileen told him they'd been to the hospital, had somehow gotten meds to dull his pain, and they'd said Harold would be dead in two weeks. They had no money, no anything, just each other, and here they were at the end of the road and the end of their ropes. Of course, they were squatting here illegally, and Declan wondered why the police hadn't rousted them yet. He figured some cop must have been listening to Prisca, too.

Declan knelt near the couple. He said, "I'm Declan. I brought you some water and food. Is there anything else I can do? Do you feel safe here?"

As Eileen began removing items from one of the bags, Harold reached out a hand toward Declan and seemed to be trying to say something, but Declan couldn't make it out. He barely had a voice. "He's saying thank you," said Eileen.

"Would you like me to send a priest to say prayers?"

"Oh, yes. Prisca will come."

"You know her?"

"She comes often."

"I wish there was more that I could do."

"You've done a lot," Eileen said.

As Declan headed back to the RV, his mind was awash in thoughts. Why was there such suffering in the world? Funny thing was, Declan thought, despite the presence of such need, the commitment he'd seen this morning at the hut was undaunted. He realized, with such clarity that he stopped there in the weeds, forgetting his concern about snakes, that he was now a part of all that. He turned and looked back at the dark doorway of the motel room. And he wished he could visit again.

When he returned to the hut, he sought out Prisca to give his report to her. When she saw him, she said, "How'd it go?"

"Uh, good. I guess. I admit I was scared."

Her eyes seemed to bore into him. "What were you scared of?"

"It was a dangerous area."

Prisca nodded. "It can be dangerous."

"It was also sad."

"Yes," she said.

"So, you visit Eileen?"

"Yes."

"You kinda set me up for this, didn't you?"

"Do you regret going?"

Declan looked around at all the busy workers. He felt a surge of joy that he was a part of this. "I'm really glad I did. But I'm not sure I did okay," he said, hoping for some reassurance.

But Prisca just nodded and smiled. "So, what do you think about how you did?" she asked.

"I'd like to do it again."

"That's what I hoped you'd say."

"Prisca," he said, "you have to deal with situations like this all the time, I suspect."

She nodded.

"How do you do it? I mean, how do you keep going? It's all so sad."

"It is sad work, but it is joyous work, too. You experienced that."

"Yes."

Prisca looked hard into Declan's eyes. "I keep going because of a love and a source of energy that far exceeds anything I can accomplish on my own." She put a hand on his shoulder. "And as great as the need is, this love keeps sending people to help. Today, Declan, it sent you."

Declan's throat tightened.

"Thank you, Declan, for coming today."

Declan struggled to find words.

Prisca patted him on the shoulder and pointed to a group doing a woodworking project. "I think those folks over there could use some help."

Chapter 47

Julia's mind was awash with a swirl of troubling thoughts. She was unable to hold onto one of them long enough for any understanding to crystalize before the next troubling thought crashed in: their near deaths yesterday and all the terrifying and inspiring images that replayed; Jenny—dear God—and her own move back to Milwaukee; her growing connection to Declan and their inevitable parting soon.

Then there was the tragedy of Elizabeth, who stood next to her, packing food bags for distribution to the needy. Packing the bags consisted of selecting a wrapped sandwich from one pile, a container of fruit from another, cookies, and a soda. This would normally be a monotonous job, but at this moment it was about all Julia could handle.

She studied Elizabeth, just as Pam approached.

"How's it going?" Pam said.

Elizabeth looked at Julia as if expecting her to speak, but Julia stayed silent, wanting Elizabeth to say something.

"Good," Elizabeth said.

"Say more." Pam's brown eyes burrowed into Elizabeth.

Elizabeth shrugged and looked down. "It's good to help."

Pam waited, her gaze unwavering.

Elizabeth continued. "I mean, I didn't think there was anything I could do."

"I hear you did quite a lot yesterday."

Elizabeth turned her attention back to the food bags.

"You fought back yesterday," Julia said to Elizabeth. Then she turned to Pam. "She threw herself on me, put herself in the line of fire, just before I was about to die. She pleaded with this person pointing a gun at us, begged her to spare me."

Julia paused, as Elizabeth continued to stuff food bags, then continued. "That person somehow heard those pleas. Elizabeth saved our lives."

Elizabeth turned to Julia with searching eyes.

After a moment, Pam said, "I believe God wants to heal the broken hearted, and we are called to be a part of that work. There are still a lot of broken hearts around. It's hard and frustrating, and sometimes it seems like there's no hope. I don't know why there is still such pain. But I do know we are called to do something about it. Yesterday, Elizabeth, you did something about it. And right now, preparing these food bags, you're doing something about it, too."

They stood in silence until Elizabeth said, "I know people help. But sometimes the pain doesn't go away."

Pam seemed to ponder Elizabeth's words. "And yet you did something heroic yesterday."

"I couldn't let them hurt Julia."

"Why?"

"Because she's been kind to me."

"I wonder why she was kind to you."

Elizabeth looked at Julia. "Because she's a good person."

Pam said, "I'd say it's because you're a good person, too."

Tears filled Elizabeth's eyes. "You talk about hope, but I'm not sure there's hope for everyone." She began to pack another bag.

Julia turned toward Pam, waiting for her response. But Pam said nothing. No wise priestly words, no palliative consolations that Julia might have expected. Instead, Pam stepped in next to Elizabeth and began packing bags. There were tears in her eyes, too.

Julia picked up a wrapped sandwich and placed it in a bag.

Chapter 48

They continued to work until it was getting late. Finally, Ken set down an old blender he was trying to rewire and said to Declan, "Looks like it's about time to wrap it up."

Declan looked up to see people putting tools away and returning food items to cabinets. There was a lot of laughter, even though Declan suspected everyone was, like him, exhausted. A few of the people pulled on jackets and headed for the exit, but most of them picked up hymnals from the table near the door and made their way toward the far end of the hut, toward the chairs and the stage.

Declan stepped over to where Julia and Elizabeth were finishing their work. "I guess we can leave now."

They watched what was going on up front, where people took seats in front of a simple table, covered by a green runner. A candle sat on each end of the runner, surrounding a large loaf of bread and a tall cup.

Navarro began noodling at the keyboard.

Prisca and Pam stood behind the table. Stoles hung around their shoulders, over their work clothes. Prisca's stole was a deep forest green. Pam wore a colorful stole of brilliant reds, blues and greens that caused goosebumps to rise on Declan's arms. It was the same pattern as Declan's blanket—her grandmother must have made it for her. Pam's flute was tucked under her arm.

Ken lit the candles. Then Navarro paused his noodling, and the room was quiet.

Declan looked at Julia and Elizabeth. Without words they each picked up a hymnal and moved toward the folding chairs.

An hour later, as the three of them left in silence, Declan couldn't find words to describe what had happened.

He'd taken a seat and tried not to catch anyone's eyes. He would get through this by just following what everyone else did.

Then Navarro's powerful voice resonated throughout the hut, with words that Declan would remember later, especially, "His eye is on the sparrow, and I know he watches me."

There were prayers and readings and beautiful words from Prisca, followed by Pam playing a haunting melody on her flute.

Declan knew what communion was, but he'd never witnessed it in person, much less received it. It seemed strange. Was there some qualification, some preparation needed to receive it? As others came forward to receive the bread and wine, he stayed back. Then Prisca saw him and extended her hand with a come-on wiggle of her fingers.

He stood in front of the table and looked down the line at the others. Julia, Elizabeth, Greg and Ken, and Navarro were there with others, their hands extended. There were hands of all kinds: Elizabeth's gnarled hands, Ken's calloused hands, Julia's delicate hands. It seemed like everyone was invited.

Prisca said words that Declan didn't understand about God, but as she placed a piece of bread in his hand, something happened to him, which he also didn't understand. More than Prisca's wiggling fingers inviting him in, it was like the universe's wiggling fingers, maybe God's wiggling fingers, were inviting him in. He struggled to form an explanation. All he could come up with was the memory of the starry sky at Pam's house, but he was no longer merely an observer, he was now a part of that universe, somehow connected with everything and everyone.

When Pam stepped in front of him and offered him a sip of wine from the cup, he didn't want to look up. He didn't want her to see his tears.

Then he looked down the line again and it was like others were there, too. Eileen and Harold were there. But more. Alana Selkirk was there, next to Justin and the man with the shaved head. There was Gerald Bender, the program manager from Washington. On the other side of Bender were people he couldn't fully see. But then one of them leaned forward and looked directly at Declan. It was his father.

Declan wiped his tears, just as another person leaned forward. Her smile was not the haunting smile he'd seen through the ER window. It was a smile of pure joy.

So what if he couldn't write some fancy physics equation to describe what he experienced? Perhaps the most important things in life aren't meant to be subjected to analysis—things like the golden sunrise hues of the Chiricahua pinnacles or the catchlight in Julia's eyes.

What came to him were Pam's words back in Oklahoma that he could now begin to grasp. "You are loveable."

Outside, he turned toward Julia and Elizabeth but had no words.

"What an amazing day," Julia said. "There is one thing left to do."

Chapter 49

Near sunset, the three of them stood on a thin crusty layer of ice left by the first light snow, facing a modest tract house in Columbia Heights, on the north side of Minneapolis. Terror filled Elizabeth's face, as she looked first at Julia then Declan. "I never thought I'd be here again."

They'd left the Chiricahuas three days ago, after another day at the hut, and driven straight through. If it hadn't been for their time there, they had all agreed, they wouldn't be standing here now.

"I still think this is a bad idea," said Elizabeth, both of her hands clamped tightly on Julia's arm. "I should've never given you her name."

"I know this must be scary," Julia said. "Twelve years. But she didn't say no when I called her." Calling Elizabeth's daughter had been difficult. Who knew what kind of emotional mess she'd be stirring up? Before they left the Chiricahuas, Prisca and Pam had met with the three of them, encouraged them to do it, said prayers for them, then sent them off. What courage Elizabeth had, Julia thought, to agree to follow through on this. To go home again to confront her past, after all this time. It would be hard and risky, but they had all agreed it was the only path forward.

Elizabeth had said again, as she had out in the Grottos, that the door was closed. After all, her daughter had told her that she was no longer her mom, that she wished it had been her who'd died, that she never wanted to see her again, that the very sight of her or hearing her voice brought back the awful memories of Angie's death. Don't ever call me again, she had said, when Elizabeth had persisted in calling during those first weeks.

With Pam and Prisca's encouragement, they'd come to realize that just because the door is closed doesn't mean it's locked.

"What if she's changed her mind? She's had several days to think it over." Elizabeth was pulling back.

Julia looked at Elizabeth. They'd gotten her new clothes along the way and had worked on her hair. She looks pretty good, thought Julia. "You won't know until you go up there and knock."

"Will you go with me, Julia?"

Julia wasn't much more confident about this than Elizabeth was. She swallowed hard. "Of course."

"Okay," Elizabeth said. She took a couple steps toward the front door but then pulled back.

"We can do this, Elizabeth," said Julia.

"Julia, whatever happens, I want you to know how grateful I am for you."

Julia thought about her own mother, who was barely speaking to her, and had to work to keep the tears from coming.

Then they went to the door. It was a small house, probably built back in the sixties. On a front porch, outdoor furniture was covered with tarps for the approaching winter.

Elizabeth's hand trembled as she pushed the doorbell. Nothing. She shot Julia an apprehensive glance.

"Push it again," said Julia.

Elizabeth did, then stepped back, perhaps ready to flee.

The door opened and a woman about Julia's age stood there, wide eyed with a look of fear. They stood and looked at each other for a while. Elizabeth couldn't meet her daughter's eyes. Julia had to force herself not to look away. The daughter's face was red from crying. Then she took Elizabeth's shoulders and pulled her close. "Mom, I am so, so sorry."

Elizabeth shot Julia an uncertain glance. Her daughter continued, "I never thought I'd get you back. I've needed you. I've missed you. I know I treated you so badly. I was wrong."

"No, you weren't wrong."

"You were a wonderful mother… Mom, I've needed you so much … I've been trying to find you for years … Oh, God, Mom, I thought you were dead. Mom, I was wrong." Her words came out in breathless gushes. "But now I see. My dear mother, can you ever forgive me? I've dreamed about this moment. About what I would say." She looked down, as she gasped, as if struggling for air. "Do you think that after all this time, we might have a chance to start again?" There was a look of complete helplessness on her face. Julia had to look away.

"But I killed—"

"—No, you didn't. It just took me a little while to realize that, Mom."

"My dear daughter, you are the most important thing there is to me."

As Elizabeth's daughter took her mother's hand and guided her into the house, she said to Julia, "Why don't you come in, too?"

Julia shifted from one foot to the other, suddenly feeling wobbly. Maybe she should stay to provide moral support for Elizabeth. She placed a hand against the door to steady herself. She shouldn't stay. Whatever was going to happen next had to happen between just the two of them. "Oh, no, we have to hit the road. It was great to meet you."

Elizabeth turned to look at Julia and extended a hand, which Julia gripped hard. "I'll never forget you," said Elizabeth.

Julia couldn't speak. She stepped forward and gave Elizabeth a quick hug. Then she turned and left.

At the curb, she was still shaking. Declan was beside her now, his arm around her. She laid her head against his shoulder.

"That was a wonderful thing you just did, Julia," he said.

Then she lost it. Loud sobs gushed out, as she fell into his arms. Finally, she raised her head, sniffled and wiped the back of her hand across her eyes. "There's so much I don't understand. Why has this happened to a good person like Elizabeth? Why did she have to experience all this for so long?"

Julia saw the tears behind Declan's wireframes. He opened his mouth to speak but then just shook his head. After a while, he said, "I don't know." He shook his head again. "They say physics is the study of reality, but after all my study, it seems like I understand reality even less."

Still holding on to each other, they turned and looked toward the house. A light had just come on behind a large, curtained window. "The purpose of our trip was never to return some secret object to an army base, was it?" she said. "It was to bring Elizabeth home."

Chapter 50

Declan had just told Julia that he now understood reality even less. But that wasn't quite right. It had been true a few days ago, as he shivered alone in that Wisconsin campground. But then he found himself somehow in a new place. Giving when he had thought he was empty. Sharing when he had thought he had nothing left to say. Moving and exploring when he had thought there was no place he wanted to be.

Pam had told him around that campfire in western Oklahoma that when his hands were empty, he might be ready to take hold of the world. He didn't understand her words at the time. Maybe *take hold of the world* meant to conquer the world, but now he knew differently. It meant love the world, extending his empty hands to surprisingly discover that they contained something to give.

He looked at Julia. How much of what he had learned was because of her. Maybe the most beautiful place he had been was right here on this crunchy layer of old snow on this drab evening in these drab suburbs. Next to her.

The tears she shed for Elizabeth were also for the whole world, and they were real. No, he didn't understand, as Julia had asked, why there is so much suffering. But he was beginning to understand that if there was going to be hope for the world, it might begin with tears in the eyes of people like Julia.

He closed his eyes and he was back in that dark motel room with Eileen and Harold. He'd knelt beside them and set the bags of food down and said a few words, but then he had nothing more to say. He had stood to leave. But he got halfway to the door then stopped. He had no idea what to do, but he sensed he needed to do more. He turned and sat back down on the floor next to Harold.

They sat in silence for a while, a silence that reminded Declan of those last days in the hospital waiting room, while Emily was on the ventilator and he was not allowed into her room. Chaplains visited him. Some of them offered words of consolation and guidance, but he remembered few of those words now. What he remembered was the one chaplain who was simply present, waiting with him in silence, crying with him.

Declan sat quietly next to Harold.

Eileen said, "You don't have to stay."

"I know," Declan said. He trembled with uncertainty. What should he say? How long should he stay? He didn't want to overstay.

Harold interrupted the silence periodically with his coughing.

Eileen said, "I wish I had something to offer you."

"It's okay," Declan said.

Even as his eyes adjusted, he could barely see in the dark room. Eileen and Harold were nearly motionless shadows. The only motion he saw was a mouse skittering along the wall.

After a while, Harold emitted a soft grunt, nearly inaudible.

Declan leaned toward him. "What?"

Eileen put a hand on Harold's shoulder. "He's trying to tell you that he's grateful you're here."

Declan couldn't speak.

Now he looked down at Julia, there beside him on the gray snow. Tears still streaked her face, as her eyes continued to be locked on the house. She had taught him how to trust, how to give. She had said the real purpose of the trip was to bring Elizabeth home. That was true. But it was also for him to meet her.

His voice was shaky as he began to speak. "Julia," he said.

She looked up at him.

"I—"

Julia's phone beeped. She pulled it out of her Levi's, then looked at him with a mixture of joy and apprehension. "It's Jenny!"

As Julia climbed up into the cab to take the call, Declan stepped away from the RV. He could not bear to hear Julia announce her decision to her daughter. He pulled Pam's blanket tighter around him—he no longer owned a coat—remembering Pam's face as she presented it to him back in Oklahoma. That was just a few days ago, but it seemed so far in the past now. She'd said something about how he needed some nice things to happen to him.

He stared into the drab uniformity of the evening. Patches of ice on the sidewalk meant he'd have to watch his footing. He could see Julia, animated inside the cab, talking with Jenny. Dear Lord, she would be moving back to Milwaukee soon. Into this. What was he going to do? California? He shook his head, and his shoulders slumped. The physicist could plunge into some interminable analysis, the kind of thing a physicist does best— measure the thermal conductivity of the rose but never run his fingers along the velvety surface of its petals. He could analyze this objectively, keeping his feelings at arm's length. An objective analysis that would lead to nowhere and miss the main point. Why not just name it? He hadn't so far. Not even to himself. He looked back at her again, up inside the cab. Now she was laughing. His throat tightened.

Here she was laughing, looking forward to her future. And here he was, falling in love.

Chapter 51

Julia hadn't talked to Jenny since that terrible afternoon in Tucumcari, when Jenny hung up on her. Since then, Julia had done a lot of soul searching, and she had her speech well-rehearsed. She'd tried to call Jenny twice, once leaving that cryptic message: "I have some news." Then she had decided not to be the needy, desperate mom and wait for Jenny to call her. Finally, here it was, and she was still shaking from her farewell to Elizabeth. But she was ready for this conversation, and she knew what she had to say.

"Hey, mom, what's up? Sounds like something important." Jenny sounded fine—no hint of the bad way the call had ended the other day.

"Sweetheart, I've been doing some thinking, and I've made some decisions. I realize that I haven't been the best mother to you, that I—"

"Mom, you're—"

"No, hear me out." She took a deep breath then continued. "I've been too caught up in my own needs. I haven't been there for—"

"Stop it, mother. That's not…look, I said some things the other day, but you've—"

"I know, Jenny. Guilty as charged. And I want to—"

"Mom," Jenny shrieked, "will you just be quiet for a minute? Of course you're there for me. I know it. Sometimes I say some shit, I know, but you've got to let me blow off some steam, and not get all freaky over it, okay?"

"Okay," Julia said meekly. "But please listen. I have a new plan. Okay? Hear me out. I'm going to move back to Milwaukee, get a place where I'll be permanently, and you can have a—"

Jenny cut her off. "Mom, do you have any frigging idea how cool you are? How much I admire you? You're my mom, the struggling novelist, on her own traveling around the country in an RV. Among my friends, you're kind of a celebrity. My cool mom, the modern-day hippie. You're who they all want to be.

"And here's another clue, in case you need it, which it seems you do. Every summer I get to travel to some cool getaway on the ocean or the mountains, some destination kind of shit that most people just dream about. And I get to hang out in an RV next to a waterfall or whatever. I'll take that any day over some claustrophobic shoebox in Midcity, USA."

Julia laughed to herself. This kid of hers was pretty amazing.

"Look mom, I want to live my life to the full. I know I'll make some mistakes, and I know you'll worry about me. But, Mom, hear this: I want you to live your life to the full, too."

Julia couldn't speak.

"Mom, I'm so proud of you. You've struck out into the unknown. You have been so courageous. I don't want you to go back now. I remember when I was in high school—you were wrapped up in decorating the kitchen, worrying about the garden—you were pretending to have a life, not actually living a life. Maybe I need to say it again: I want to live a life, and Mom, I want you to live a life, too. I'm happy to see you when you visit, and I'll come to where you're camping." Then Jenny's serious lecture mode switched to a softer, almost laughing tone.

"Gotta admit, there's a little swagger when I tell my friends about my amazing mom."

"But, Jenny, I have to do what's right, not just what my emotions and my hormones are telling me to do."

"Mom, you are doing what's right. So, you met some guy at a campground. I think that's great. Don't underestimate the importance of what those hormones are telling you."

This got them both laughing.

Geez, thought Julia, I must really be out of it. Now I'm getting relationship advice from my daughter. "Oh, Jenny, I'm so proud of you."

"Don't get carried away again, Mom. But thank you."

"And Jenny, I want you to know that I support whatever you decide." She knew Jenny's plan to take a year off was still out there on the table, but at this moment there was something more important. "Whatever I think is the best path doesn't matter. What matters is that I know what a person of integrity and intelligence you are. Whatever you decide, I'll support."

"But Mom, I'll always want your advice."

Julia laughed. "I'll try to only give it when you ask me for it."

"I'm sorry about what I said about you being a camp host. You—"

"It's okay, sweetie, what you said is—"

"No, what I said was wrong. I know I made some smart-ass comment about Harvard not offering a major in campground hosting, but—"

Julia laughed. "That was actually pretty funny."

"You know I got my sass from you." Jenny laughed.

"I know."

"Just want to say that if Harvard did offer a major in campground hosting, you'd be a professor for sure."

"Not sure that's a compliment, but I'll take it."

Finally, Jenny said, "I love you, Mom."

"Oh, sweetheart, I love you, too."

After the call, Julia was beaming, as she stepped down out of the Minnie Winnie.

Declan stood there, looking cold wrapped in his Indian blanket. "Well, what did she say?" he asked.

"I guess I'm going to Florida," she said.

Chapter 52

Declan was aware that his mouth was hanging open. Also, that he probably looked ridiculous wrapped in that colorful blanket. "You mean you're going back to Milwaukee after your Florida gig?"

"I'm not going back to Milwaukee at all." She was glowing.

Declan was still trying to put this together. "But you told your daughter that—"

She shook her head. "She doesn't want me to move back to Milwaukee. Said I'm a modern-day hippie, and she likes that."

Suddenly, Declan didn't feel cold anymore. "So, you're going to continue being a campground host?" He was still trying to make sure he understood.

"Yep. Until I run out of money."

"And you're going to continue writing?"

Julia's glow faded. "I'm not sure. I've got to review all that. Your talk about literary fiction … I just don't know if I'd be good at it."

Declan smiled. He remembered her words to him about dancing at the KOA. "So, you're not trying it because you're no good at it?" he said.

She obviously remembered, too. She let out a little laugh, then nodded her head.

"I personally think you'd be good at whatever kind of novel you want to write."

"You do?" She stepped closer to him. "But you've never seen any of my writing."

"But I've seen you."

She licked her lips and swallowed, like her mouth had suddenly gone dry. Her eyes now had questions in them. "So, that's me. I guess you're headed out to California." She looked around at the bleak surroundings. "Not that I could blame you."

"That's what I told Conor. I guess …" He trailed off.

"You guess what?'

"I guess that's contingent on whether I find a better opportunity."

Those questioning eyes continued to bore into him. "I said you should be a teacher. You'd be so good."

"Maybe I'll do that. Eventually."

"What do you mean 'eventually'?"

"I've heard Florida is nice this time of year."

Now her mouth fell open. "That's true," she said.

"But I don't even have a car."

"You could take a bus." He loved that twinkle in her eyes.

"Yeah, but busses are usually crowded."

"Hmm. That's true." She put the tip of her index finger to her lips.

"If I had a nice RV, that'd be the ticket."

"Yeah, they're nice."

"Know where I could find one?"

"There are RV dealers everywhere."

"But I don't have much money."

"That could be a problem."

"Maybe I need to get a job."

"Yeah, that sounds like a good plan. What do you have in mind?"

"Well in the long run, teaching, like I said. But I'll probably need some more classes."

"But what about the near term?"

"I'm feeling ambitious. I was thinking maybe assistant campground host."

Her eyes grew large and misty. "Pretty ambitious."

"Oh."

"That kind of professional position has some demanding qualifications."

"Yeah?"

She stepped closer. "And just what makes you think you're qualified for such a position?"

He trailed a finger down the side of her cheek as he studied her face, then he cradled her face in his hands and delicately kissed her. Then he pulled her into his arms and kissed her deeply. His knees felt wobbly, and they stumbled backward until they were pressed up against the RV.

Julia was breathing hard when they finally pulled away. Shaking her head slowly, she said, "I have to admit, you do seem to have some significant qualifications."

Declan suddenly turned serious. "I've got to tell you, I've only got about forty K and no income."

"Forty K?"

"That's approximately. I don't check my account often. I know that's not much."

"That's probably more that I've got. I don't check often either."

"But I don't need much," he said.

Julia ran her fingers along his stubbly cheek. "Actually, there's quite a lot that I need." She took his hand and led him into the RV.

If you enjoyed Heart of Rocks, please consider posting a customer review at Amazon or Goodreads.

Acknowledgements

It is a pleasure to thank my editor, Elizabeth Evans, who made major contributions to this novel. You can learn more about her work at elizabethevanseditorial.com.

Thank you to my gifted and helpful beta readers: Nancy Howell, Denton Jones, Bob Pavlik, Meredie Scrivener, and Tom Scrivner. And my sister, Mary Patricia Trainor.

I am grateful to the following group, with whom I have met regularly to discuss important life issues such as forgiveness and God's love: Greg Bell, Jim Benton, Steve Bruemmer, Fr. Oswald Bwecha, Alan Forristal, Tom Herbstrieth, Mark Hilgendorf, Jack Holzman, David Honecker, Kjell Johansen, Dwight Morgan, Bob Pavlik, and Richard TenHoor.

Thank you to Tom Herbstreith, who introduced me to the beauty and magical power of the native American flute.

The quote by Steven Charleston is from Joyful Defiance, *Spirit Wheel*, p. 202.

Prisca's teaching about pinpoints in the middle of the darkness was drawn from Kate Bowler, *Have a Beautiful, Terrible Day*, New York: Convergent Books (2024), p. 199.

It is important to acknowledge the beauty of our beautiful national parks and monuments, only two of which are described in this book. It is critical that we all work to support and preserve them.

Some of the history of the Chiricahua Apaches was drawn from *Chiricahua Apaches: A Concise History*, by Bill Cavaliere, ECO Herpetological Publishing, 2022. I purchased the book in the visitor center at Chiricahua National Monument, where our fictitious friend Prisca served.

The hut is fictitious, a product of the author's imagination. However, people all over this country working quietly on the same kinds of projects that the people in the hut did.

The characters Pam and Prisca were inspired by the many dedicated Episcopal priests I have known, who are faithfully proclaiming God's love to the world.

Much appreciation to my devoted Redbone Coon Hound, Clyde, who was the inspiration for David Niven.

The communion scene at the hut was inspired in part by the account in *Take This Bread*, by Sara Miles; the concluding scene in the movie *Places in the Heart*; the first communion described in Thomas Merton's *The Seven Storey Mountain*; and my personal experience.

Heart of Rocks is dedicated to Ron, Damon, and Bob. Ron Kaiser was my friend in high school and introduced me to the beauty of hiking in the wilderness. Damon Giovanielli was an outstanding physicist and research leader at Los Alamos National Laboratory, who taught me much about scientific curiosity and integrity. Bob Pavlik was a scholar, who taught me much about the importance of friendship and kindness. I lost all three of these friends in the year prior to publication of this book. I miss them greatly.

Finally, I thank my wife Mary, who understands fiction better than I do. She was a strong encourager of this project, a dedicated reviewer of various drafts, and continues to be the love of my life.

About the Author

Jim Trainor grew up in LA and lived much of his life in the West. He now lives in the upper Midwest with his wife Mary. When he's not writing, they can often be found hiking in the wilderness. They have three grown children and a Redbone Coonhound named Clyde.

Jim is both a PhD physicist and ordained pastor. He's a former deputy director of the Physics Division at Los Alamos National Laboratory and has authored over seventy articles in physics. As an Episcopal priest, he has served congregations in New Mexico, Texas and Wisconsin. He is active as a speaker on the relationship between science and spirituality.

Jim is the author of eight books.

More information on Jim and his books at
www.JimTrainorAuthor.com